MURDER IN MONTEGO BAY

A gripping crime mystery packed with twists

PAULA LENNON

Preddy and Harris Book 1

JOFFE BOOKS

Revised edition 2022
Joffe Books, London
www.joffebooks.com

First published by Jacaranda Books
in Great Britain in 2017

This paperback edition was first published
in Great Britain in 2022

Cover art by Nick Castle

ISBN: 978-1-80405-185-6

For Mom and Dad,
Yuh done know how it go

PROLOGUE

The man looked up when he heard the purr of an engine.

He slumped low behind the steering wheel and watched as his target's white SUV slowed to a crawl and passed his vehicle. His heart palpitated as he reached for his weapon, fondling the cold steel. This job had to be quick clean and smooth. A better opportunity was unlikely to ever arise. It would provide no real enjoyment, no job satisfaction; it was a necessary act.

The target unsuccessfully tried to open the electronic gates protecting his home. The gunman smirked, knowing that the security system's controls would not respond. A small dog ran out to the gate and yapped sharply in excitement. The man's smile faded. He had never liked dogs; they were annoying, needy creatures who shit anywhere they wanted to. He pressed on the unfamiliar accelerator and grimaced as the noisy engine sprung back into life.

Sweat trickled from his neck down his back as his chest heaved and fell. Inhaling deeply, he could smell his salty odour mixed with fear and adrenalin. He stared through tinted glasses at his target, a young brown-skinned man who

1

alighted from his vehicle to inspect his security system. The target showed no indication of being disturbed by the noise of the engine as he forcefully pushed the heavy gates aside.

The gunman lowered the car window. He inhaled again, more deeply this time, taking in the fresh, clean air. He advanced towards the target who was heading back to his SUV and hit the brakes. Three explosions followed; two bullets for the man, one for the pup.

The gunman scrambled from his car, tugged at the victim's limp wrist and checked that the job was done. More explosions rang out as the gunman jumped back into his vehicle. They were not from his gun. The shots ricocheted off the car's bodywork and he heard the distinct crack of the rear windshield. Startled, the gunman slammed down on the accelerator and sped away.

CHAPTER 1

Sunday, 19 July, 6.05 a.m.

Detective Raythan Preddy wanted a hot cup of ganja tea, a large one. Sleep had eluded him last night, and now he was driving along the deserted roads of Montego Bay with no time for his usual therapeutic brew. His body was missing the vital energy that came with rest just when he needed to be at his productive best. Relaxation would need to wait until the "unwanted spike in crime" — as once described by the police commissioner — had retracted. Twenty minutes earlier an incoming phone call had all but confirmed that crime was in no mood to retreat just yet. Carter Chin Ellis, heir to the Jamaican Chinchillerz empire, was dead.

The distance between Preddy's Ironshore apartment and the Red Hills district was less than ten miles of pretty good road with not a pothole in sight. To the untrained eye everything on the route appeared to be perfectly in order, yet it was not. The city of Montego Bay was a tale of two extremes with a delicate balance in the middle. The tourist side brought the Caribbean sea, an unending blanket of shimmering silver, which turned many shades of blue as soon as the sun came up in a cloudless sky. Palm trees everywhere with their fronds splayed like giant feathers covering their trunks, and endless miles of white sand. That was the magnificent side espoused by the glossy brochures enticing visitors to the parish of St. James.

Then there was the flip side: an unhealthy dose of guns, drugs and scamming. That side rarely reached visitors to The Rock whose adequately guarded hotels shielded them from anything that did not match the Jamaica Tourist Board's output. The ugliness remained blotted out by the dazzling sun, the crunch of warm sand and the blare of reggae music. The locals saw it though. Those people unwilling or unable to leave their unstable communities lived it on a daily basis. The gangs in particular focused on the outer, unfashionable districts where unemployment was an occupation and there was no such thing as social security, save that provided by the gang leaders.

Preddy was thankful a middle ground existed. Most residents would only ever read about crime or watch reports on the news, without directly being caught up in it. In the daytime there was no discernible change in people's behaviour. They worked, shopped, swam, strolled in the park and otherwise led completely normal existences. At night they went to bars, movies, parties and wherever their social lives took them. Once home they affixed solid padlocks to iron grills caging all possible entrance points, and those who could afford it enabled their electronic security systems.

Preddy reached for the radio control knob. As to be expected on a Sunday morning, the voice of a ranting preacher filled the air space, predicting that the wicked would burn in Hell and God would withhold his blessings from blasphemers. A tabby cat decided to use up one of its many lives and ran out in front of Preddy's vehicle, startling the detective.

"A whe de rass," he muttered, as he swerved to avoid it, and then immediately apologised to God. Too late. There would be no blessings on him this morning, and he was really going to need help whether it was to come from on high or on the ground.

The detective had worked for the Jamaica Constabulary Force for over eighteen years. It was tough, yet even at its hardest stage he had never regretted his choice of career. A failed raid had set his superiors' nerves on edge and tested his resolve for a while though. He licked the bile from his lips as the visions of shots, screams and dead bodies that occupied his nights flashed through his mind yet again.

Pelican Walk was not a large police station compared to some of the others in Montego Bay, but it benefitted from high-calibre detectives, sergeants and constables, some of whom had up to twelve years of service. The detectives were members of the Major Crimes task force, which formed a primary part of the Area One geographic division, covering the western parishes of Westmoreland, Hanover and Trelawny, as well as St James. Its remit was to reduce major crimes, particularly murders, in the region.

Preddy glanced at the dashboard clock. The two female detectives he had called earlier would now be making their way to Red Hills. He had somewhat hesitated before placing a third phone call. There was a new, temporary addition to Pelican Walk, a police officer on secondment from Glasgow, Scotland. Detective Sean Harris, a redheaded, white male approaching fifty with nearly two decades in law enforcement. For the past two weeks the foreigner had cut his teeth on the Jamaican style of policing and spent a great deal of time reviewing evidence of violent crimes with other officers. Preddy was reserving judgment on Harris. Although Preddy was always open to a fresh take on things, he was not entirely comfortable with this green-eyed outsider, but the superintendent had indicated that Harris must be given high-level work to do and chances were it would not get much higher than this.

* * *

The scene that greeted Detective Preddy was not unfamiliar. Furious, half-dressed residents on the roadside complaining loudly about murderers holding the community to ransom and demanding that the police catch the criminals. Had Red Hills not been such a wealthy area, tyres would probably be burning in streets blocked by rusty white goods and placard waving residents. As it was, both people and traffic were temporarily prevented from contaminating the crime scene by reams of yellow and black caution tape strewn across the road from lamp posts to trees.

The abandoned SUV stood with the driver's door open as if waiting for its owner to return. A Scene of Crime van was parked about twenty feet away. Crime scene investigators, decked from head to toe in white, were photographing the vehicle and the roadway, camera lights flashing every few seconds. They took notice of tyre tracks, spent bullet shells and anything that looked remotely like evidence before carefully placing the items into transparent bags.

Two media vehicles from rival stations were parked at the end of the road, their dogged reporters mingling with the vocal crowd. Though dressed casually, Preddy knew that the reporters would soon spot him. Most reporters easily recognised him as a police officer even if they had never met him before. His appearance and stature fit the mould of a law enforcement leader. Tall and well-built with a poised bearing that conveyed self-assurance and control, his mahogany-brown skin was clean-shaven, with salt and pepper hair cut short against his scalp. Whatever he wore, be it plain clothes or his jogging gear, it sat well on his athletic frame. He enjoyed jumping out of bed before the sun came up to go cycling or running. Admiring glances frequently accompanied him and he would usually acknowledge female watchers with a wave when he was off-duty. On duty, he had no time for flirting, no matter how attractive the temptress.

Preddy had no intention of dishing out comments to anyone as the media relations team was empowered to feed the hungry reporters and they knew how to do it without getting their hands bitten. Past experience had shown news folk to be masters of misinterpretation and he was not entirely convinced this was accidental. The last time he told a reporter that he was "making good use of the limited resources available," the reporter wrote that he had "issued a heartfelt appeal for more resources." This had not sat well with the police high command. He brushed off a pushy reporter and swooped low to navigate the fluttering tape, emerging purposefully on the business side.

"What we have here?" Preddy's question was aimed at Detective Kathryn Rabino.

Rabino was a slim woman with a long Brazilian hair weave and obvious false lashes. At first sight she could appear shallow, but she was a genuine professional, trained to never blink first. Rabino spun around and acknowledged her superior, resisting the urge to correct his language. Her boss was a Jamaican's Jamaican and would never give up his Patois.

"Carter Chin Ellis, deceased. Two gunshot wounds to the right side of the head," said Rabino, who was a stickler for the Queen's English unless riled or engaging in a joke. On those occasions, Patois really was best. "The car is registered to his brother, Lester Chin Ellis. It's the same vehicle that was pulled over early this morning off the highway by Timmins and Franklin. The brothers were taken to Pelican Walk for drunken behaviour. The parents know all about it, sir."

Detective Preddy frowned as he lifted the cloth and looked at the body. He had so hoped there had been a mistake. The death of any young person was a terrible blow. But the murder of Carter Chin Ellis, from a prominent and respected family, would be treated as an outrageous attack by the monied class and as a tragedy by everybody else. The killing of a poor person never elicited the same frenetic reaction from prominent citizens as the death of a rich person. Add to the pot that Carter had been killed shortly after leaving Pelican Walk police station and the public would eagerly stir. The calls for justice would be much louder than usual. Preddy covered up the young man's body.

Everyone on the island knew the Chin Ellis family, composed of a Chinese man, a Black Jamaican wife and two sons.

Their empire had grown from a single ice cream shop thirty years ago to a state of the art, fast frozen-food operation with outlets in each of the fourteen parishes. It was hard to find someone who had never eaten in a Chinchillerz at some point in time and the detective himself was not immune to the draw of their yoghurts and smoothies.

"What is dat over dere?" asked Preddy, pointing to a small mound of blue tarpaulin.

"The victim's dog was also shot dead, sir."

Preddy walked to the gates, frowning.

"Why did he step out of de car outside his gates?" he asked his colleague.

"The security system was disabled. We assume it was the perpetrator's handiwork," replied Rabino, pointing to the exposed wires on the control panel which looked freshly cut.

"Eyewitness reports?"

Rabino's long fingernails deftly flicked over a page of her loose-leaf notepad. "A witness was in his front garden, sir. Said he saw a silver Subaru Outback drive up beside the victim. Partial registration, a six at the beginning, couldn't see the rest. He heard about five or six shots. The shooter came out for a few seconds, then the car sped off. He's not sure whether it turned right or left when it reached the end of the road. Said he bent down behind the wall."

"And him sure it was an Outback?"

"So he says, sir," she reported, swinging her mane back. "Said he saw a guy, medium-build, with a hood over his face and dark glasses, in a black shirt and black pants. Couldn't make out any features. He believes the suspect's car trunk has bullet holes in it. Like it got shot out before."

Preddy sensed movement at his side and turned to discover Detective Javinia Spence. Spence was a small, perfectly groomed officer who wore her natural hair in shoulder-length braids that curved into a bob around her ears. She had a sharp mind and an even sharper tongue. He was forever reminding her that diplomacy was the best way to stay ahead on the force, but Spence viewed diplomacy as something of a chore to be undertaken only when absolutely unavoidable. He could not imagine where she would be now if she was not such an effective officer.

"Any other witnesses?" he asked her.

"Some residents say dem hear up to a dozen shots. Some say dey thought it was thunder. Some hide under bed. Nobody see a thing, sir," explained Spence, with a disbelieving expression. "But if police did come up here shooting dem woulda report say dem see everything."

Preddy understood her frustration. All eyes would now be on the police, including those of the diaspora, that population of Jamaicans a million or so strong that mainly lived in the USA, Canada and England. Some of whom contributed to Jamaica in the form of money, food, clothes and education, as well as investments. Others had nothing to contribute but venom and watched the island with perverted glee to identify as many problems as possible, worshipping their residential visas and vowing never to return. The Jamaican Americans in particular annoyed him. Most of them kept quiet about the thousands of violent deaths that took place on the land to which they had pledged their allegiance, but as soon as a murder happened in Jamaica, they were all over social media. He had no time for them and would love the freedom to respond to some of the vitriol.

Preddy noted the blood splatter on the road as he walked towards a crime scene officer and took a transparent plastic bag containing the spent shells. He studied the bits of metal closely before turning his attention to the large crowd. The eager spectators were pressing against the straining caution tape, smartphones held aloft, emboldened that the police officers were concentrated near the vehicle. Most hoped that their indiscipline would be rewarded with a good close-up shot of something interesting to put on the internet. They photographed the crime scene officers as they went about their work and shouted inane questions, which were ignored.

"De body can go up to Cornwall. Get de car taken to de lab," said Preddy. "Where is de man who gave de statement?"

Rabino closed her notebook and looked around. "Right there in the red merino beside the wall."

Preddy strolled over to the skinny, middle-aged man whose dry knees peeped out under his long yellow shorts. "Is dere anything dat you forgot to tell de detective, sir?"

"'Bout what, officer?" The man's eyes flickered from the male detective to Rabino and back again. "Dat me come outside to water me flowers? I know say dat wrong, what wid water restriction."

Preddy jangled the bag of spent shells, forcing the eye-witness to focus. "Don't play wid me," he warned. "So far you have been very helpful, but now is de time to speak, man. Or come to de station."

The man's shoulders drooped and his lips suddenly required regular moisturising. He rubbed the back of his neck and stared down at his sandals.

"Different shells," stated Preddy. "You fire shot at de gunman car, didn't you?"

"Yes, sir," he mumbled eventually. "I did run out after him. I know you going want to see de gun. I'm telling you from now dat it don't license, so gwaan arrest me!" He held out both puny arms in front of him.

"A so dem love do!" shouted a woman from the road-side. "Dem don't want we to protect weself. Dem arrest de good people dem and make de criminal dem gwaan!"

Preddy moved around so that his back faced the opin-ionated woman and he beckoned to Rabino. "Our witness wants to make an addition to him statement. And him have some equipment to hand over."

A determined male reporter ventured through the caution tape and was forcefully pushed back by a watchful Spence, even though he was twice her size. Preddy walked towards the victim's house, where Detective Sean Harris stood questioning one of the female residents. Most of the houses in the Red Hills area had considerable kerb appeal and this vast property was no different. For the likes of Carter Chin Ellis, money was no object and none had been spared.

Preddy greeted Harris politely, just as the Scotsman thanked the witness and began moving away.

"You get anything interesting?"

"She heard the gunshots, but stayed in her bed, petrified by the sound of it," Harris replied. His deep voice carried a strong Glaswegian accent and Preddy wondered whether the interviewee had been able to fully understand him.

"We need to get a statement from Lester Chin Ellis," said Preddy. "Find out where dey were before de arrest and whether dey had any trouble."

"Aye, sir. I'm told that he's being held pending bail."

"Him don't post bail yet?"

Harris shrugged. "I was thinking the same thing maself. I was told he's from a very wealthy family. He's probably been in lock-up a few hours now."

"Okay, what else we know?" Preddy asked, making a mental note to find out why Carter's brother had not been given station bail.

"Another witness heard the gates squeaking as they were being opened," Harris reported. "Then there was a dog barking, screech of tyres, explosions. The witness ran to the window. He couldnae see what the shooter was doing, but thinks he might have been checking tae see if Carter was dead."

Preddy nodded. "Dem rob Carter?"

"We cannae tell if anything is missing because Carter wasnae booked in when he was taken tae the station. He and the officers who arrested him settled their differences and he was let go without charges. His valuables appear tae be on him: wallet with ID and credit cards, Rolex watch, gold charm ring and a smartphone." Harris waved the various evidence bags as he spoke.

The phone in Preddy's pocket vibrated against his chest as if awakened by Harris' words. He took it out and glanced at the screen before replacing it, seemingly irritated. Harris noted the movement, but said nothing, being already of the view that Preddy never shared more information than he considered necessary.

Preddy pulled on a pair of white latex gloves and opened one of the packages. He took out the expensive-looking ring and held it up in the air, admiring the dazzling glint of the sun's rays on solid gold metal.

"What does dis tell you?" he asked.

"That robbery wasnae the likely motive?" Harris ventured.

"Dat's what I was thinking," said Preddy.

"Or dat de gunman get frighten and run away before he could steal anything," suggested Spence, joining the detectives with Rabino at her side.

"Possibly," murmured Preddy, as he replaced the jewellery in the bag.

"I'll get the shell casings to ballistics," Rabino offered. "You were right, sir. The witness believes he hit the gunman's car more than once. I took a Beretta and some 9mm bullets from him."

A crime scene officer tapped Preddy on the shoulder. The detective spun around and looked at the officer expectantly.

"Sorry to interrupt you, Detective. De superintendent wants to speak to you."

"I know he does," Preddy frowned. "I'll call him back in a minute. Dis time of day he'll still be on line two."

"Not anymore, sir. He's at Pelican Walk, in de conference room on de second floor." The officer looked around cautiously, making sure that the reporters were out of earshot and then leaned in closer towards the detective's shoulder, whispering in his ear. "Me hear say Lester Chin Ellis get beat up right dere at de station dis morning. Him face black and blue and Super sound super mad!"

CHAPTER 2

Sunday, 19 July, 1.58 a.m.

Lester Chin Ellis was feeling the night heat and failed to catch the car keys flung in his general direction. He shook his head at his younger brother while bending wobbly knees and fumbling in the dim light to retrieve them. Carter grinned and hauled his agile body into the passenger seat of the white sports utility vehicle, reclining immediately. Lester closed the door and put the key in the ignition, welcoming the rush of cool air that flooded in. The engine hummed quietly as he reversed from the parking lot of Reingold's Sports Bar, negotiating through the mass of badly-parked expensive cars.

The sports bar was a popular weekend venue for the monied types — Black, brown and white alike. Some had genuine foreign accents, others affected ones. There was a choice of English Premier League football or NFL games on the various giant screens. Once the credit cards went down on the bar the clientele would feast on alcohol-rich cocktails and finger buffets of festival, jerk chicken, roast breadfruit, escoveitched fish and sweet potatoes. Young wealthy revellers danced energetically to the latest Billboard Hot 100 tunes with bottles and glasses held aloft. At one point earlier that night, the brothers had wrapped their arms around each other's shoulders while each tried simultaneously to swig beer from a bottle held by the other. Most of the content was spilled down their chests in the process, although neither appeared to notice, let alone care.

"Drive up, boss," urged Carter. It was relatively early to be leaving the bar, but duty called. He closed his eyes and nestled more comfortably into the plush seat. "Home time."

Aged twenty, he was the younger by two years and considered himself the more handsome of the two brothers, although this was always roundly disputed by Lester. They were both slim men with the same caramel brown skin, and slender eyes that spoke of mixed heritage. Carter was more solidly proportioned than his older brother as he favoured an hour of push-ups every morning, otherwise it was easy to mistake one for the other.

"You can always drive, you know?" Lester suggested.

"No, man, it's alright . . . go on."

The brothers were part-educated in Jamaica, part in the United States and like most Jamaicans who had been directly exposed to American ways or watched too much American television, they had adopted an American drawl which could not be attributed to any particular State. Carter would be returning to university in Miami once the summer was over, which was still quite some time away. Majoring in finance and marketing he was enjoying the opportunity to study abroad and learn on the job at home. Nothing beat being able to put the visionary theories learned elsewhere into practice. He relished sitting in on board meetings and learning how the family business ran. Lester had just completed his studies in nutrition and food science in New York. He, too, enjoyed the benefits of having a growing empire to practice his initiatives on. He believed that so much could be done with the bountiful fruits of the island, yet very few people were capable of grasping this idea.

The heirs to the Chinchillerz empire were rich beyond most Jamaicans' wildest dreams. Both sons had been well aware of their privileged backgrounds from a young age, knowing that they would never have to work for another person if they did not want to. With lifestyles begrudged by many, they had been given everything that they had asked for from childhood and plenty that they hadn't. Bicycles, motorbikes, dune buggies, jet skis and cars — anything new and hot off the conveyor belt was theirs. As soon as they hit eighteen, each son had been allowed to buy his own expensive and spacious house as befitted youngsters of their social stature. Lester's was a waterfront villa with a sweeping panoramic vista at Sandy Bay in the adjoining parish of Hanover. Carter chose to make his home on a high elevation in Red Hills which granted a spectacular one hundred and eighty-degree view of the Caribbean Sea and the western hills.

Lester glanced across at his brother, watching the hint of a smile that flickered across Carter's face from time to time. As youngsters, he had always doted on his baby brother; he taught him how to fly a kite, ride a bicycle and use a catapult. As teenagers, Carter had done his bit in return, accepting payment to do his brother's homework, lending him anything he needed and helping his rebellious self sneak back indoors after parental curfew. He glanced at the clock on the dashboard, which revealed that it was nearly 2 a.m.

Friday night was for staying out all night if they chose to, Saturday night was not. The brothers stayed at the family home most Saturday nights and accompanied their parents to church on Sunday mornings. Neither Carter nor Lester was particularly religious, but the display of unity was good for the family and those who were always watching the family. People needed to see that they remained humble and grounded, regardless of the trappings of wealth. They would dress in their finest Italian-made suits and engage in banter with their father as to whether earrings were appropriate attire for young men at all, much less young men attending church services.

"What are we going to do about the old people's twenty-eighth anniversary?" asked Lester.

Carter groaned, eyes still firmly closed. "It's next month, isn't it?"

"Eeh-eeh. A few weeks from now."

"They don't need a thing," Carter mumbled with some pride.

The Chin Ellis elders certainly needed nothing, and their standing, particularly in Western Jamaica, was second to none. They owned a huge villa on the Doubloons at one of the most prestigious spots in the Freeport area of Montego Bay, as well as classic cars, a yacht, a helicopter, a small plane and plenty of other toys. Not an unknown status for Jamaicans of European or Asian heritage, although much less common for the descendants of Black Africans. The Black element of their blended family put them on just about the right side to avoid the much-repeated accusations of foreigners taking over Jamaica. The Chinese element would always attract the suspicion of those who contended that the Chinese and the whites owned everything of worth on the island and benefitted from preferential treatment.

Their powerful vehicle suddenly swerved violently and a driver screamed obscenities at them. Carter's eyes flew open as his body lurched forward, the seatbelt holding him firmly in position. He tried to focus on his surroundings on the poorly-lit highway and noticed that Lester had just blown through a red stop light.

"Wow! Take time drive!"

"You just told me to drive up!" Lester glanced into the rear-view mirror and spotted a set of rapidly approaching blue lights flashing. "Oh shit!" He stepped on the accelerator.

Carter glared at his brother. "You mad, bro? Stop the car."

"I don't have time for them. Make them go and find something to do."

"Stop Lester! Just give them some money and they'll let us go on."

"I didn't walk with cash money tonight, youth. And they won't take credit cards."

Lester slowed down and pulled the vehicle over while the blue lights followed him into a narrow side road. Lowering both front windows, he waited, watching keenly through the mirror as the shadows moved around behind him. The police officers eventually emerged from their vehicle. One carried a breathalyser kit, the other appeared to have his hands free. They ambled towards the brothers' SUV as if they had all the time in the world. The shorter officer with the kit moved towards the driver's door while the other man took up a position outside of the passenger door.

"Good night, sir," said the officer closest to Lester. "Have you been drinking?"

Lester's eyes gave the lawman a split second of disdain and then stared ahead through the windshield. The officer moved closer, taking in the alcohol stains on Lester's shirt. He reached for the keys, turning off the ignition.

Lester frowned and slammed his hand on the steering wheel. "What's your problem? You see us doing anything?"

"Have you been drinking, sir?"

Lester kissed his teeth loudly, a long drawn out screech guaranteed to cause annoyance to the target. It achieved the desired result.

"Step out of de vehicle, please, sir."

There was no movement from inside the vehicle for a few seconds. Carter wiped a small bead of sweat from his brow as he glanced from his brother to the officer. He pressed the button for the internal light and the interior of the car lit up.

"Look, all of us know what's going on, you know," said Carter.

The second officer put one hand on the passenger door, the other on his gun belt and leaned into the vehicle. His eyes were flat and fixed and his jaw rigid as he stared into Carter's face.

"What you say? What do we know? Talk, no?"

Carter held up both palms in a conciliatory gesture and smiled ruefully at the officer who continued to stare him down. "Sorry, officer. My mistake."

Lester twisted his body and lowered his head to peer at Carter's officer. "Leave my brother alone, man! We cannot help you tonight."

"I'll ask you again to step out of de vehicle, sir."

Lester turned and studied the smaller officer this time, taking in the bursting uniform and stern face. There was no doubt in his mind that the officers knew exactly who they had detained. "Who knows what will happen to me if I get outta this car, officer? It would be better if you tell me to follow you to a safe place."

The policeman reached into the vehicle again and snatched the keys. He opened the driver's door as far as it would go and pulled forcefully on Lester's arm. Carter leaned over and managed to grab onto his brother's shirt, but the officer had already secured a firm grip on Lester. Carter collapsed sideways over the empty driver's seat. He soon found himself being dragged out of his own door by the taller officer, who by now had removed his gun from its holster and was pointing it towards the ground.

"Come on, man! What are you doing?" exclaimed Lester, trying to wriggle out of the officer's grasp.

"Stop that, man!" shouted Carter, eyes blazing. "I want your name . . . and yours, too!"

"Name? Dat is de least of your worries, I'm telling you," said the taller officer, who spun Carter around and hand-cuffed his wrists despite his protests.

"Both of you are under arrest for reckless driving, assaulting a police officer and for being drunk and disor-derly." The officer holding Lester cuffed him too and pro-ceeded to read each brother his rights while marching them towards the police car.

CHAPTER 3

The Pelican Walk conference room could hold meetings of up to thirty officers and Preddy could only assume that Superintendent Brownlow chose this room for a two-person meeting because it was furthest away from the heart of the station. Less foot traffic, less prying eyes. Dark wood tables were pressed together to form one gigantic unit, surrounded by matching heavy chairs. The thick red curtains were drawn, which reduced the natural lighting considerably. With only two occupants, the room felt particularly imposing. If the superintendent put a dividing screen between them, it would pass as a confessional. *Forgive me, Super, for I have sinned.*

Preddy looked at the photo the superintendent pushed across the table and silently cursed the officers who had allowed this to happen on his territory. The ugly weal stood out on Lester's swollen cheek, a wide purple mark that looked completely out of place on his pale brown features. Part of his top lip was cut and his open mouth displayed a small space signifying the loss of part of one tooth.

The detective had seen pictures of Lester before, at functions and grand openings, cutting ribbons and shaking hands with dignitaries, a good-looking young man with a confident smile and smart appearance. The two brothers lurked week after week in the colourful social pages of the national media. There was always something to laugh or smile about in Chin Ellis world, until now.

"An inmate attacks Chin Ellis and everyone is oblivious. Nobody heard a disturbance. Nobody saw anything," the superintendent huffed. He was an extremely overweight man whose suit used up a whole lot of khaki and whose voice never needed artificial amplification. "What am I supposed to tell Commissioner Davis?"

The superintendent sat forward in his chair, hands clasped together, elbows lodged firmly on the table. The superior officer would have achieved the dramatic pose he had planned but the table legs were uneven and rocked under pressure, despite his valiant attempts to disguise his efforts to hold it firm.

"You think I can tell the commissioner that no-one knows anything about it? Somebody must know something!"

"Sir, I can assure you dat I am going to get to de bottom of it," said Preddy. "We only had a few officers on duty in here at de time."

"And when are you going to do that?" The superintendent fixed Preddy with a dark glare. "The parents are already talking to the media. They only found out we were holding one son when they were told that the other son was dead."

Preddy winced. "I understand, sir." He was mortified that the officers had made such a spectacular mess of what sounded like a minor traffic case, but he would ask the hard questions of them later.

"I cannot believe we had Lester Chin Ellis in a cell with God-knows-who. Why wasn't he bailed immediately? We suddenly have room for people like him?"

Preddy maintained a straight face. "We can find room for anybody who deserves it, sir."

The superintendent bristled and studied the detective's demeanour. "Oh, really? You know more about our facilities and resources than I do?"

"No, sir." Preddy cleared his throat. "I understand dat a large quantity of hard drugs — cocaine — was found in de car, so we can make dat known to de public in due course. Lester is not some innocent, misjudged young man."

Preddy had no time for drug dealers of any complexion. He had served on various anti-crime task forces, including a short and useful stint at the Criminal Investigations Bureau. The anti-narcotics campaign was a source of particular pride, leading as it did to the successful prosecution and extradition of a number of major cocaine traffickers who had established bases on the island and in the United States.

When it came to marijuana though, he experienced mixed feelings. Destroying whole fields was a nonsense when it could be reaped and used for medicinal purposes. As usual, North America had got in on the act first and growers were making millions, while Jamaica was content with setting fire to what could become its most lucrative export and borrowing money from the IMF. The small time ganja dealers were still around and always would be, particularly with the recent decriminalisation of ganja for those found with up to two ounces. That infraction was now a minor ticketable offence. This would save a lot of wasted manpower spent prosecuting the smokers of herbs that custom, tradition and even religion deemed relatively harmless. Tourists wanted to be able to smoke the weed in peace, too. If only everybody would just drink the tea, the problem would be solved.

Superintendent Brownlow leaned back in his chair with his hands spread over his protruding stomach. "Let's keep quiet about the drugs for now. I am not so sure that it is in our interests to try and bring any drug charges against him. We cannot afford to have the general public and the business community turn against us at this stage."

No, we certainly cannot have dat, Superintendent, thought Preddy. *No more hobnobbing with influential, high-living, society types. No more black-tie balls and gala dinners, and certainly no invites to parties, christenings and weddings. We must get the upper echelon back on board by releasing the coke-snorting, spoiled, rich kid with a smack on the wrist and condolences on his bereavement.* The superintendent was a good man at heart, but he was also a shameless social climber.

"Commissioner Davis wants this dealt with, and dealt with quickly. One assault and one murder in the same family on the same day!" Brownlow groaned and stuck his nails into the table. "You and I both know that the commissioner has you firmly on his radar since the Norwood catastrophe. If you don't think you can handle this case, Preddy, tell me now."

Preddy tried to blink away the images that immediately clouded his mind. He wished that people would stop mentioning Norwood. Three men had been killed that night in Norwood district. Not innocent men by any accounts, as all were involved in some way in the attempted murder of a police officer who had since been left in a persistent vegetative state. Preddy was in charge of the officers who went to the tenement yard to arrest the men in connection with the outrageous attack on the officer. It was the worst tactical decision of his career as he had spectacularly underestimated the pent-up rage of his fellow officers who had witnessed their injured colleague's speedy deterioration. Nobody wanted to be the invalid and everybody wanted to avenge him. The mission had ended badly. It was not the sole blemish on Preddy's illustrious crime fighting career, but it was a monumental one and the only one that had attracted international, albeit temporary, attention, and one that Commissioner Davis would never forget.

"Something in your eye, Detective?"

"Touch of hay fever, sir."

"Should I be worried that you clearly have to think about whether you can handle it?"

Preddy coughed. "No, sir. We have a good lead on de murder. We are trying to trace de suspect vehicle, a silver Subaru Outback. I have a strong team of detectives on de case and I'll be working very closely wid dem."

"Which detectives are working on it?"

"Kathryn Rabino, Javinia Spence and our Scotsman, Sean Harris."

"Ah."

The superintendent hauled his ample frame out of the chair and waddled towards the louvre windows. Preddy studied the man's broad shoulders, taking in the rolls of skin on the nape of his neck. The last time he had seen his superior in the flesh was only two weeks ago, yet the man seemed to have put on even more weight in that short time. That was what vacations in foodie cities like New Orleans did to you. The Super had a liking for beers and fried foods, and a great dislike for any form of exercise. The man would drive to the end of the road to collect a newspaper rather than complete the simple fifteen-minute round trip on legs. *Yes, Super would have been in his element in the jazz city, sitting back, listening to music and savouring unhealthy delights*, thought Preddy. Today he looked just one fried plantain away from a heart attack. For all his quirks, though, Brownlow was a thorough law enforcement officer and Preddy had no doubt about his wish to clean up the parish of St. James.

"It's a start, I suppose," the superintendent said eventually. "We really have to move on this."

"You will get my preliminary report on what happened to Lester Chin Ellis within twenty-four hours, sir."

The superintendent's huge body did not move, but his head snapped round, making his neck look even more rolled. "Make it twelve. I'll need a response for the family's press conference tonight."

"Press conference, sir?"

"Press conference, Preddy."

"Yes, sir."

Preddy took the lack of further movement from Superintendent Brownlow as an indication that he should leave. He closed the door quietly and walked down the hallway, pausing momentarily to collect his thoughts. Through the glass windows, he stared at the seamless blend of cloudless sky and turquoise sea. In the distance a few sailboats were visible calmly traversing the horizon. Closer still flowed a large volume of highway traffic, racing both ways, barely acknowledging the speed limits. A perfectly manicured green lawn ran the entire length of the highway's median strip decorated with evenly placed miniature palm trees. It should have been a calming sight for most drivers. As usual, though, impatient racers sounded their horns a nanosecond after the traffic lights changed from red to green. Luckily, Pelican Walk had a long driveway, which helped mute the vehicles' noise. The cars were followed by busloads of tourists blissfully unaware of the degree of ugliness that had taken place a few miles from the beauty of their gated enclosures.

Somewhere out there, a murderer had brought all eyes to Preddy's cherished city and now his own colleagues had unhelpfully turned the spotlight on themselves. He prayed that their only lead would turn out to be a solid one. The next forty-eight hours would be crucial and he had no doubt that the commissioner, who had shown him no love in the past, would be paying close attention to his progress.

CHAPTER 4

As expected, the Chin Ellis murder was lead story on the national seven o'clock news.

"*... TVJ News understands that the dead man has been identified as Carter Chin Ellis, son of Terence and Ida Chin Ellis and heir to the Chinchillerz group of companies. Eyewitnesses say he was gunned down in a hail of bullets at around 5 a.m. on Sunday morning by an unknown assailant. Police are urging anyone with information about the shooting to contact the police at 919, 131 or the nearest police station. We will now go over to the grounds of the Old Hospital Park in Montego Bay where the family are holding a press conference.*"

Preddy sank into his leather sofa and used the remote to increase the volume. The last eleven hours had been dedicated to making enquiries about matters relating to both Chin Ellis brothers and he did not want to miss a thing. He set the DVD recorder then picked up a notepad and pen.

Terence and Ida Chin Ellis stood behind a tall, well-built man in an expensive suit and tie, whom Preddy immediately recognised as a bumptious corporate lawyer. Neville Higgs could always be counted on to appear whenever the family was acquiring a new site or purchasing another business, never forgetting to have his firm's logo prominently displayed in the background. Just last month, he had told reporters about the imminent purchase of a large dairy farm in the parish of Westmoreland. Crime was not really his arena, but the attorney was not one to let an opportunity for public exposure go begging.

Beside them stood Lester, whose bruised face still looked decidedly unphotogenic, making it a massive draw to rabid photojournalists. Shots of him in this state had never been obtained before and probably never would again. Large, furry microphones of varying colours were inches from the faces of each person and adjusted to satisfactory heights. Preddy was surprised that the family felt it necessary to hold a press conference so soon. The public perception would likely be that the police and the family were on different sides, particularly as no senior representative from the force was invited or present. It was inevitable that the public would side with the family when they were looking at walking-talking evidence of police negligence.

The detective was glad he was watching the proceedings from the comfort of his home and not in the station, or anywhere else, with Superintendent Brownlow or Commissioner Davis. Wherever the brass were, they would be glued to TV screens with their media consultants, identifying claims to rebuff and working on statements that would sound positive and reassuring to the public.

Preddy scribbled short notes as the participants spoke. The lawyer elaborated on the terrible and tragic situation in which the family now found themselves, with the murder of their youngest son and the assault on the elder. He appealed to the public to contact the police with any information they had on the murder. This pleased the detective, until the lawyer said that if the public were afraid of contacting the police, they should contact his law firm, Higgs & Partners instead. Preddy's scowl deepened as Higgs went on to criticise the police for allowing Lester to be assaulted while in their custody and invited the police commissioner to carry out a swift and unbiased investigation into the matter.

Thankfully, the family acceded to the police request not to offer a reward at this stage. Preddy had no doubt that any reward would have been sizeable and attracted hundreds of unwanted calls. He did not have the resources to deal with the volume of work his team would be under and they could do without the added distraction of idle callers. The family had warned that if the police investigation did not proceed satisfactorily they would revisit their position about the reward.

Preddy was also grateful that the broadcasters had refrained from giving a description of the suspect vehicle. There was no reason for the murderer to be alerted that the police had a lead. It had been a hard sell, because the reporters had arrived on the scene at pretty much the same time as the officers and knew about the car.

When invited to speak, Lester rearranged the microphones closest to him and pointed at his damaged face. "You see this? I was attacked, punched in the side of the face for no reason! I was just standing near the cell bars trying to get the attention of an officer, as I wanted a glass of water. No officer responded to my calls! None of them!"

"Did you see who hit you?" asked a reporter.

"No, I did not see the face of my attacker. There were three other men in the cell occupying two bunk beds. All of them appeared to be asleep when the officer threw me in there, although I think I saw someone move on the top bunk of one bed. After a while, I heard the sound of feet thudding to the floor behind me, but before I could spin around I received a blow to the face, which made me dizzy, you know?"

"And what happened after that?"

Lester frowned. "I don't know much about what happened after that, except I felt a further blow to my face that hurt my jaw. I must have passed out. For how long I couldn't tell you, but when I came to, I was lying on the lower bunk with pain shooting through my head and an officer standing over me."

Preddy had already heard that the prime suspect among the cellmates had denied beating Lester. The man said he was barely awake and did not even see who had joined them in the cell. His bruised knuckles did not support his pleas of innocence, but the duty solicitor insisted that his client's injuries were caused earlier when a police officer had dragged the suspect from his bicycle and he had fallen onto the concrete pavement. The lawyer insisted that his client's only offence was telling the officer not to call him "bwoy" when the officer had used the derogatory term to get his attention.

The other two inmates both denied all knowledge of any altercation. One claimed to have been too drunk to even remember the night in question. He only knew of his incarceration because his cousins who bailed him out told him about it once he had sobered up at home. The other inmate seemed to be borderline schizophrenic and spoke non-stop when questioned. Unfortunately, his answers bore no relevance to the questions asked and included a lot of references to rat poison and matches. It was clear that he would not be a credible witness and Preddy felt some discomfort about how any of these men came to be locked up in the beginning.

Preddy had ascertained that Officer Wilson was on the desk and Officer Nembhard patrolling the cells at the time the brothers were brought into Pelican Walk police station. Apart from his own team of detectives, the other officers at Pelican Walk were not under Preddy's direct control, yet as the highest ranked officer at the station, he did offer them all assistance and guidance when necessary. All attempts to obtain information from Wilson and Nembhard were thwarted, because Nembhard insisted that he had to attend an all-day prayer meeting and Wilson had declared himself ill. Preddy was deeply annoyed, but as neither man was assigned to any of his cases, he could not order them to return his calls. Religion and sickness were two ruses commonly used by officers who felt entitled to a day of rest, regardless of what was going on in the island. He had already phoned the superintendent to warn him of this snag and they agreed that no officers' names or details would be released to the press and no assumptions would be made about what did or did not happen. Still, Preddy felt slight unease about what the superintendent and commissioner would actually say in public.

When the press conference was over, Preddy watched it again on DVR. He hastily completed his initial report and emailed it to his superiors, hoping that it would be satisfactory for the time being. There were still unanswered questions, not least of which was the identity of the person who had really committed the assault on Lester Chin Ellis, although he had a feeling that the man with the bruised knuckles would eventually make a full confession.

The detective realised he had not eaten a thing all day, which might explain why his temples were pulsating unabated. The rich smells emanating from the kitchen reminded him that the domestic helper had cooked a meal earlier on. An advert came over the airwaves as he made his way to the stove and he grinned as he scooped up his food. "What are you wearing 'Jake from State Farm'?" He never got tired of that one. Soon he was re-seated with a plate of rice and peas, curried chicken and macaroni cheese, which he doused in hot pepper sauce.

The next news story told of an argument between two teenage cousins over the leaving of an empty ice-tray in the freezer compartment of their home. This resulted in the death of one cousin as the other had ended up stabbing him three times with an ice pick. Although the killer had desperately hailed a taxi and taken his victim to hospital, it had been too late.

The detective shook his head and switched to CVM, the other local news channel, where he found more on the Chin Ellis incident. A rent-a-mouth academic lawyer was confidently proclaiming that Lester should sue the government for damages as the police owed him a duty of care and had clearly failed to live up to their responsibilities. *As if the Chin Ellis family needed any encouragement from a non-practising phoney when their own arrogant lawyer had no doubt got the monetary aspect covered*, thought Preddy. The academic opined that badly needed investment in the island would now be at stake, because investors would be scared off if they thought the police were ineffective at crime-solving or, even worse, complicit in crimes.

The camera then panned to a vox pop being conducted in the streets relating to the safety of police stations. Those locals who were unperturbed by the microphone and eager for their few minutes of fame used the opportunity to berate the police and to claim that this had happened before and would happen again. The detective gritted his teeth when one interviewee said that the lock-ups islandwide were not fit for purpose and Preddy had a feeling that the person had a more in-depth knowledge of the force than the everyday man on the street. Behind the scenes, INDECOM, the Independent Commission of Investigations charged with investigating police behaviour, would be keeping a close eye on the case and Preddy hoped that any conclusion they reached would match his own. The officers had clearly taken their eyes off the ball, but they were not bad men.

He turned down the set and made a call to his ex-wife, who lived in Runaway Bay with their teenage children, Annalee and Roman. The children were at Karate class, although they were due to return home shortly. Since it was the summer holiday, he liked to have them stay with him for a few days each week when work permitted.

"Sorry, I can't have dem over tomorrow," he apologised. Expressing this regret was nothing new. She used to complain that there was no point planning for family weekends away and she was right, as inevitably something would come up and he would never refuse the call of duty. "Things get heavy at work so dem going need to wait a while."

"Dey will understand," she said sympathetically. "Everybody hear de news, you know. Is long time I don't go past Pelican Walk station and see it dere now pon TV. Dem need to fix up de place man, and put little paint pon it."

Preddy allowed himself a wry smile. A man had been assaulted inside. The cracked windows and the flakiness of the blue and cream paint outside were unlikely to concern the brass or the public half as much, but trust his ex-wife to focus on the small things.

"I'll mention it," he lied. "Tell de kids to call me before dey go to bed."

"Alright, dem soon come. I hope you not going talk to dem 'bout no murder?"

Preddy clenched the phone hard and kept his voice even. "I want dem to get a good night's sleep, so no, I won't be doing dat."

"I know dem going want to watch de ten o'clock news to see if you on dere."

"Dey can watch it," he said. "I won't be on dere, but de commissioner should be and maybe even de security minister himself. Let dem watch."

* * *

Commissioner Davis stood with hands placed firmly on the podium, wearing his best "trust me" face and his official khaki suit. He had made sure to apply foundation and concealer before getting in front of the TV cameras. If he was going to be lambasted by the talking heads, he would at least make sure it was not for his appearance. He surveyed the eager press correspondents with his chin held high, glasses resting on his nose. A lot of them he knew well and trusted. There were one or two he knew well enough not to trust and there were others he had never seen before. Beside the commissioner stood Superintendent Brownlow, looking equally resolute and prepared to defend the honour of his men if necessary.

Preening his chest, the commissioner started off by denouncing the assault on Lester Chin Ellis and then informed the viewers that he had called for a complete review of all lock-ups in each parish. Preddy groaned inwardly. Not this again. He imagined that at that very moment a chorus of outrage was echoing throughout all the police stations on the island. Everyone already knew the state of the lock-ups and no complete islandwide review was remotely necessary.

Some of the smaller stations were so old they were burgled repeatedly as thieves easily made their way in by prising rotten iron bars from the windows or removing rusty zinc from the roof, and leaving with any electronic equipment they could find. A few stations had CCTV cameras in lobbies, cells and interview rooms. Those fortunate enough to have them, regularly complained that they malfunctioned, froze or showed grainy images. A lot of stations, particularly the rural ones, did not have even one CCTV camera anywhere on the premises. There was not one single station that had not previously reported shortage of space, broken furniture and crumbling ceilings.

The detective clearly recalled that a complete review had been ordered two years ago when a policewoman in the parish of Hanover had fallen through a rotten ceiling and landed in an interview room downstairs, surprising both the interviewer and the suspect bag-snatcher, who moments earlier had uttered the fateful words "Jah lick me down if a lie me a tell!" Terrified, he had confessed his guilt after picking himself up and dusting himself off. The shocked policewoman had ended up in hospital for two weeks with a broken ankle, fractured rib cage and multiple bruises.

Most of the public would be appalled to see the conditions under which the men and women who were charged to protect and serve spent their time. Preddy thought about the new mahogany desk that was placed on the detectives' open-plan floor the day before Sean Harris arrived from Glasgow. Everyone had their eyes on it, but it was promptly allocated to the secondee along with a matching chair. The only reason the white man did not get his own office was due to the lack of space. The detective was thankful that his team had not responded negatively to this open display of favouritism. Instead they treated it as a joke and discussed whether bleaching their skins and sending photos to the commissioner could get the whole station refurbished.

Camera lights flashed as the commissioner declared, "Our main responsibility is to make sure we have an effective and efficient police service in this island. We want the public to have confidence that we are here to protect and serve them, and that what happened in Pelican Walk early this morning is not the norm in St James or anywhere else in Jamaica. We will be looking at what needs to be done to avoid any further repeat, what training has to be implemented and how much it will cost. We already have a comprehensive approach to policing and we will build upon it. Rest assured that we will monitor the performance of the entire Jamaica Constabulary Force to ensure that the agreed objectives are being met."

A reporter whom the commissioner did not recognise challenged him. "Commissioner, what is going to happen to those officers who cannot or do not comply? Year after year, the public complains about police behaviour and yet no officers ever appear to be dismissed."

"As you must know, the JCF operates under considerable pressure for many reasons, not least of which are budgetary restraints and the need to make significant savings. There would be no point in us jumping to dismiss officers and then using taxpayers' money to pay wrongful or unfair dismissal lawsuits. Legal representation does not come cheap."

The commissioner turned away from the reporter and focused his attention back on the amassed gathering. "We are fully committed, *fully committed*, I say, to maintaining high performance levels despite internal and external challenges faced by officers."

Another reporter whom the commissioner did recognise got to his feet. "Commissioner, would you say that overall the public have begun to lose confidence in the police service?"

"No, Edwin. You and I have discussed this before," he replied. "We will keep pursuing our goal to reduce crime levels and ensure that people feel safe and satisfied with the service we provide. The Jamaican people must know and accept, however, that we cannot effectively do our work without public support."

"Are you ready to charge anyone with the assault on Lester Chin Ellis?"

"That investigation will be concluded as swiftly as possible, of that you can be sure," said Commissioner Davis confidently. "Persons will be interviewed in a timely manner and statements will be taken."

"What about the murder of Carter Chin Ellis? Can you tell us anything about where you are with that?"

The commissioner looked at the superintendent, who quickly leaned towards his microphone. "At this time we have no comment to make as the investigation has just commenced," said the superintendent. "What we would like to repeat is our sincere heartfelt condolences to the Chin Ellis family on their tragic loss. As the commissioner said, we cannot do our jobs without the public, and I would invite any member of the public who has any information on the matter to contact the police in confidence."

Preddy felt a twist in his stomach as he wondered whether a scapegoat would eventually be needed in this instance and whether they would come after him again. Maybe they would get him this time. Gaining notoriety as a police officer in Jamaica was one thing, attracting the attention of the international media was quite another. It was true that the high command would not want to fight legal battles with their officers, but they were not above reaching a private compromise with officers they wanted out of the force. As a high-ranking detective, Preddy's position meant the world to him and everything else jostled for a secondary position. Even when he was not physically at work, his mind was usually on the job. He was by no means ready to be pensioned off or otherwise disposed of. He would have to nail the murderer of Carter Chin Ellis or die trying.

CHAPTER 5

Monday, 20 July, 8.00 a.m.

Morning dawned blue and bright, with no indication that all was not well in Montego Bay. The start of the working week was an ordinary day for many, but for the detectives who worked around the clock it would be yet another hectic day. Although it was only eight o'clock, the sun was already making its intense presence felt. Having managed to fit in an early morning jog, Preddy had returned home to steep a handful of ganja leaves in boiling water with a dash of sugar. Now he could feel the adrenalin pumping through his veins, reminding him that his passion for the job would never diminish, whatever the challenges.

Preddy drove the four miles from his home with the air conditioner on full blast and arrived at Pelican Walk ready to tackle whatever was thrown at him. He climbed the stairs two at a time, as usual, and strode into the meeting room where his presence was awaited. Inside were the two officers who had arrested the Chin Ellis brothers in the early hours of Sunday morning — Oneil Timmins and Everton Franklin. Detectives Spence, Harris and Rabino were at the other end of the room talking quietly together. Preddy placed his briefcase on the table and began to greet the occupants. Within a few seconds, his eyes filled with water and his throat constricted. He quickly backed out of the room and, from a safe distance, peered inside.

"What is dat smell? Does anybody else feel like deir eyes burning?"

Spence looked at Rabino and grinned. "You lucky you never come in here earlier, sir. De place so grey, you woulda blind!"

"If you never choked to death first," added Rabino, fanning her face with a notebook.

"Sorry, sir," stammered Harris, his pale face rapidly turning a bright shade of red. "I sprayed some mosquito repellent . . . maybe tae much?"

"Oh," said Preddy from the doorway, "well . . . er, next time, Detective, I think we should agree dat if de room gets sprayed it has to be done at least twenty minutes before anybody enters. Is dat okay?"

"Aye, sir. I do apologise."

"Guess you won't need a mint, sir?" said Spence.

"I'm okay." Preddy coughed a bit as the potent chemicals dried out his throat. He re-entered the room and stared pointedly at the two arresting officers. "Timmins, Franklin. Let's hear it. What happened?"

"First of all, we never do anything to either of dem, sir. Carter Chin Ellis was released without charge because his blood alcohol test was borderline and he apologised for his behaviour," explained Timmins, the shorter officer. "We had a diplomatic chat wid him in reception. He was very polite and humble and we saw no reason to charge him."

"Except de drugs," said Spence.

"At dat time we never know 'bout any drugs," Timmins responded. "We never search de car."

His colleague Franklin continued, "He asked if Lester could be let go just dis once. I said no. I told him his brother could apply for bail before de magistrate on Monday morning and he, Carter, could come back Monday wid enough cash for bail."

"Carter asked if someone could take him back to him car." Timmins looked sheepish. "I told him we don't offer chauffeur service, he should call his daddy. De last thing I saw was him trying to hail a taxi."

"Did you see a taxi pick Carter up?" asked Preddy.

"No, sir. When I next looked out of de window, he was gone," Timmins replied.

Preddy stared him down. "Why we never let Lester out on station bail though? Why him have to wait till Monday for magistrate?"

Timmins and Franklin exchanged glances. "Sir, you would have to have been dere to understand," said Franklin earnestly. "Lester Chin Ellis was feisty, cursing and swearing. Passing all kinds of dirty remarks 'bout we. He was not cooperating wid us and his blood alcohol test was way over de limit."

Timmins said, "I heard Lester tell Carter not to call de family lawyer, because de lawyer would report everything to de old people. Carter said he would find a lawyer for him because if he represented himself he wouldn't get bail or de bail would set at a hundred million dollars. Dey were laughing and joking. Nothing was wrong at all, sir."

And now something was. Preddy stared up at the stripping ply board ceiling, noting that even more of the plasterwork had come away since the last heavy rains. They needed a good roofer to add a new temporary zinc barrier until money could be found for decent storm-proof tiles. The last cut-price roofer clearly knew nothing about securing property from the powerful elements.

Preddy sighed deeply. He could not record that Lester had been mouthy and disrespectful. The report was bound to end up in unfriendly hands eager to divulge to the public exactly how vexed officers took revenge on the insolent. Twenty-four hours inside inhospitable cells normally cured the exuberance of even the most arrogant of detainees. There were tales of phantom beatings delivered by inmates and officers, but it had never happened at Pelican Walk and would never be tolerated on his watch.

The detective returned his gaze to the two officers. Permission had been granted to check their disciplinary records and he vowed to do so as soon as the files arrived on his desk. He was aware that a lot of people viewed the police as licensed thugs, and suspicion of involvement in the beating and the murder would quickly move towards the officers, even as they protested their innocence.

"What happened after Carter left?" asked Preddy.

"We went back out on duty shortly after, sir. Opposite direction to Red Hills too . . . Lilliput way," Timmins replied. "We never go anywhere near Lester and we never tell anybody to do him anything. We never follow Carter and shoot him."

Preddy did not know Timmins well enough to be able to judge his honesty and he was not picking up any vibes one way or the other. "Which officers did you see in de station when you got here wid dem?"

Timmins looked thoughtful. "Most of de officers were out. Dere was a disturbance up de road when a gas tanker caught fire. It was a busy night, sir. Wilson was on de front desk and Nembhard was around, too. I didn't see anybody else. Both of dem will tell you dat dere was nothing wrong wid either of de Chin Ellis brothers when Franklin and I left here."

"Is it true dat you refused to give dem your name?" asked Preddy.

Timmins glanced at the floor. "What, sir?"

"Lester Chin Ellis was on TV last night claiming dat you both refused to give your names."

"No, sir," replied Timmins, shaking his head from side to side. "Nobody asked us 'bout any name."

"No, sir," agreed Franklin. "Nothing 'bout name was mentioned."

Preddy allowed the two officers to leave and then turned to Detective Harris. "Can we get reports from Nembhard and Wilson? Interview dem separately, please. I have a feeling I should have done just dat wid those two."

"They're naw indisposed today then, sir?" asked Harris.

"I passed Wilson downstairs," Preddy replied. "Nembhard should be around somewhere. He couldn't still be praying to him God all now."

"I'll make a report of what de officers just said," offered Spence.

"Thank you," said Preddy. "Rabino, you're wid Harris. I need to go meet de Chin Ellis family."

"I wouldnae mind meeting Mr and Mrs Chin Ellis," said Harris, getting to his feet.

A taut smile appeared on Preddy's face. Rabino and Spence exchanged knowing glances.

Preddy picked up his notebook and keys. "Nembhard and Wilson are tired of me, Detective Harris, I'm sure dey will welcome a fresh face and new voice."

"Just like we do," said Rabino with a friendly look in the Scotsman's direction.

"Heh," muttered Spence.

"Later, people," said Preddy.

* * *

Detective Preddy drove west along the busy Top Road on his way to interview the Chin Ellis parents. The road's official name was The Queen's Drive, but no true Montegonian ever called it that. Its highest point was at least eighty feet above sea level. From this high vantage point he could see some parts of the low-lying Gloucester Avenue, more commonly known by the locals as Bottom Road, or by the uninitiated, tourists mainly, as the Hip Strip.

As he drove, he caught glimpses of the foam-covered waves toppling over each other and melting back into the sea. The magnificent view was blocked in part by high walls, dense foliage and long-abandoned independent hotels that failed to compete with the coastline chain hotels and their all-inclusive offerings. With towering water slides and bouncy diving boards in the sea, scuba diving, water ski-ing and sailing, they were a big draw. And then there was the copious amounts of food and drink around the clock. It was little wonder the visitors left their cold, rat-race lifestyles behind and flocked to the water front. Preddy could only hope that the tourists made it their business to venture out leaving the man-made entertainment behind and see some of the natural attractions of the island, the mountains, caves, mineral springs and waterfalls.

As he rounded a corner on his final approach towards his destination, he absorbed his favourite view of Montego Bay: the Freeport area, which stood out on a reclaimed peninsula in the middle of the blue-green sea. The most conspicuous buildings on the Freeport were the oatmeal-coloured twin towers of the exclusive Sunscape Splash hotel, surrounded by an impressive array of upmarket residential apartment blocks and townhouses. Behind the accommodations, the undulat-ing green hills and mountains created the perfect backdrop to the scene. Yachts, catamarans and kayaks navigated the waters around the Freeport, which also served cargo freighters and cruise liners all year round. Within seconds the remarkable view was gone as Top Road started its decline until it joined the low coastal boulevard that led to the Freeport itself.

Soon he was heading into the luxury oceanfront com-munity that was the Doubloons. The protected enclave of the wealthiest of residents, who had worked hard for their comfort, security and peace of mind. A beautiful area, where the water appeared to change colour depending on where one stood. In some places a spectacular greenish blue, in others almost a transparent light blue, and elsewhere a dark navy blue. Preddy's eyes were now drawn upwards to the surrounding hills rising from the earth, dark green, thick vegetation interspersed with three-storey mansions. Probably the only place in Jamaica where the super-rich surveyed the equally rich down below with no hint of property envy. The higher-ups enjoyed an uninterrupted view of both land and sea, yet were far enough away to avoid the hustle and bustle of the port.

The multi-million-dollar Doubloons villas came complete with a security guard outpost manned twenty-four hours a day. A shaved head attached to a uniformed body appeared as soon as Preddy's unmarked vehicle rolled close to the entrance. The detective turned off his air conditioner, wound down his window and waved his badge at the man who raised the long iron pole barricade. Preddy slowly drove past a few sprawling properties and eventually pulled up at the Chin Ellis home.

It certainly met the description he had been given. Even from outside it was staggeringly large, with two double garages and plenty of parking spaces for a dozen more cars, as well as a helipad. There was an annex to one side, which he supposed was the helpers' quarters that all villas appeared to have as standard, usually home to a maid and or a gardener. The only relatively small structure on the premises was the swimming pool, although Preddy wondered why they needed a pool at all when the house was mere footsteps from this extraordinary beach. Beside the pool was a thatched bar and next to it a steel drum cut in half, lined with charcoal, and covered with a barbecue grill. Plenty of jerked meats were surely prepared right there.

A detached building appeared to be a guest cottage strategically placed right on the beach so that it was possible to sit on the floor of the verandah and relax with both feet emerged in the warm sea water. There were no animals to be seen. Although many Jamaicans kept dogs for protection and to alert them to intruders, Preddy suspected that several of the Doubloons residents were well-armed themselves.

The detective pressed the bell, listening to the loud chimes reverberating behind the huge mahogany door. A closed door: pain on one side, apprehension on the other. He enjoyed the intellectual challenge of his job, gathering of evidence, investigating, teamwork and the satisfaction that came with solving a troubling case. The dark moments were many.

41

They came when faced with gun-toting criminals equipped with better fire power, when a jury gave an astounding "not guilty" verdict, when sentences handed down to the guilty were ludicrously light. And then there was this, discussing the deceased with distraught relatives.

The door was opened by the patriarch, Terence Chin Ellis, who greeted him with a scant glance through glazed eyes and a handshake. As he entered, Preddy looked around the grand entrance, admiring the exquisite interior, professionally laid-out minimalist furniture and decorative floral arrangements. The few sculptures in the hall were clearly artist-commissioned statement pieces. He recognised the engraved names of some of the artists from exhibitions he had attended at the art gallery in the city centre.

There were plenty of family photographs throughout the hallway, some of the whole family, some featuring just the two sons. Photographs of them as young children, teenagers and, eventually, as adults. Plaques of awards won by the family business were on prominent display in the sitting room.

"Take a seat, Detective," murmured Terence. "Ida is getting some drinks. I'll just go and help her."

Preddy preferred to study the surroundings instead. It was unusual for any business to successfully serve the rich as well as the less well-off, but Chinchillerz catered for those with money to burn as well as those without bank accounts. Visiting ambassadors, dignitaries and politicians all received the elite food service. The company supplied five-star hotels with luxury ice creams and any type of frozen dessert required, made from local cows' milk, fresh fruits, pure cane sugar, herbs, nuts and vegetables. For the standard products sold in the lower budget range, the company substituted powdered milk for fresh milk and used imitation flavourings instead of the real thing. They supplied products for grand openings as well as for national sporting events, school fairs and church cookouts.

All this from the fine fruits of an abundant land, Preddy thought. His children were doing reasonably well academically, although Roman had a tendency to stray from homework and concentrate on sports too much. They had not yet set any real career goals for themselves and, as most teens, they were mainly focused on today. Already, Preddy was beginning to think he should encourage them to become entrepreneurs rather than to work for other people. Then again, modern day empire-building in Jamaica took a great deal of money and he would no doubt be expected to provide it.

The detective pulled out a chair from under the dining room table and turned it to face the sofa on which now sat the gilded home owners. He was not one for sitting on a sofa to interview people as it made him feel more relaxed than he should be. Reclining or sampling home comforts did not square well with the need to be alert and it always raised concerns when interviewees offered him beer or rum punch, even if they were just being hospitable. Luckily, Ida Chin Ellis had only placed a long glass of ice-cold orange juice in front of him.

She must be in her late fifties, he mused, looking at her unlined face, *and still an attractive woman*. Her eyes were hooded, which he put down to a lack of sleep and crying. Her natural, greying black hair was held together with a single plait, which was tied up in a bun at the nape of her neck. She sat kneading her hands in her lap.

"I know dis is very hard for you, but dere are a few questions I need to ask," started Preddy. "Anything you can tell me to help wid de investigation will be good."

"We have both spoken about it, Detective," Terence said wearily, glancing at his wife. "Sometimes I feel like my head is going to burst. We don't know who would want to kill Carter."

Preddy nodded sympathetically in his direction. Terence had strong East Asian features with thinning, grey hair, pale brown, almost-white skin, very narrow eyes and extremely thin lips. The detective could only recall seeing photographs of Terence in the business pages, never in the social pages.

Indeed, Terence Chin had been happy to promote Ida Ellis as chief spokesperson for the business empire, while encouraging his sons to enjoy the social limelight. It was common knowledge that his parents had not welcomed his choice of bride at first, preferring for him to choose "one of his own," but with her strong work ethic and keen belief in family, Ida had gradually won them around. The merger of surnames was for sound social as well as business reasons and Terence liked to introduce himself as Mr Ellis, as there were more than enough Chins on the island. This did not deter the locals from addressing him as "Misser Chin" and his wife as "Miss Chin," but he had long accepted that this was inevitable. Even if his surname had been Lee, Sang or Yin, the Jamaicans would still have called him "Misser Chin."

Photographs of Terence around the house allowed Preddy to see a man with a cheerful and approachable disposition. At this particular point in time, he understandably looked strained and totally disconnected. The detective flipped open his well-worn notebook.

"We have also considered whether anyone had issues wid Lester. As you know, Carter was driving Lester's car and it could be dat de gunman thought he was Lester," said Preddy.

The couple looked at each other briefly before turning their attention back to the detective.

"No, sir." Ida looked taken aback. Her voice was very soft. "Those boys will have their secrets like everybody else, but I never saw or heard about any of them at war with anybody."

"They don't keep bad company," Terence agreed.

"How often did dey come here to visit you?" asked Preddy.

"They come most weekends, you know," said Ida, breaking into a weak smile. "Sunday morning they go to church with us then eat a big dinner with us. Later in the evening, they and their friends usually go down by the beach house and play music and do young people things."

"So dere is nobody you can think of dat might have a grudge against either of your sons? Any friend dey might have fallen out wid recently?"

Ida shook her head and lowered her eyes, lost in thought. Her husband kept his focus on the detective. "There was that racing driver he was competing with. What's his name again? Oh yes, Kirk Grantham."

"Can you tell me more about him?"

"Carter and Kirk were rival members of the Race Drivers Club for motor car drivers, you know? There had been fierce competition between the two of them for years. Both wanted to be champion driver of the year and there were only a few more races to go in this season." Terence shook his head as he spoke and Ida took his hand, rubbing it gently. "Carter won the championship two years ago, and Kirk got it last year. Carter was just ahead of Kirk on points this season and I saw that bad blood was developing between them."

"Did dey ever fight?" asked Preddy.

"Not a fist fight. A brief sort of scuffle did break out between them after the last race a month ago, when Kirk followed Carter underneath the sponsors' marquee to curse him. Kirk said Carter tried to cut him up on the track in a dangerous move that could have ended his life." Terence stared ahead as if picturing the scene. "Carter brushed him off. Carter said it was a fair move and that there would not have been any danger if Kirk was able to handle his car like a real man. That really riled Kirk! I'm not too sure who started the fuss, but it was just pushing, shoving and shouting."

"Have dere been any other incidents since den?" asked Preddy.

"They've met only one time since then, at a party, although they didn't acknowledge each other." Terence dabbed his eyes. "I told him to shake hands with Kirk and let bygones be bygones, but he refused. He said that when he won the championship he would shake Kirk's hand and wave the trophy in his face."

Ida looked at her husband. "You didn't tell me any of this," she said in an accusatory tone. "You didn't remember to?"

"I remembered, yes," he replied quietly. "But I would have never told you anything. I didn't want to worry you and anyway, boys will be boys."

"Do you think he could have killed my son, Detective?" Ida asked tentatively.

"We will certainly look into all leads, ma'am."

The couple could think of nothing else to tell Preddy despite his gentle coaxing. The detective closed his notebook and stood. The matriarch walked him back through the long reception hall towards the front door. He moved to shake her hand and she clutched his with both of hers. Her hands felt surprisingly strong, although her small frame suggested she was not that powerful.

"Please find whoever did this to my son, Detective. Please."

"We will do our very best to get justice for Carter. You can trust me on dat," Preddy promised. He glanced up the stairs. "Would you mind if I take a quick look around your son's bedroom?"

"Yes, you can look." Ida turned her head over her shoulder and shouted, "Miss Janie, where are you?"

A short, plump lady entered the room and looked in the direction of her employer. "Yes, Miss Ida?"

"Show the gentleman to Carter's room."

Preddy started to follow the maid upstairs before turning around briefly. "Oh, do either of your sons have life insurance policies?"

"No, Detective, that was something we all discussed years ago but didn't bother with. Not even Terence or I have any." Her eyes darkened suddenly. "We're not going to kill each other over money, Detective Preddy."

Even millionaires kill each other over money, he thought, but he just nodded and continued up the stairs. Carter's bedroom was extremely spacious with a stunning en-suite bathroom. Preddy's own bedroom was reasonably large, but this was more than twice its size. The king-size bed looked strangely small in the vast expanse of whiteness surrounding it. The room was extremely neat and Preddy suspected that the maid was tasked with giving it a thorough cleaning before Carter's return each weekend. At the bedside table, Preddy bent and retrieved a photograph that had been set face down with a

46

paperweight on top of it. The photograph was of Carter and a pretty Black female laughing with their heads close together.

"Who is dis?" he asked.

The maid craned her neck and peered around Preddy's broad shoulders. "A Zadie dem call her. Me call her Miss Merton. Is Carter girlfriend."

Preddy straightened up, holding the picture. He had not heard from Zadie Merton, and usually girlfriends tried to find out what the police were doing about the murder of their other halves. She had not appeared at the family press conference either. He held onto the photo and continued to browse through the room, his every move watched by the hovering woman. Eventually, he closed the door and glanced at the open door opposite.

"Is dis Lester's room?"

"Yes, is Misser Lester room."

Preddy put his head around the door. It looked quite similar to that of his younger brother, oversized and very white. There were photographs of Lester and Carter, and Lester and friends, both male and female. Lester posing happily with a smiling Terence beside classic cars, on the steps of a small plane and in front of a superyacht. Preddy stepped inside to take a closer look. A large model glider sat on a long shelf, surrounded by aviation books and maps. On a coffee table sat aviation glasses, a few recipe cards, religious tracts and personal finance books. The detective thumbed through one book and replaced it.

The maid looked on uneasily. "Misser Lester don't love when anybody trouble him things, you know."

"Yes, I understand," said Preddy, retreating from the room. "Oh, and don't worry, I'll ask Miss Ida about keeping de photograph."

CHAPTER 6

"We've got a possible lead on the suspect's vehicle, sir. Look at this guy, Marcus Darnay," said Harris, swivelling around in his brand new chair, oblivious to the jealous stares of the detectives across the open-plan floor. "Lives right here in Mo Bay. Seems tae have quite a criminal record."

"Dat name is familiar," said Preddy, as he walked towards the Scotsman.

"Looks like a right dodgy so and so," added Harris.

"Well, we won't judge him on whether he can enter Mr Universe, Detective," replied Preddy with a tight smile.

Preddy stood over Harris's shoulder looking at the heavy set, insolent face that filled the computer monitor. The tiny dreadlocks, the wide eyes set far apart over a broad nose bridge, the square stubble jaw. Marcus Darnay was a drug dealer who once referred to himself on customs documents as a pharmaceutical entrepreneur. Here was a man who was intimately acquainted with the criminal justice system and known to all the local judges. Incarcerated more than once for drug-related offences, and a few times for theft, he always seemed to spend little time in jail.

It was deeply frustrating to Preddy that the police force went to great lengths to apprehend criminals like Darnay only for the courts to fail to give them the sentences they deserved. Sometimes it was the prosecution who blundered and the defence would scupper what should have been a straightforward cruise to conviction. Past experience taught the detective that there was no point insisting on a prosecution with purely circumstantial evidence as the jury would rarely, if ever, bite. Their demand for real evidence was based partly on mistrust of police and Preddy knew that the JCF had no-one to blame but themselves.

There had been no suggestion of Darnay being involved in a murder before, but this was the natural progression for some hardcore criminals, particularly where drugs were involved.

"Darnay owns a silver Subaru Outback matching the description with a license plate starting six four seven one," said Harris.

"Do we know where he is?" asked Preddy.

Harris smiled. "Aye. Invited him in for a chat and he agreed tae come."

Preddy looked surprised. "Dat should be something. Darnay turning up voluntarily to speak to de police."

"Well, we won't judge him, will we, sir," said Harris.

Preddy was not sure if he detected a snide tone in the Scotsman's voice and decided to ignore it. With that strong accent anything could be misconstrued.

"Maybe he has turned over a new leaf, sir?" suggested Harris.

"Not Darnay, he is a career criminal," replied Preddy, shaking his head. "He'll just have moved on to de next type of profitable crime."

"I told him tae ask for Detective Spence when he comes in."

"Och, did ye now?" Spence turned to face the man who had taken to delegating interviewees to her and her expression could not be described as friendly.

Harris gave her an apologetic look. "Sorry, I forgot tae tell ye."

"What time are we expecting him?" asked Preddy.

"In about an hour, sir," said Harris. "I'll be down at the lab though, if that's okay with ye?"

* * *

Preddy was on the lookout for Darnay and was disappointed to see the suspect turn up in a taxi and not in his own vehicle. It would have been too good to be true. He would need to work much harder than that to get Darnay. He retreated to the sparse interview room to wait for the new arrival. Spence was already seated and drumming her fingers on the off-white plastic table. Preddy sat in the empty matching chair beside her and positioned another one on the opposite side of the table.

"Me 'fraid to come to dis place, you know," Darnay announced sarcastically, staring at Preddy as he sidled through the door and took up a seat. "Me never bring a bodyguard and me know dat you will beat me, kill me."

"You are perfectly safe here, Mr Darnay. You have my word," Preddy replied.

"I don't want your word, Misser Police Officer, 'cause I know what it good fah," Darnay retorted. "Everybody done know say you a Dirty Harry!"

Preddy was used to this and did not flinch. He held the interviewee's gaze and said nothing. Darnay leaned forward aggressively and Preddy noted two prominent tattoos on his arm. Names and birth dates of children he guessed.

"Turn on de TV camera! A dat me want!"

"Dere is a CCTV camera right over your head, Mr Darnay." Spence pointed and Darnay's eyes followed her direction. He was not to know that despite their best efforts the camera rarely recorded properly. "Thank you for coming in to see us. We are glad you could make it."

"I heard dat you want talk to me and I have nutten to hide." Darnay settled back in his chair, jeans-clad legs spread apart, one arm slung over the backrest and the other hovering around his crotch. He leered openly at Spence. "Ask me what you want ask me, natural lady, me well glad fi see you, too."

"We are grateful, Mr Darnay," she smiled at him. Marcus Darnay, God's gift to women because He just couldn't be asked. "Where were you on Saturday night?"

The conversation was largely disappointing. Darnay was at the Orchid Bar all night on Saturday until dawn on Sunday morning. He did not know Carter or Lester personally and denied owning any type of gun. The car, he said, was stolen a few days ago and he had not yet got around to reporting it. Neither of the detectives believed this for a minute, but as it was not a crime to fail to report a stolen vehicle, there was nothing they could do. Preddy wished there was such a crime. If a victim did not have a valid excuse, such as being in hospital or off the island, they should be charged with the crime of failure to report. Too many people were using the convenient excuse of being robbed when asked about their vehicle's involvement in a crime.

According to Darnay, he could always find transportation to get around if he needed to. There were plenty of cars in his garage workshop that were either already fixed or in the process of being fixed when their impoverished owners conceded that they could not pay for the service. Reporting the theft of the car had been the last thing on his mind and he expressed his gratitude to the detectives for reminding him about it.

Preddy was sceptical of Darnay and his garage. The idea that this criminal could ever have a legitimate business was not credible. Darnay was not stupid enough to take the car there and even if he did, it would have been expertly dismantled into a million pieces by now. The detective knew that there were many places off the beaten track where a car could be successfully hidden and there were also many precipices over which it could have been pushed, never to be seen again, so thick and deep was the bush. It could even be at the other end of the island by now, parked up in some remote village where unsuspecting residents walked past it every day. Maybe someone had already painted it and changed the license plates. But then there were the bullet holes. If the Red Hills witness was as good a shot as he thought he was, there would be bullet holes and those were not that easy to disguise.

* * *

Preddy stood in front of the whiteboard in the evidence room. With his black marker he wrote the names of the persons of interest, as Rabino and Spence looked on intently. *Marcus Darnay, Zadie Merton, Kirk Grantham.* He hesitated briefly, and decided against writing down the names of any of the officers at Pelican Walk. The team already knew who they were. There would be too much bad blood if any of the officers discovered that they were under investigation and it would be prudent to file that information in his mind where no feathers could be ruffled and no cliques formed.

"Is Harris not back yet?" asked Preddy, glancing at his watch.

"No, he went to look at Lester's SUV. It's parked up at the lab, sir," Rabino replied.

"Dat white man, you see." Spence kissed her teeth. "Look from when him gone."

"Don't be so mean, he might find evidence," said Rabino with a grin. "He must be good for something or he wouldn't be here."

"So you say." Spence sounded unconvinced. "Foreigner can come here and do as dem please."

Preddy did not take the bait and concentrated on the whiteboard instead. The Glaswegian should have returned by now and Preddy could not imagine what his colleague was still inspecting at this hour.

"Darnay. We need to find his car. Get a clean sweep of dat garage," Preddy tapped the suspect's name. "Can we ensure all parishes know we are on de lookout for dat car?"

He waved a photograph at the team. "Zadie Merton, Carter's girlfriend. A very elusive lady who is not interested in our investigations. Not returning calls to her cell phone. Keep trying her."

"Get dis, sir: Grantham does have a Subaru, too, but a metallic bronze Forrester wid a different registration," said Spence. "Starts wid a four."

"Interesting, Terence Chin Ellis was somewhat suspicious of him," said Preddy.

Rabino tapped her pencil on her notepad. "You can speak to two people who saw the same car drive past them in broad daylight. One will say it was red, the other will swear it was blue. Numbers are always a bit off."

Preddy moved the marker down to Kirk Grantham's name and drew a circle around it. He took out his cell phone and pressed away for a few seconds, studying the large screen. "Hmm. De weather forecast for the next few days is looking fine." He smiled broadly. "Who would like to accompany me for a day at de races on Wednesday?"

"Caymanas Park?" asked Spence, her eyes brightening.

Preddy smiled. "No, not horses, Spence. Nice try."

"Right up my street, sir," said Rabino. "I love all that Formula One stuff."

"Well, it's not quite Formula One," said Preddy.

"She just loves de fine young men and de rippling muscles. De cars don't mean nothing to her," Spence teased. "You'll be able to let dat weave down, and flutter dose lashes, girl! Let it all hang out!"

Rabino laughed and threw a scrunched up sheet of paper at her. "You talk too much! I love watching racing cars."

"Well, I guess dat's settled den," said Preddy.

CHAPTER 7

Wednesday, 22 July, 11.30 a.m.

There was no better place to interview members of the Race Drivers Club than at their primary race course, and for this Preddy and Rabino travelled to an open meet at Dover Race Track just north of Brown's Town in the parish of St Ann. The detectives were indistinguishable from anyone else travelling to Dover. Preddy was comfortably dressed in grey chinos and a short-sleeved bush jacket. Rabino wore blue jeans, a loose T-shirt and tucked her hair away under a broad-brimmed straw hat.

The club had a large and active membership of mainly young, highly competitive males, although there were a few fearless female drivers too. They raced motorcars at over a hundred miles an hour for medals, trophies and the considerable prestige that went with being crowned champion driver of the year. Preddy's eyes moved around the track, noting the families and friends of the drivers milling around near the starting line, wearing T-shirts emblazoned with the subject of their support. Among them were proud, excited fathers eager to watch their offspring demonstrate brawn and exuberance, and anxious mothers, watching with their eyes half-closed most of the time, trying to keep their stomachs from leaping to their chests.

Competing engineers gathered around their team's car, working feverishly on last-minute tinkering to keep the turbo-charged machines on the track. Preddy watched the enthusiasts gather and was pleased to see that the large crowd comprised a good deal of Black Jamaicans as well as the light-skinned people he had expected to find. Out of many, one people and all that.

Some fans stood, others sat on rocks and grass way up on the banking, high-wire fencing preventing them from getting too close to the track below. A variety of coloured umbrellas were dotted throughout the crowds, providing the grateful holders with somewhere to hide from the unrelenting sun. Preddy decided there and then that he would have to bring Roman and Annalee to this remarkable place before the summer was over. The teenagers relied on electronic entertainment way too much.

There was no chance for the detectives to interview Kirk Grantham before the race started, although they had identified him having a pep talk with his team. Kirk had long spotted the detectives, having been advised by his entourage that the police were there asking about him. He had no doubt about what they wanted. The fact that Carter Chin Ellis was gone definitely made the season better for him as far as his chance to claim the championship was concerned. It was inevitable that the detectives would come. He pulled down his helmet and climbed into his car.

The competitors lined up, engines revving and emitting a strong odour of motor oil mixed with petrol. The tricked-out car that Kirk competed in looked nothing like the suspect vehicle and although Rabino had scoured the parking area, she found no trace of the wanted car. The parking attendant informed her that although Kirk did have a Subaru, he had arrived at the race track in a burnt orange jeep driven by his father.

The detectives watched as the flag went up and the race was on. Seven men, one woman, ten laps and lots of gas. The baying crowd waved their arms and blew vuvuzelas loudly. Preddy had planned to try and mingle with the crowd and ask questions, but he had not bargained with the noise generated by the masses as their idols sped around the track. Instead, he tucked his notebook into his pocket and enjoyed the action with everyone else. One glance at Rabino told him that she was enjoying it too, as she stood on tiptoe and tried to keep the lead car in sight. A car managed to run off the track and into a tyre wall, with the driver emerging furious, but unscathed.

Kirk Grantham came in first, as expected, leading the other competitors by a good few seconds. The victor punched the air in delight while his team members hugged each other and cheered loudly. Kirk waved triumphantly at a man who was leaping and giving him the thumbs up. The detectives waited until his enthusiastic supporters had offered their congratulations and begun to filter away before they approached him.

"Kirk Grantham?"

The driver whipped off his helmet and turned to face the police officers. He certainly looked younger than twenty-four and was much smaller and darker than Preddy had imagined, with an appearance more befitting a jockey.

"Yes, that's me."

Kirk took a white towel from his father, who was his aged reflection, and wiped the perspiration from his face. In exchange, the man took the helmet from him and tucked it under his arm. Preddy held up his badge.

"I'm Detective Preddy and dis is my colleague, Detective Rabino. We were hoping we could ask you a few questions."

Kirk Grantham turned and started striding towards his sponsor's tent, beckoning the officers to follow him. "Sure. It's about Carter Chin Ellis, right?"

"You were expecting us?" asked Preddy.

"Well, I knew that somebody was going to call my name at some stage. Me and Carter were always at war . . . racing war, Officer. I had nothing personal against the man."

"Do you own a Subaru Forrester, Mr Grantham?"

"Call me Kirk," he replied pleasantly. "Yes, I do. It's parked at home in Falmouth. Why?"

"Where were you last Saturday night, Kirk?" asked Rabino.

"In Port Antonio with my family. We stayed at a guest house and came back to Mo Bay late on Sunday . . . isn't that right, Dad?"

The older man walked over to his son's side and nodded. "It's true. All of us spent the evening at a restaurant on the marina and then back to the guest house, had a few drinks and off to bed."

"You drove your own car?" asked Rabino.

"Yes, most of the way. Dad took over the wheel from Oracabessa until we reached. What is it about the car?"

"Do you have any idea who might want Carter dead?" asked Preddy, pointedly ignoring the question.

"No, Officer. We were never friends, but he was a good rival to have, you know? He helped me push myself. I'm not glad he's gone at all. The other drivers are good, but they're just not in the same league as Carter."

There was nothing in Kirk's voice or body language that betrayed any emotion towards Carter, and Preddy wondered at the young man's composure. He studied the cool driver who smiled and waved at an adoring female fan blowing kisses at him. Power being the ultimate aphrodisiac Preddy could hardly blame Kirk for making the most of it.

"What did you think about Lester?" asked Preddy.

"Lester?" The smile swiftly disappeared from Kirk's face. "He can't drive to save his life. I was glad when he gave up competing last year, although he still comes down here to annoy us all the time. Telling people how to drive, like he knows anything about cars."

Preddy tried to keep his eyes on Kirk's face, but the young man made a show of using a towel to cover it and rubbing vigorously. "You sound like you don't like him, or is dat putting it too mildly?"

"Nobody likes him. Well, except Carter, Miss Ida and Terence. Terence is a nice man though. I feel sorry for him." Kirk threw the towel towards his father who caught it deftly.

Rabino took out a photograph and held it out. "You know this man?"

Kirk turned his head to look at it. "No. Who is he?"

"His name is Marcus Darnay," she replied.

"Marcus Darnay," Kirk repeated slowly. "No, don't know him."

The elder Grantham took the photo from Rabino. "He looks like somebody I've seen before."

"You can remember where?" asked Preddy.

"No, I'm not so sure." He stared off into the air. "You know what? This guy did come here once, came to look on Carter's car."

"Eeh-eeh? I never saw him," said Kirk.

"Yes, man. This is him. Is he dead?"

"No, Marcus Darnay is very much alive," said Preddy. "When last you see him?"

"It's only one time I saw him and that was a good few months ago now," said Mr Grantham. "Something was wrong with Carter's engine and that man came to look on it, but the team engineer sent him packing."

"Why did he send him away?" asked Rabino. "Darnay is a mechanic, you know?"

The man shrugged. "Not everybody can fix these types of car. A special engine is inside and if you don't know what you're doing, you will make it worse. If you're not on a team, you're not supposed to touch the cars."

Rabino retrieved the photograph and slid it into her pocket. "You know if Darnay and Carter had an argument over the car or anything?"

Grantham senior shook his head. "I never even saw them talking to each other." He looked closely at Rabino. "Look here, your father is the politician Andre Rabino?"

"Not a politician, he's an attaché, but yes, that's my father."

"That's why you sound so speaky-spokey. You sound just like him!"

"I like to think so," Rabino smiled at him. "Thank you very much."

The detectives gave the Granthams their business cards, thanked them for their assistance and left them enjoying well-earned celebratory drinks. The cheers echoed in their ears as they made their way back to their vehicle.

"What are you thinking?" asked Rabino.

"I didn't warm to Kirk Grantham, but I don't think he's our man. He's not de right build, has a good alibi and he's believable," said Preddy as they walked. "De thing is, he clearly has no love for Lester and we can't get past de point dat de gunman may not have known dat his victim was not Lester."

"So Kirk got someone to do it?" Rabino mused. "He has no sympathy, but he grabs me as being just a tiny little guy using a powerful machine to big up his ego and nothing's wrong with that. He didn't come over as a cold-hearted conspirator to a murder though, even if Lester annoyed the hell out of him."

"I agree," said Preddy. "On the other hand what we do know is dat Marcus Darnay is a liar."

Rabino nodded. "We can link Darnay to Carter now. What did Carter do to make Darnay mad enough to kill him?"

"It's not enough. Darnay is no fool and he'll probably say he didn't even know whose car he was looking at," said Preddy, as he removed his car keys from his pocket. "We need more. Wonder if I can get Lester to talk to me?"

Rabino looked sceptical. "He looked well-vexed on TV, sir, what with that big bruise on his face. You really believe he will talk to you?"

"Well, I'll just have to be as humble as possible and see."

Rabino stopped walking and stood hands on hips looking at her superior. "Humble? Really?"

Preddy grinned. "Get into de car, Detective Speaky-Spokey. And don't make me write you up."

Kirk Grantham watched the detectives as their backs disappeared in the distance and wondered how on earth his car had come to be of interest to them. He downed his orange juice, heavily laced with the sponsor's champagne, and wiped his mouth. Maybe it just looked like a criminal's car, although to him it was a suburban family vehicle. He certainly had not seen many like it on the island, not of that shade anyway. Maybe he had better take it back to Port Antonio if it was suddenly going to become hot to the police. The last thing he wanted was police trailing him anywhere and shooting him in a case of mistaken identity. Preddy, he recalled, was known to have a trigger finger and he did not want to be on the other end of the detective's next shooting spree.

CHAPTER 8

When Preddy first met Lester Chin Ellis he was relieved to see that the bruising on his face had reduced considerably. The press would, of course, keep recycling the original photograph as they were only interested in seeing injuries, the more shocking the better, and had little interest in the return of his unblemished features.

"Mr Chin Ellis, I am Detective Raythan Preddy and dis is my colleague Detective Sean Harris. First of all, I again wish to offer our sincere condolences on de death of your brother."

Lester sat across from the two male detectives in the interview room. He was dressed in black jeans with white polo shirt opened down to his chest revealing a thin gold chain. A large designer watch enveloped his left wrist and gold rings adorned two fingers. His black silky hair lay curled against his scalp. He sat upright with arms resting evenly on the table and leaned forward slightly as if preparing to chair a board meeting with his subordinates. He stared at Preddy in silence, barely moving his head.

"On behalf of de entire Pelican Walk community I wish to apologise for de treatment you received here," Preddy continued. "It is our policy to care for de welfare of any persons in our custody and we really regret something went wrong dis time."

"Your lawyer can tell my lawyer what went wrong. You'll soon get the bill too." Lester opened his mouth widely and pointed at a barely chipped tooth. "This alone is going to cost you ninety thousand."

"Sorry to hear about dat. I am sure de lawyers will do deir thing and I truly regret it has come to dis."

"If it's not the police doing the beating, it's the criminals beating up innocent people," complained Lester. "Looks like nobody is safe in this place again. Look at what I got, when all I wanted was a glass of water."

Preddy had already taken a dislike to the pretentious young man. Just hearing him pronounce it "warder" as opposed to "wata" irritated him.

Harris tapped his pen on the table. "Mr Chin Ellis, we were hoping ye might be able tae assist us with our enquiries. Do ye know if Carter had any enemies?"

Lester fixed his eyes firmly on the speaker taking in the vivid red hair and green eyes, then returned his gaze to Preddy. "So, they had to send a white man from foreign to watch you because you can't run things?"

Preddy felt the jab right under his ribcage and it hurt, not least because he wondered the same thing himself. This order to accommodate a foreigner was the first of its kind. Prior to this he could pick and choose who to welcome. Young cadets were sometimes assigned to train with him or his team, usually only for a few weeks during the course of the year. When Superintendent Brownlow had first raised the matter of seconding Harris to Pelican Walk, Preddy had suggested that the Criminal Investigations team based south of the city might be more to the Scotsman's liking. The suggestion was batted aside by a strangely stubborn super-intendent who insisted that Harris had a lot to contribute to Pelican Walk and would work there until such time as Commissioner Davis decided otherwise.

It took some effort for Preddy not to glance sideways at Harris and he half hoped the detective would answer the question for his own benefit. Harris remained silent, his expression blank while twisting his pen between his fingers.

Preddy said, "We welcome whatever assistance we can get, Mr Chin Ellis, wherever it is coming from. Now, can you tell us if you and Carter had any trouble on Saturday night, before . . .."

"How do you mean? Of course, we had trouble! Your officers were the trouble. They dragged us down here for nothing. Talking about drunkenness and assault and some foolishness."

"I was going to say: before you were stopped by de officers. Were you aware of being followed?"

"Yes, by your guys!"

Although Lester's reaction disturbed him, Preddy decided to give him the benefit of the doubt. The recently bereaved could not be second guessed when it came to their behaviour and who knew what internal pain and suffering the young man was enduring.

"We really are trying to help you and your family, so if dere is anything you can tell us?" Preddy coaxed him.

"Anything at all, sir?" added Harris. "We really do want tae catch the killer."

"No, I don't know anything. The only people who seem to have anything against my family are you people. Everybody else knows and loves my family. My family built up Jamaica! You know how many people we employ and train and edu-cate, eeh? You know how many people from foreign want to come do business with us? Everybody wants to come and join us, buy us out or collaborate." Lester turned his impassioned face towards Harris. "You're not going know, but he can tell you: the Chin Ellis name is king in Jamaica! Everybody knows Chinchillerz!"

"Aye, I have heard of ye," said Harris. There was no hint of admiration in his tone. "Slushies and slurpees or something."

"Are you for real?"

As Lester's eyes narrowed, Preddy quickly interjected, "What about Carter? Girlfriends, ex-girlfriends?"

"Carter had plenty of girls. None of them were special to him. All of them thought they were something special though."

"Well, if ye could just write down the names of any of them that ye remember that would be a great help." Harris pushed a notepad and a pen towards him.

Lester took the pen and began to scribble. Preddy watched as his hand moved across the page. That gold watch probably cost a year of a detective's salary and he could not even guess at the value of the rings.

"I see you have Zadie Merton. We can't seem to get hold of her. Your mother seems to think she was Carter's only girlfriend," said Preddy.

"I don't know about that. Carter talked to a whole heap of girls," Lester replied. "That one came by the house a few times. Nice enough Black chick."

"What about male enemies? Did Carter have any arguments with any men about women or money or anything else?" asked Preddy.

"Carter barely even argued with me, much less with other people. He was not that type of person. Only that idiot racing driver I ever saw him really argue with, Kirk Grantham. The workers loved Carter. His friends loved him . . ." Lester's voice trailed off, seemingly drained.

"Have you ever seen dis man before?" Preddy placed a photograph on the table.

"No, never seen him before."

"Ye need tae take a good look at him," pushed Harris.

"His name is Marcus Darnay," said Preddy. "He's a mechanic and we thought he might have worked on Carter's racing car."

"I don't really know Carter's mechanics." Lester leaned over and looked closely. "Wait. I believe I saw this man's picture in the paper one time. He got jail time for dealing drugs or something."

"We found some drugs in ye car. A whole lot of drugs in fact, approximately two pounds of cocaine. What can ye tell us about it?" asked Harris.

"What drugs? Any drugs in my car, is you put them there! I don't know anything about any drugs!" Lester's voice rose. "So now you put drugs in my car and you're going to say that we upset a drug dealer and he killed Carter? Or what, that Carter was a drug dealer and ripped his customer off?"

"Calm down, sir," said Harris. "Naw officer put any drugs in yer car."

Lester rounded on the Scotsman. "I know how things work out here, even if you don't know! You just came from foreign and maybe this is not how things go in your country."

"Even if ye personally didnae know about the drugs, do ye think they could have belonged tae Carter?"

"You know what? I'm done talking. My lawyer will talk to you." Lester got to his feet. "You better be careful you don't slander my family name, because that's a big-big thing!"

"We'll be in touch, I'm sure," said Harris politely. "Sorry for yer loss."

Preddy stood and opened the door, moving aside to allow smooth passage for his departing visitor. Lester did not fit the mould of any cocaine kingpin Preddy had ever come across, and he had come across a few. Hardened criminals were known to be moving the drug in and out of the country, mainly via small fishing vessels and yachts, although some had taken to disguising the goods in shipping containers sent on cargo freighters. Besides, a couple pounds did not prove that he or Carter had a budding empire.

"We thank you for coming, Mr Chin Ellis."

Preddy watched as the interviewee checked the time on his expensive arm piece, holding it aloft for an unnecessary amount of time before striding out of the room and disappearing down the hallway.

"He's naw a very nice chappie, is he, sir?" Harris remarked once the door was firmly closed.

"I wouldn't want to drink wid him, but people react differently to grief. Some cry, some get mad or defensive and others show little reaction." Preddy studied Harris' expression and wondered if the slight against Chinchillerz was deliberate or whether Harris had read nothing about the products manufactured by the company. The foreigner's green eyes gave nothing away.

"What did ye make of his reaction tae the mention of drugs?"

"Difficult to say. He seemed genuinely surprised, but people lie all de time," Preddy replied. "We going need to tread carefully fi true. Dat family has a lot of money and can afford to keep people quiet."

"Money can buy ye a lot of things, but it cannae buy ye humility that's for sure."

"Too true," Preddy nodded. "You get anything from ballistics?"

"Aye, sir. The bullets are forty calibre, so I guess we're looking for a semi-automatic pistol. I understand they're now quite common?"

"Unfortunately, you're right." Preddy inhaled deeply. "I better go brief de Super before him come looking for me."

"Do ye need any help with the briefing, sir?"

Preddy stared at him. The question sounded innocent enough, yet he wondered what sort of double act Harris envisioned. "Sort of like Ity and Fancy Cat?"

Harris frowned. "I'm naw following ye, sir?"

"Dat you are not. See you later."

* * *

"None of dese women have called to ask about Carter's case?" asked Preddy, standing alongside Rabino's desk.

"Not one of them," replied Rabino, running her eyes down Lester's list. "I checked the names with the victim's mother and the only one she recognises is Zadie's. She is adamant that Carter did not have another serious girlfriend to her knowledge and Carter was with Zadie for around a year."

"Yet he turned her photograph face down," said Preddy thoughtfully. "And for some reason Lester doesn't believe Carter was dat serious about her."

Spence looked up from her paperwork and grinned at her boss. "Well, I know some men like to pretend and gwaan a way when dem like a girl and don't want dem friend to know. How is Valerie by de way, sir?"

Preddy smiled and averted his gaze. "She is fine. Try and talk to de girlfriend. I don't understand why she's not returning any calls. Tell her if she does not talk to us we will put her face on TV and in de newspaper."

"Speaking of which, did you see today's paper?" Rabino held it up.

Preddy looked at the large picture of Pelican Walk station, next to a photo of the minister for national security. The detective speed read the story. As expected the point scoring had begun, with rival politicians having a field day at the expense of the grieving family. The opposition party lay all the blame for the constabulary's current embarrassment squarely at the feet of the ruling party. The ruling party claimed that they inherited a service which had now, in the main, been transformed and met most of its targets including gaining the respect and co-operation of the public. The national security minister stuck to the party position that the Lester Chin Ellis incident was a one-off and vowed to get to the truth of the matter swiftly and publicly.

In a related story immediately below was the photograph of a distraught woman waving a piece of paper — a missing persons report. She was the mother of one of Lester's inmates. The names of the three inmates under suspicion had recently been announced sparking claims of injustice and a cover-up. The irate mother said her son was a schizophrenic and she had searched for him for days, asking for him at every station in the area, including the very lock-up in which he was held. Her son was at Pelican Walk all along. The police response was that the man had given them multiple names when asked to identify himself, including proclaiming himself to be Haile Selassie, and he had no identification on his person.

Yet, thought Preddy in frustration, *the officers had not allowed the woman to take a look at any of the detainees nor shown her photographs of any of them.* It was beyond him why some officers could not follow simple procedures, but this was something that would have to change.

CHAPTER 9

Wednesday, 22 July, 7.20 p.m.

Zadie Merton balanced the supermarket basket on her hip and fumbled for her phone in her bottomless pit of a designer handbag. More missed calls. The number was unidentified, yet she knew exactly who it was. If they kept on at this rate the phone's memory would be filled up with voicemail messages and unable to hold the ones that she really wanted to listen to. Damn police. She had nothing to give them. They hadn't been too concerned with speaking to her before when she wanted to report threats or assaults, and now they were suddenly keen to discuss the death of Carter Chin Ellis. If she were dead would they be so quick to start harassing him?

She had less than two hours to food shop, get home and get changed for work. She pursued her mission through the wide overflowing aisles, picking up bottles of wine and vodka without looking at the prices and throwing in a few bags of banana chips and chocolate bars. Being able to eat and drink whatever she liked was a blessing. No matter how high the calories or how unhealthy the food, it never affected her enviable shape. Friends teased her that being nineteen and quite active, she could get away with it, but in a few years it would all go downhill. Soon she would have cellulite and overhanging belly skin like everybody else, they warned. Zadie had confidently proclaimed that it would not be so. Her own mother was similarly built and even after having four children could still get away with wearing clothes marked small or petite.

Carter had asked her to go to the gym with him, choosing an elite local gym where business professionals worked out and where he could stock overpriced Chinchillerz natural smoothies. She hated going to the gym and would never understand how people, particularly women, could enjoy running on treadmills and lifting weights for hours, perspiring and breathing heavily. She had forced herself to face it three days a week lifting the lightest weights possible when she realised that it pleased Carter to see other men and women follow her movements.

She was well aware that men found her particularly appealing because of her buxom figure with a tiny waist and broad hips that she accentuated by wearing heels as high as possible. Her straightened copper-toned hair fluttered around her shoulders, held back today by a thin hair band. She had quickly learned what effect she had on men. Even a couple of male teachers at high school had tried it on with her, subtlety not being their main subject. It was one of the reasons why she had decided to abandon school before graduating and to date she had no regrets. All those earnest girls with a long list of subjects on their framed certificates and still no meaningful jobs. Even those who managed to make it to university would be lucky to get anything better than a mediocre call centre job or a basic admin position. As she took out her wallet and reached for cash she glanced at the uniformed cashier who smiled brightly back at her. She wondered what education this middle-aged woman had and how she made ends meet with a supermarket job.

Like most people on the island, Zadie had watched the extensive news reports of Carter's murder. It felt like an out of body experience for her, watching the cameras zoom in on a road that she had driven on and a house that she had slept in.

She even recognised some of the neighbours standing around idly surveying the scene. As the whole thing seemed so surreal to her, she could not imagine how it must feel for Carter's family.

Phoning his grieving parents was always at the back of her mind, but she resisted the temptation, afraid she might say something she shouldn't. As far as the parents knew, she and Carter had been a happy couple until the end and there was no reason for them to be told otherwise. She had seen his parents on TV talking about how wonderful their son was and she expected them to say nothing less. Terence was quiet but seemed nice, and although she had only met him a few times he always made her feel welcome. Miss Ida, she was not quite so sure about. It was clear to Zadie that to this no-nonsense lady her boys were in a class of their own and any women dating either of them should count themselves very lucky. She still remembered how Miss Ida had refused to believe her when she complained that Carter had slapped her across the face. Not her son, she had said, and Carter of course had denied it. Lester had been a bit off at first, but he turned out to be a good listener, quite a nice guy really.

Zadie picked up her bag of groceries and said goodbye to the cashier. Sometimes bad things happened to good people and sometimes bad things happened to bad people who pretended to be good. As her great-granny used to say "If a man put him hand on you make sure him can't use dat hand again." Zadie smiled to herself. Gran-gran always knew best.

She placed her shopping bags in the back seat of a taxi and climbed in. Once she had made herself comfortable, she took out her phone. The smile disappeared from her lips as she listened to Detective Rabino's message in stunned silence. Put her photograph on government TV for the whole nation to see? How dare they even suggest such a thing? Her hands shook as she punched in the detective's number and waited. She was not going to attend any interview and they needed to leave her alone.

* * *

It was approaching eight o'clock and Detective Preddy was nearly ready to go out for his date. He had rarely taken his wife out on dates during his marriage, which he regretted. As he stood in the modest Ironshore apartment purchased three years ago, after his divorce, he was determined to get it right this time. It was a comfortable place with an open-plan kitchen-dining area, a study room that doubled as a private office, a balcony, two sizeable bedrooms and a second bathroom. The second bathroom was non-negotiable when it came to buying a property, being particularly necessary for when the kids came to stay. He had visions of what teenagers could do in the room unchecked and he fully intended that they would clean up after themselves. Annalee had discovered make-up and he had no wish to be cleaning up multi-coloured products from the tiled walls and floors.

When he was young, there was one bathroom in the ancestral home in Darliston and his mother took great pride in keeping it spotless. In fact, he could recall being told that they were one of the first people in the little district to have a properly plumbed and fully functioning bathroom inside the house. The neighbours' bathroom consisted of a small outhouse with a huge steel bathpan and a hose fed in through the window leading from a standpipe in the yard. Whenever the pipe ran dry the children would collect water from a well half a mile away and sometimes he would go with them, enjoying the challenging rocky route. The neighbours also had a pit latrine with no basin. Instead a blue plastic keg caught rainwater and a cheese pan was used to scoop water for washing hands. His parents still lived in the family home and he phoned as often as he could, although he rarely completed the fifty mile round trip because of work pressures. A visit was long overdue and he needed to take the children with him.

Preddy closed the bathroom door and padded his way barefoot to the walk-in closet in his bedroom. He retrieved a short-sleeved, pale blue cotton shirt noting that it was roomy around the middle and hadn't hung so loose a few months ago. A navy blue pair of slacks added to his attire and his smart-casual look was finished off with a pair of canvas slip-on shoes. He eyed the grey sneakers that stood ready and waiting to go on a morning jog and realised they were likely to be forsaken in the days ahead. Nothing beat working up a sweat before the sun had risen, before the traffic was out polluting the clean air, and he enjoyed the challenge of racing against the clock feeling the rush of adrenalin that came with it. He could run in peace for miles around the relatively quiet streets of his middle-class neighbourhood which was home to hundreds of expatriates and business people. Still, work came first and if something had to give, it would be the early morning jogs.

Preddy lightly patted a strong smelling cologne on his chin. Come what may, he was going to find time to see Valerie and have a proper relationship. His body moved involuntarily as he thought about Valerie. They first met many years ago in the days when they worked together in the government forensic laboratory, where he began his career in crime management as a lab technician. Both were married to other people then, but there was a clear attraction from the start. She was funny and witty with a dimpled smile and a throaty laugh. They were colleagues, just good friends with easy banter passing between them, although both had known that there was much more to it. Eventually he had joined the JCF, as although he enjoyed analysing evidence, he wanted to be in the thick of things and the two stayed in contact over the years.

He still remembered his delight when she told him she was thinking about getting a divorce, how his heart had leapt, but he managed to maintain a poker face while consoling her. Every time he looked at her he wondered how her husband ever thought their relationship would work if he stayed in Kingston running a private forensic lab and she moved to Montego Bay to open a second establishment. It meant she only travelled back to the family home on Friday nights and returned to the western coast on Mondays. This was fine with

Preddy as it meant he could see her Monday to Thursday when time allowed, although they agreed to be as discreet as possible for now. She lived less than fifteen minutes' drive from his apartment and he had once absent-mindedly taken a turn into her road with his son who had wondered where they were going. It was a close call, but Preddy had evaded a tricky situation by claiming that he had just wanted to view the outside of a property that was new on the market.

Preddy had never imagined himself in this type of relationship, but it worked for them as they both knew the score. He always enjoyed the time they spent together particularly walking along the sea side at the edge of the water, allowing the warm water to lap over their toes, while cool salty breeze blew against their faces. He could talk to Valerie about anything and everything, although inevitably they always ended up speaking about the topic that had united them in the beginning: crime and evidence. She was his ideal kind of woman; natural, bright and ambitious, a person who understood what it was like to work under such intense pressure day after day, sometimes with no demonstrable results to show for it.

Four days had passed since he had last seen her, although the two spoke every day. He smiled wryly. Last Saturday night to be exact: they had done a soul concert and dinner, before he returned home alone to endure a restless night, unaware of the mess that he would wake up to on Sunday morning. Now that her divorce was proceeding, their relationship would soon be out in the open, although a few people were already aware of it, and he was looking forward to introducing her to Annalee and Roman one day. Valerie would still need to travel back to Kingston each weekend for the sake of her son who was due to start sixth form next term. Teenagers could be particularly tricky at the best of times, let alone when a family shake up was imminent and it was best that immediate change was not imposed on the youth.

Roman was thirteen and Annalee eleven at the time that his divorce had been finalised, but he and his ex-wife had gradually got the children used to the idea of separate homes in the year before that. He was grateful for the fact that they were able to do the split reasonably amicably, having agreed that the relationship was over. Although he did think the child support was on the steep side, he had no wish to rock the boat. The last thing he wanted was for his children to believe he did not wish to fully support them and besides, the payments did not leave him poverty stricken. It was better to hand over the money for his children's benefit than to give it to the predatory lawyers.

Preddy set the security alarm and turned the lights off, leaving only the sitting room light on. Although the apartment felt relatively secure, he preferred not to give any prospective thieves the blanket cover of darkness under which to case his residency. Very few burglaries occurred in this area of the community, but, as usual, he double locked the front door before walking down the external staircase and strolling off into the moonlit night.

CHAPTER 10

Thursday, 23 July, 9.20 a.m.

A mass of empty coffee cups surrounded the three detectives who sat around their desks comparing notes and awaiting the arrival of Preddy, who was unusually late that morning.

"Tell us about Glasgow, Detective Harris," said Spence. She tried to swirl her chair around to face her new colleague, but it creaked and moved grudgingly. "All we know is dat it is in Scotland, which is not in England, and dat it cold bad."

"Yes, tell us what would make us want to go to Glasgow." Rabino sat upright and stared at him over the top of her monitor.

Harris smiled. "Ye got me there. Okay, I'll admit the weather is nothing tae crow about. It's the largest city in Scotland with about six hundred thousand people, if ye like huge places. We've got loads of restaurants, museums, art galleries. It's great for nightlife and shopping."

"Shopping? Do you know how many Jamaican dollars there are to the pound? We won't be doing much shopping," said Rabino. "If I never used to travel with my father back in the day, I would never have been able to get on an aeroplane and go anywhere."

"Is not a joke. De fare alone make me eye water." Spence opened her eyes wide as she spoke. "I have never made it further dan California and I paid my own way. Detective Harris, you lucky you get free plane ride to come here. Nobody not going pay for us to go Scotland."

"Not even to as far as Kingston," Rabino smiled. "It's a whole big thing to claim gas allowance for the car. A plane ticket would give them a heart attack."

"Ye might get seconded one day, ye never know."

"And we might win de Super Lotto at de next draw too," said Spence. "You must prefer to stay in de office and work all de time when you over dere? It must be better dan walking around in de ice?"

"It doesnae snow all the time, ladies," Harris defended the character of his misunderstood homeland. "And believe me ye get dressed for the weather and ye get used tae it. We are allowed tae wear coats, scarves and gloves ye know."

"But if you have to make a phone call outside you would have to take off the gloves," said Rabino, cringing at the thought. "You cannot press the numbers with gloves?"

"Believe me, it's naw that hard. Uncomfortable sometimes, but naw so hard," Harris laughed. "Ye do it without thinking about it."

"Bwoy, me never want to experience dat." Spence shivered. "Me couldn't bear it."

The door opened and a cheerful Preddy bounced into the room. The female detectives exchanged meaningful looks as their superior clasped his hands together firmly and beamed around the room.

"Give me some good news no, people?"

Rabino grimaced. "Darnay's garage is clean. No sign of the car or any parts of it." She rolled up an open bag of mints and aimed it at Preddy. "Catch this, sir."

Preddy caught it and popped two mints into his mouth. "Good news, anywhere?"

Harris wondered why Rabino's generosity did not extend to him, but decided to ignore it as Rabino had been nothing but friendly towards him so far. The other female he was not so sure about. "We've compared notes from Nembhard and Wilson's interviews, sir. Cannae see anything out of place." Preddy took the documents from him and pulled out a chair.

"Sorry, sir. De prosecutor says she can't run wid de narcotics thing," said Spence shaking her head. "She says we don't know where de drugs came from."

Preddy groaned loudly and placed his forehead on his desk. It was the only possible charge he had left against Lester, having dropped the drink driving charge because the breathalyser was found to be old and miscalibrated. The charge of assaulting a police officer had already gone. Having listened to the arresting officers' tale she had decided that the case sounded contrived and too flimsy to stand up in court. Neither officer was hit or even pushed. There was a brief struggle when Lester refused to step out of the vehicle, but the brothers had put hands only on each other, not on the officers. Those sorts of charges had never managed to gain traction in the past.

Now their last possible charge for drug possession would not stand up either. Preddy knew exactly why the prosecutor had shied away from a drug charge, but he felt obliged to send her the files anyway. The SUV was left unlocked and unattended on a side road for a good few hours during which time the brothers were at Pelican Walk. The defence would claim that anyone, even the police, could have stashed the drugs in the car before Carter returned and drove it home. Once the prosecutor had spoken, the chance of a change of mind was slim. That was just how it worked unless the commissioner appealed to the Director of Public Prosecutions herself and she was not known for ignoring her prosecutors' recommendations.

"Wakey, wakey," said Rabino.

"I'm wide awake. I've had my tonic." Preddy raised his head and gave a wry smile. "I'm just wondering how long we've got before de walls start closing in."

Inevitably the Chin Ellis family, the public and the media were bound to turn against the police once they realised that no charges would be brought against Lester. The pressure on the lawmen would ratchet up a notch as one brother had been assaulted, the other murdered, and the officers could not justify the arrests. There was only one likely outcome to this and it would involve the government being forced to pay out millions to settle claims for wrongful arrest and false imprisonment, in addition to assault and battery. This was all taxpayers' money, as the JCF had no separate coffers of its own.

Once the news did get out that all possible charges against Lester had been dropped, the response from the Chin Ellis family was swift: if money was what it would take, then money was what the family would give.

"De phones don't stop ring all day," complained Spence that afternoon as she slammed down the receiver. "And not even one sensible call. People want to know if dem can claim de money by telling how much shot dem hear. A what kind of foolishness dat?"

"That's what ye get sometimes when ye offer big rewards," agreed Harris. "Although the announcement clearly said 'for information leading tae an arrest.' Can we get any more hands on deck tae weed the callers out, sir?"

"Not at dis time," said Preddy. "We're just not going to get any more resources. De calls will soon die out when de idlers give up. Until den we'll just have to manage."

The seasoned detective exuded outward confidence that he did not feel, but it was his duty to keep the team alert and driven. While ten million Jamaican dollars would not make anyone rich, it would sound like a fortune to the locals barely surviving on the minimum wage. The idea of "nothing ventured, nothing gained" would take over and so they would continue to ring. Everyone had a cell phone nowadays and a lot of people had more than one. They might not be able to find money for many of life's necessities but they would always find a way to obtain credit for their phones, even if that money was relayed by friends and family abroad. It had been his experience that offering reward money too early in a case simply led to a lot of wasted man hours, and this was the unwelcome result of having drawn the ire of the Chin Ellis family. He would have to work twice as hard to regain their trust and co-operation.

Preddy left his team manning the phones and made his way to his office. He liked working in the open-plan area, but also appreciated having his own quarters to retreat to. It was a large enough room for a police station of this size, with a solid wooden desk and sturdy chair in the centre, and a separate table which could seat four people comfortably, although they would have to borrow mismatched chairs from adjoining rooms. Filing cabinets sat in each corner and criminal law books adorned the shelves on the walls. A large window provided considerable light and the half-drawn blinds kept the sunlight from being too overpowering.

He lowered his athletic frame onto the chair and read the interview reports of Nembhard and Wilson. Officer Wilson said he had not left the front desk from the moment the Chin Ellis brothers entered Pelican Walk station. Officer Nembhard swore he had patrolled the holding cells on a regular basis and said most of the inmates appeared to be asleep in their bunk beds. Even the three who shared a cell with Lester seemed unconscious, although one of them did turn over when the cell door clanged shut. According to Nembhard, Lester had played down his injuries in the immediate aftermath of the assault.

Preddy sighed and picked up another report. Jerry Knight. The inmate with the bruised knuckles was now formally charged with the assault on Lester. Although the detective had hoped for a quick resolution to this case, he feared that it would not happen. The wheels of justice turned slowly on the island and the court system was just not equipped to deal with instant trials. A huge backlog of criminal cases existed, caused by ill-equipped courts, lack of court staff, overworked prosecution lawyers and police officers, as well as vanishing witnesses and incomplete files. Then there was the defence lawyers' strategy of demanding case management hearings at every possible opportunity. It could be many months before the assault case against Jerry Knight got heard, but at least it was a pretty strong one.

Preddy's attention was drawn to a large orange envelope sitting at the corner of his desk. He stared at it. The divorce petition from his wife had been dropped off at his office in a similar envelope and he still remembered the feeling that overwhelmed him back then.

Being forced out of the Runaway Bay home within six months of spending hundreds of thousands of dollars making it comfortable for the family had been painful. Creating a more spacious living environment was supposed to help the strained relationship, as they could retreat to their own zones when the need for peace and solitude took over. The children could also get away with increasing the volume on their TV shows and games without being accused of disturbing their parents. Although Preddy had convinced himself that things were improving between them, he knew deep down that much of the blame lay with him. It was his own fault for working as he did and neglecting his wife, who found temporary comfort with one of the local carpenters he hired to work on their home. A man who quickly vanished unpaid when he cottoned on to exactly whose wife he was playing with.

The words on the front of the envelope were typewritten and addressed to him personally, marked "private and confidential" in bold. He wondered if the letter had come from the police high command. Maybe his progress was too slow for them? Or maybe they were just tired of seeing his face? There were no stamps on the front. The back of the envelope gave no indication of where it had come from either. It must have been hand delivered.

He carefully tore the envelope open and retrieved a single large photograph accompanied by a typewritten letter on plain paper with no letterhead. It was only a few lines long without signature. The writer stated that the marks to the side of Lester's face were made by a blunt unknown object, not by a fist. The note was obviously written by an educated person who was involved in the medical field and had personal access to Lester Chin Ellis. The detective deduced that it had to be from a private medical facility, as the wounded Lester had refused the attention of Pelican Walk's own on-call doctor.

Preddy immediately went to question the young office assistant whose job was to sort and deliver mail. The youngster had no idea who had dropped off the envelope. A pile of letters were in a bag at the door of the station when he arrived and he just sorted them out and delivered them. Preddy knew that the chances of identifying the doctor who had treated Lester was slim. Charges had been laid against Jerry Knight and any questions about the incident would now have to go through the respective lawyers. If he asked the prosecutors to find out who Lester's doctor was, they would demand to know why the interest and question the relevance.

The detective stared at the photograph while trying to envisage what object the inmate could have used in the attack. There should have been nothing in the cell, as all personal belongings were removed when suspects were booked in at the front desk. He frowned and tapped the envelope on his desk. The doctor and patient confidentiality code was sacrosanct and whoever wrote the note would never come forward voluntarily.

CHAPTER 11

Tuesday, 28 July, 2.30 p.m.

The funeral of Carter Chin Ellis took place at the local Roman Catholic church in which he had been baptised as a baby. Only family and close friends were invited, yet there was a noticeable gathering of hangers-on and spectators, most of whom were inappropriately dressed in tight colourful leggings and T-shirts, while others were clad in shorts and vests. Some of the invited mourners were bedecked in ostentatious jewellery that appeared quite out of place in the church yard.

Preddy had convinced the Chin Ellis family to grant the detectives permission to discreetly attend the funeral service, using the excuse that they were providing added security. His real intention was to see if anyone caught his eye as being particularly out of place.

The interior of the church was sensitively decorated with specially imported pure white oriental lilies, gladioli and carnations. The wooden pews were packed with solemn faces, many of whom had flown into the island for the service. At the front stood the solid white casket which would remain open until the start of the service to allow mourners to pay their respects.

The local Chinese business community was out in force, and it occurred to Preddy that he had never seen so many Jamaican Chinese of all ages congregated in one place. He could identify quite a few of them whom he recognised as owners of various businesses including opticians, pharmacies and supermarkets. People that he used to say hello to when he walked the beat many years ago, although he doubted that any of them would even remember him. Back then few owners would ever respond.

Rabino and Harris were strategically placed at the rear, surveilling the mourners as they gave heartfelt eulogies. When the ceremony was over they followed the extremely long procession to the family plot in the adjoining town of Reading for the interment. Spence was already in Reading keeping a watchful eye on the arrivals, ready to accost anyone who appeared dangerous. Carter's parents stood weeping into their handkerchiefs as their beloved son's coffin was lowered into his grave. Miss Ida's glasses fell from her face, narrowly missing the deep hole and were quickly retrieved by her husband, who wiped his wife's face tenderly and replaced the glasses over her nose. She gave him a grateful half-smile. Lester, whose face was a picture of abject misery, stood on the other side of his mother with one arm across her shoulders. He dabbed at his own reddened eyes from time to time and squeezed his mother's hand.

Preddy patrolled outside, surveying the grounds, his eyes invisible behind the dark shades necessary to keep out the blinding sunlight. Beneath his jacket he was armed and ready for the unexpected. He hoped that the criminals had enough respect for the dead not to interfere in this private, overwhelming moment of grief, or at least had the good sense to realise that the police would likely be present.

Preddy found himself next to Harris. "Notice anything strange?" he asked.

"If ye mean the dazzling multi-colours and the tight revealing clothes, I'll have tae say, aye." Harris removed his shades and polished them with his handkerchief before setting them back on his nose. "Blinding stuff out here."

Preddy was not sure whether Harris meant the weather or the women, but he had detected a twinkle in the foreigner's eyes. "Dat's Jamaica for you. We like to be different."

"Ye are certainly that."

Suddenly, Preddy craned his neck having recognised a familiar face in the crowd. He had not expected to see this man. Not even the dark aviator shades could disguise Marcus Darnay's heavy set features. He was in deep conversation with another man who Preddy remembered from his days on the lottery scam taskforce. That team was created solely to investigate electronic crimes that had blossomed out of control in a very short space of time, catching the police and public completely unaware. Technology had done great things for Jamaica, however the parish of St James had become the headquarters of the advance fee fraudsters who targeted vulnerable people, usually retirees, mainly based in Canada and North America. These unwary people would either be emailed with a congratulatory message notifying them that they had won a large lottery prize, or telephoned if the scammer had been industrious enough to procure an international phone number.

Preddy could just about get around the idea of the victim being scammed the first time around, but he was baffled that the victim would then wire more money because of some alleged snag and maybe even a third set of funds if the scammer said it was the final requirement. It came as no surprise to anyone on the force that a new anti-lottery scam bill became law. Everyone was aware of the pressure being brought to bear on the island by powerful countries whose citizens had suffered most. As far as Preddy was concerned St James must remain famous for its breath-taking beauty and not be diminished by the ugliness that some worthless citizens would like to smear on it.

The detective could think of no reason why Darnay and his cohort would be at a high profile funeral like this, particularly when he had denied knowing the family. The two criminals stood at quite a distance from the mourners, dressed appropriately enough in black suits and ties. Either Darnay was getting careless or he was supremely confident that the murder could not be linked to him.

Preddy left Harris and continued to scope the crowd until he spotted a crying man carrying a scrappy bouquet of wildflowers and kicking a car tyre. Preddy removed his glasses and made eye contact with Spence then gestured towards the man. She nodded almost imperceptibly and slowly made her way through the crowd toward the suspect. Preddy watched as they spoke, wishing he could lip read. The man stopped kicking the car and stood weeping quietly with his head slightly bowed, while Spence stayed beside him.

The repast was due to take place at the Doubloons where all hangers-on would be prohibited from entry, and Preddy made a decision not to venture onto the premises since the family had already hired extra security guards for the complex. Unknown to the detective, someone else was also busy surveilling the crowds that afternoon, someone seated in a car a good distance away and watching keenly through powerful binoculars.

* * *

The noise of high-pitched voices echoed long before Preddy was in touching distance of his front door. A tantalising odour of boiling coconut milk and thyme hung around the doorframe. He smiled broadly while pushing the door open and stepped inside accepting the disarray in a manner that only an indulgent father could.

Every inch of kitchen work surface was taken up by pots and pans as well as a variety of vegetables and spice bottles. Fourteen-year-old Annalee was going to show her father the latest dish that she had mastered and he was not looking forward to it. It was not that he doubted his daughter's ability to cook. She and her brother successfully assisted him in cooking pots of food for the homeless persons' kitchen from time to time. His problem was that Annalee was preparing a vegetarian meal and Preddy was a meat and fish sort of man. Sixteen-year-old Roman had also rolled his eyes when told that dinner would be courtesy of his sister and would be missing a vital red ingredient. He lay sprawled on the floor playing games on his phone, making no effort to assist the hardworking cook who loudly demanded that he pass the kitchen towel. The overhead fans and the air-conditioning unit were all on and Preddy turned off the unit before reaching towards the nearest window.

"JPS," was all he said.

Annalee squealed loudly when it went off and turned to smile at her father. "Don't you mean JCF, Dad?" She ran and hugged him with floury hands, leaving an imprint on his shirt.

"No. I meant what I said, madam. When you can pay JPS light bill you can turn everything on." He leaned over and kissed her on the cheek. "Roman, what a gwaan?"

Roman looked up and grinned. "Me cool, Misser Officer!"

The children had not seen their father for a week and the initial plan was to go out for a meal. That plan was scuppered by the forecast of heavy rain, but although the skies were heavily overcast and the humidity unbearable, the rains did not come. Having to stay indoors was annoying at the best of times. Having to stay indoors without meat was even worse, on this Roman and his father agreed, and when Annalee took a break to make a phone call, Preddy showed his son a large margerine tub containing jerked pork hidden in the back of the fridge. If all else failed there would be pre-cooked meat tonight.

Roman had never seen Annalee use a grater before this evening and he expected to hear her yell when the coconut slipped as it surely would. She did stop a few times but there were no yelps of pain, she just gritted her teeth and started again more carefully. Preddy had offered her the use of a high-speed blender which she turned down as she was determined to cook coconut rundown in the way that her grandmother cooked it. He knew that it was his mother who had suggested this meal, rather than his ex-wife who, like him, would just use the blender or add water to the powdered product, time being precious and all. He was glad that his daughter was trying out the good old-fashioned methods of cooking as they always tasted better.

When the meal finally arrived on the table the presentation was immaculate. Annalee had produced an impressive meal of boiled yellow yams, cornmeal dumplings and green plantains, served with gungo peas, cho-cho, red peppers and escallion cooked together in coconut rundown. Roman gave an exaggerated bow towards his sister before taking up a seat at the table. Preddy soaked his cornmeal dumpling in the coconut sauce and savoured a mouthful, nodding appreciatively at his daughter.

Familiar reggae music played in the background and they sang along to the songs even when they did not know the words and laughed at their mistakes. They agreed to toss a coin to see who would undertake the mammoth task of washing up which Preddy lost by flicking a fake double-headed coin and calling tails. As he put away some of the uneaten food he smiled at the sight of the margerine tub that never made it out of the fridge. Nice one, Annalee.

* * *

"You alright Dad?" Roman peered at his father through the half-darkness.

Preddy rolled over and blinked at the slender silhouette reflected in his bedroom doorway. Gradually his eyes made out his son clad in his pyjama bottoms with his phone glued to his hand. The detective had briefly forgotten that the children were staying overnight with him, not that the knowledge would have deterred his dark dreams.

"Alright, son. I wake you up? Sorry, about dat," he mumbled. "Is Annalee okay?"

"Yes, she still a sleep. Me no hear no movement from her room."

"You go back to bed son, everything cool."

"Eeh? You sound like somebody a beat you," said Roman. "Is not de first time I hear you bawl out so."

"I'm fine, honestly. Gwaan go get your sleep, man. Nothing is wrong."

Roman departed reluctantly. As soon as the door shut, Preddy sat up in bed and wiped his wet brow with his forearm before reaching over the side table for the reading lamp. The clock told him it was nearly 2 a.m. He was getting used to this now, waking up at least once a week to the sound of bullets and people screaming. It had been like this ever since the bloody raid and the detective wondered when things would ever return to normal. All offers of counselling were rejected because he had assumed that with time the visions would go away, but they had not.

The plan had been to arrive in Norwood with a show of force and take the wanted men by surprise. Coming quietly would be the only logical way out of their predicament — that was the thought anyway. Instead, the men failed to acknowledge the officers calls to come out with their hands up and movement was heard inside. A shot rang out from an unknown source. It caused a panic ripple effect within his six man squad, resulting in the officers kicking down the door and firing blindly. Even as Preddy shouted at his men to hold fire, he watched as the youngest of the outlaws, at a mere eighteen years of age, collapsed to the floor in a pool of blood.

He had held the dying youngster's head up and begged him to breathe while witnessing him taking his last breath. The walls inside the house were pock marked with bullet holes, while blood and brain matter were spattered throughout. It was a sight he could not erase from his mind.

Another image that refused to fade was the face of the sole survivor who had stood in a corner hands above his head, urinating uncontrollably and begging for his life while awaiting execution. Death did not come to him that moment only because Preddy had stood in front of him while waving his men away. Even when hidden behind the sturdy detective, the man still screamed and pleaded not to be killed, so strong was his fear. At Preddy's insistence, he reduced his cries to stifled whimpers. It was only when taken out of doors that the survivor fell completely silent. Outdoors he had good reason to believe that he would not be mown down in full public view.

Two of Preddy's team were injured by ricocheting bullets, although it was later discovered that the shots came from weapons in the hands of their own colleagues. The suspected men did not have guns on them and this was mentioned more than once in the follow-up reports in the media. Preddy had made the point that this was unknown at the time, and days later the officers had located the stash of guns buried under a thick stone slab in a chicken coop mere metres from the house.

Preddy reached for a glass of water on his nightstand and downed it in one go. He folded his arms behind his head and lay back watching the shadows of the tree branches playing on the ceiling. While his eyes were open the nightmares would stop.

CHAPTER 12

Wednesday, 29 July, 10.00 a.m.

Preddy and Spence spent the early hours at Chinchillerz head-quarters speaking to the staff. Ida and Terence had approved the visit and agreed not to be present. It was an opportunity the detectives could not afford to miss, not least because the police needed to be seen to be working on the case.

None of the staff members had ever been interviewed by the police before. Some found it thrilling, others found it terrifying, and the rest were happy to escape from their work stations for an hour. They gathered in the combined space of the canteen and games room, which came complete with pool table, flat screen TVs and bar. Some employees were dressed in office wear, others in gowns with white mesh caps covering their hair. The detectives were allowed to make a statement, requesting help and information in identifying possible suspects in Carter's murder. Business cards were handed out. Employees who wished to speak with the detectives on a one-to-one basis were invited to phone or visit Pelican Walk station as soon as possible.

The detectives were then taken on a tour of the extensive factory floor with its giant walk-in freezers, cooling machines and countless plastic containers of varying sizes and shapes. Preddy had never seen so much gleaming metal in his life — stainless steel pipes and tubes were everywhere. Every piece of shiny machinery was whirring away demonstrating efficiency and precision. The work surfaces and floors were spotless. Rolls of food labels sat on the shelves carrying the distinctive red and orange logo of Chinchillerz. The aroma that permeated the air was a mixture of many fruits, some of which were easily identifiable, others not. Pineapple was the most distinctive, with soursop a close second and mango quite heavy in there too. Crocus bags full of citrus fruits were stacked upon each other in one corner. A conveyor belt transported huge watermelons from one side of the factory to another where a machine resembling a guillotine bobbed up and down in anticipation. Long stalks of sugar cane were fed into a crusher by hand and the resulting juice caught up in a giant glass bottle. Whatever drawbacks were affecting the world outside, the multi-million dollar operation of the Chinchillerz empire was functioning at full throttle.

Miss Ida's secretary showed them to the top floor of the three-storey administrative block which was quieter and even more modern. Light poured in through the wide skylights, giving the broad leafed plants below much needed energy. The family members had large offices next to each other, partitioned by solid walls, although the doors were made of transparent glass and all carried a name plate. Terence's office was at the end, Ida's next to his, then a wide space occupied by a juice fountain and a stack of ottomans. Beside that chill-out space was Carter's office which adjoined Lester's. On the opposite side of the corridor were offices belonging to the directors of finance, marketing and operations. All were male and tried to not raise their eyes from their file-strewn shiny desks as the detectives sauntered past.

"Can you imagine if Pelican Walk did look like dis place?" whispered Spence in awe.

"If only." Preddy gave her a rueful smile. The public sector and the private sector would never play in the same league, let alone on the same field.

Spence thanked the secretary for her assistance as she escorted them back to the carpark. As the detectives drove away, Preddy was aware of being watched by various members of staff. One employee in particular had caught the detective's eye earlier and the man was now visible in the rear-view mirror, watching keenly — Arroun Fisalam, chief finance officer.

Lester Chin Ellis also watched, unseen through the tinted windows of his chauffeur driven car which passed Preddy's car on the long driveway. This was to be Lester's first full day back at headquarters since the death of his brother, although he had popped in briefly once before to ensure that the incoming and outgoing deliveries were running to schedule. There was also the matter of the building of a children's playground on land abutting Chinchillerz car park. The workmen needed supervision. If they moved on to another project he would have difficulty getting them back and he really wanted the playground to be completed for the children.

His parents had not fully returned to work either, although they still conducted vital business from the confines of their home. It was at their insistence that he was being driven around by a chauffeur, despite the fact that his physical injuries were long healed and his mental scars would not be worsened by him driving a car. Eventually, he had just given in. They were great parents and it could only be a good thing that he did not have to personally anticipate the actions of erratic drivers on the road.

Lester waved at the security guard as the vehicle made its way through the masses of employee cars and company vans parked in the forecourt. He could still remember when his parents had bought the empty twenty-acre lot. Back then he and Carter had raced their dune buggies back and forth to the annoyance of the surveyors and contractors who were trying to lay the foundations. The sprawling building had taken nearly two years to build, and since the original structure went up they had added a much needed staff relaxation zone.

If people were giving their all to the business, they deserved to have somewhere pleasant to unwind in.

He recalled their mother's indulgent treatment of them throughout their childhood. She had even allowed her pre-teens to rename the business and they had had fun playing with names until finally agreeing to the change from Ice Island to Chinchillerz, although she had put her foot down at the idea of changing the logo to purple, his favourite colour at the time.

Lester alighted and strolled through the giant glass doors. He greeted the receptionist. He wished that she would stop using blue eye shadow and deep red rouge on her cheeks. She was dark and lovely enough, but spoiled her beauty with her overdone make-up. He entered the lift, nodding at employees who smiled sympathetically at him, and emerged on the third floor. He passed the offices used by his parents, which doors remained locked and lights out. A slight chill ran through him as he walked past Carter's office towards his own. The layout of the floor had been his father's idea. It was important that this tight family worked side by side and not divided by outsiders.

Lester opened his door and sank into the plush leather chair while gazing around him. The walls were decorated with family pictures in between expensive artwork. It was like a small suite rather than an office, with a long leather sofa and matching armchairs, coffee table, and small entertainment system. A lot of work was done in this room and the result of the last brainstorming session was all over the room, on the whiteboard, on the desk and on prototype artwork for posters.

Last time he had been in here the product developers had popped in bringing various blends of fruits for a possible new ice cream flavour. They had decided on a tamarind guava mixture with a hint of vanilla. The taste testing went down well particularly with Carter, who had finished off the three-ounce cup in a matter of seconds. The buttercup yellow colouring had to go though, as it looked more appetising as a much lighter shade of yellow. Try as they might they could not make anything tasty with avocado pear and had decided to scrap that idea completely. In any event, a public questionnaire resulted in a lot of negative responses to the idea of avocado yoghurt or ice cream. Avocado was a savoury treat for eating with a good plate of cooked rice or hard dough bread or bulla cake they said, and not for mixing with milk and sugar.

The sorrel and ginger flavour had not received much positive feedback either. It was missing something, but they had not yet given up this idea. As a drink, Lester loved sorrel and ginger with a splash of rum. The whole family did and there had to be a way to make it into a delicious flavoured ice cream without the alcohol. Rum and raisin had never been allowed on the menu as his parents were concerned about the church's likely reaction to them selling alcohol-flavoured desserts. Even the idea of a separate range for adults was not met with enthusiasm at all, but he and Carter had often talked about a time when their parents would have to step back from the day to day running of the company. When the young people took over, they could make things happen. Religion should have no place in Chinchillerz business, as it could only stifle progression and growth.

The silence of the room next door struck him. At this time of day he would usually hear Carter either on the phone or in a meeting, sometimes coldly berating people who had annoyed him, sometimes holding discussions with other staff members. Lester felt a thump in his chest as he realised that he would never again hear Carter's laugh or his unique voice through the thin wall. His shoulders slumped and he buried his head in his hands, rested them on the desk, and wept.

Eventually Lester sat up and wiped his face. He took a small mirror from his drawer and polished it before using his tongue tentatively to test his teeth. Others might not be able to see it, but his handsome narrow cheek boned face was slightly lopsided and it hurt when he sculpted his goatee. Goddamn police, how dare they arrest him and hold him in that filthy hellhole with the scum of the earth? Boy, if this was America. Goddamn police. Goddamn lawyers.

CHAPTER 13

Wednesday, 29 July, 12.50 p.m.

Officer Lindon Nembhard had been removed from cell duty and confined to a desk job at Pelican Walk. His unsmiling face told every officer who ventured into his area that he did not want to be there. The police high command had assured him he was not being punished and this was standard procedure, but he still felt persecuted.

It was an insult to be treated like a pariah at his own station. With a basic salary that barely covered his family's needs he sometimes ended up working fourteen hour days just to get additional overtime pay. A shortage of officers to cover so many cells was always an issue and Saturday nights were bound to be worse, needing at least four people to do his job. It just was not possible for one person to keep an eye on the cells for hours on end and everyone knew that. He needed to eat, take bathroom breaks and deal with walk-in emergencies involving agitated members of the public. Finding time to call his girlfriend and complete the odd difficult Sudoku puzzle also had to be factored in. And there was always the need to catch a little shut eye in between, although he would never admit it.

When he first joined the force as a constable eight years ago he had carried high expectations of quickly rising through the ranks, what with his high exam grades and good recommendations from supervisors. There was a bottleneck at his career level. He had climbed only one rung of the ladder two years ago and realised with a great deal of displeasure that he was unlikely to ascend anywhere else in the near future. The idea of ever making sergeant still less detective inspector had begun to fade in his mind as not many officers voluntarily left the force, and those that did were not being replaced.

He could afford to buy a small property and second-hand car for himself and his live-in girlfriend, yet could not afford to help his extended family and he dearly wanted to help his younger sisters through university. The thought of joining a private security company had flitted across his mind before being dismissed. It was a better paying job, but would not hold the same cachet as being a policeman, and there was no defined career plan in the security role.

Moonlighting in the force was frowned upon, but not forbidden, so he took jobs as a bodyguard and as a club bouncer from time to time. A muscular build and authoritative persona was enough to deter the chancers. Occasionally he would keep watch over private parties too, blending in with the patrons and looking out for pickpockets and troublemakers.

Some of his colleagues made additional money by allowing their private cars to be run as public passenger vehicles and charged the drivers a considerable amount per day to hire the car. That was a step too far for Nembhard as not only was it an illegal use of the vehicle, but the drivers drove so badly he could foresee bills for all sorts of dents and parts in the future. No, he would stick to moonlighting for now and hope that his prospects improved. God would watch over him and provide.

* * *

On the first floor above Nembhard's head, the detectives were holding a team briefing.

"Remember dat strange guy from de funeral? Not a suspect, sir," Spence announced. "He's a serial mourner. Him go to plenty funeral and behave same way."

"Is he right in the head?" asked Rabino.

"Not a thing no wrong wid him. De man is a loner. Him get caution before, but him just keep on doing it. One day him going do it with de wrong family and den we going have to scrape him up off de ground," predicted Spence in a matter of fact manner.

"The Chin Ellis parents say they dinnae know Darnay at all, nor his friend." Harris informed them. "But then again they said half the people who turned up were strangers."

"A food dem did a look. I don't know what is wrong wid some people," said Spence.

"Darnay is not in need of food though," said Preddy thoughtfully. "Him look very well fed to me."

"He must think we're idiots and won't make any connection," said Rabino, adding in Patois, "A bright him bright and bold."

"Him well bright fi true," agreed Spence.

"Yes, him bright," said Harris. The eyes of his three colleagues were immediately upon him and he smiled back pleasantly. "What? I got it. If ye are all doing Patois I dinnae want tae be left out."

Spence laughed. "We going have to take time talk now. Is not everything you hear we going want you to learn."

Preddy smiled. Harris was learning fast which was just as well. He turned his attention to a worn plaque on the wall holding a yellowed paper, the result of facing the penetrating sunlight for two years. The shiny bamboo frame remained as good as new, having been treated with non-toxic borax to render it impenetrable to termites. The plaque commemorated the work of various divisions of Area One police and was a particular source of pride as it was not easy to get acknowledged in the force unless you did extraordinary work. Much easier to get singled out for special attention if your crown ever slipped.

Preddy stood and rubbed clean a smudge on the glass. He moved the plaque slightly so that it was level. Marcus Darnay would never get the better of him. This murder would be solved. A shrill noise rang through the station and a universal groan went up from all except Harris who looked around quizzically.

"What's that?" he asked.

"Fire alarm," said Spence, stretching her bare feet towards her discarded shoes. "Don't know if it's a test or de real thing."

"Come on," said Preddy heading towards the door. "Let's get to de assembly point."

"What about the people in the cells?" asked Harris.

Spence glanced at him sideways. "I guess dey will need a hero."

Preddy smiled. "Other officers will take dem out, Detective Harris. We won't leave dem to burn."

"Can we find out if this is a drill, sir?" asked Rabino, turning off the desk fan. "I was just getting comfortable and I really don't want to go out there right now."

"Come lady, bring your shades," said Preddy grinning back at her. "We can ask downstairs."

He pulled down the blinds so that any officers passing by in the hallway could not see inside the evidence room. Blinds were also on the other side of the room attached to the window that faced outdoors. These were partially shuttered already as a barricade against the sun rather than prying eyes, as, other than the window cleaner, no-one ever climbed up that far.

The detective locked the door and followed his colleagues down the stairwell, accompanied by other officers who were also making their way towards the courtyard. They congregated under the huge Julie mango tree whose dense cluster of leaves provided welcome shelter from the direct sun rays.

Harris looked up in admiration. "Any chance we can get some of these mangoes down?"

"But of course," said Spence. "Gwaan climb it no?"

"I'll catch," offered Rabino.

"I dinnae think so. Tree climbing should be left tae young kids."

"Nobody not climbing any tree," said Preddy following their gaze. "When de handyman come him can use a stick and pick dem. You can get plenty mango."

The inmates were led out by a group of officers, some with guns drawn at their sides, all dressed in the standard uniform of black trousers with red seams running down the sides from waist to cuffs, light blue short-sleeved shirts and flat black caps. Among the group, Preddy spotted Timmins the officer who had arrested Carter and Lester and who had, whether unwittingly or on purpose, created a disastrous chain of events. A few paces behind Timmins came the disgruntled Nembhard. Preddy had little sympathy for the man's plight. If he had done his job properly the pressure on Pelican Walk would not be anything like it was today.

Timmins had noticed Preddy too and a scowl crept across his face. Who did the detective think he was? Watching him all the time, clamming up whenever he saw him approaching? Arresting lawbreakers was Timmins' job and that was exactly what he had done on that Saturday night. He was now under suspicion on his home soil when nobody could possibly have any evidence against him. Only careless fools with little training and even less sense committed crimes and left evidence, and he was nobody's fool.

"Look pon de hot sun inna de sky, me cyah go out deh!" grumbled one detainee.

"Dat's where you are going and nobody not carrying you. Walk, man!" ordered Timmins.

The resentful man dragged his feet. "Bwoy you have people just a fry inna de sun. You is a wicked set a people!"

"A true man," said another inmate, "not even one umbrella or nutten!"

"De sun good for you man," replied Nembhard. "You going have a long wait before you see de sun again if you did really stab up de man."

"Is dis a drill, officer?" asked Preddy as the group passed in front of him.

"Yes, sir," said Nembhard. "Wilson clearing de place first, den we can all go back in."

"Wilson? I didn't know we change fire officer?" said Preddy in surprise.

"De fire officer on leave today, sir," replied Nembhard.

"A him pick de right day," said another angry inmate. "Man have fi out here a bu'n up!"

"Put dem under de almond tree for a while," said Preddy, noting that the large courtyard really did not provide adequate cover for the men.

The last thing he wanted was a riot on his hands, and in any event the men were innocent until proven guilty and deserved to be treated in a civilised manner. He wondered why Wilson had taken the decision to run the fire drill in the fire officer's absence. This was surely outside of Wilson's remit and had caused an unnecessary distraction. The detective's eyes followed the marching group as they approached the nearby almond tree whose flat compacted leaves acted like a thatched roof to the welcome relief of the suffering men.

One frustrated suspect kicked out at a stray female mongrel trying to share a small spot of shade. The dog quickly scuttled to one side narrowly avoiding the boot, her wide brown eyes warily watching out for more attacks. Timmins immediately rounded on the would-be assailant.

"What you doing, man? Leave de dog! It trouble you?"

Timmins gently called out to the dog which hesitantly crept a bit closer, ever watchful of a human trick. The officer bent down and Preddy could see that he was talking to the animal although he could not hear what was said. The dog wagged her tail timidly and curled up close to the officer's feet. Timmins patted its head and the dog focused her grateful eyes on him for a few seconds before placing her head on her paws.

Within ten minutes the fire practice was over and the officers and suspects were free to make their way back inside.

The detectives waited until everyone had entered before following behind.

"Well, at least we know we can get everybody in and out quickly without anyone dying from sunstroke, so it wasn't a complete waste of time," said Rabino drily.

"Oh, we know much more dan dat, Detective," said Preddy.

They filed back into the evidence room one by one and flopped down into their chairs. Preddy was soon on his keyboard amending his notes.

"Lord, it's hot. So, did you bring any skirts with you, Detective Harris?" Rabino asked, eyeing the Glaswegian. "You must feel like you need one right now."

"Skirts? Oh, ye mean kilts?"

"Yes, same thing," she said. "You bring any?"

"Naw. I didnae think there'd be any cause tae wear them in Jamaica."

"You suppose to wear dem once a week," said Spence. "You never know?"

Preddy said, "Don't listen to her. She a ginnal."

"What's a ginnal?" asked Harris.

"A deceptive person," Preddy grinned. "A term usually reserved for tricksters rather dan hardened criminals."

"Och, I'll try tae remember that one," said Harris. "I usually only wear ma kilt for special occasions."

"Oh, dat's a shame," said Spence. She turned and stared at him intently. "Is true dat you don't wear anything under it?"

"Well, I cannae speak for anyone else, but I always wear something under it."

"I guess you must suffer from icicles forming on all parts of you?" said Rabino.

Spence nodded in agreement. "Eeh, eeh! Suppose to painful."

The female detectives both laughed oblivious that Sean Harris flushed pink. His chair scraped back as he stood upright and glared at the officers. He seemed a few inches taller than before, Preddy thought, although he was probably around five foot ten at most, about three inches shorter than himself. The green eyes flashed and took on a dark emerald tint giving Preddy a slight chill, but before he could intercede Harris spoke:

"Ye know, if we were in Glasgow, right about now we would all be marching tae the human resources department and ye would have tae explain why ye think that sexism is appropriate in the workplace."

All voices were suddenly silenced. Rabino's standalone fan purred gently as it valiantly circulated warm air. The wall clock ticked loudly, unaware of its intrusion.

"Since there is naw HR here, maybe I'll just take maself off and make a call tae the top man instead?"

The foreigner strode out of the room and slammed the door leaving an eerie quiet in his wake. The old plaque jumped and became dislodged again as if settling into its preferred position of comfort.

"Lord God! What we going do?" asked a panicked Spence. Her smile had long disappeared and she held a hand to her chest.

"Oh, hell!" Rabino blinked rapidly and looked crestfallen.

Preddy stood up and quickly walked towards the door, but before he could reach it the door creaked and the red head reappeared stopping Preddy in his tracks.

"Look pon you," Harris declared in his best Patois. "You cyah take joke?" He closed the door and disappeared again.

A collective sigh of relief went around the room. "A him a de real ginnal," said Spence, staring at the door.

"That is one strange white man," murmured Rabino.

Preddy retook his seat and allowed himself to exhale. "I don't disagree wid either of you."

He was relieved that it was a joke, although he was somewhat perturbed by it. Who knew that the mild mannered Harris could act in that way? How would they recognise what was an act and what was the true Harris? The white man could look and sound positively menacing if he chose to. If it could be channelled wisely then maybe he would prove a good antidote against the criminal element of the city after all. Preddy decided not to think too deeply about the alternative.

* * *

On the outskirts of the city, a homeless man settled onto an upturned rubber crate under a towering mahoe tree. It was a strategic position for catching hungry school children and other pedestrians in need of a light snack. He wheeled his wobbly handcart there each day, sold a few guineps picked from trees on wasteland, got drunk from the sun and slept amid the noise of the traffic. Then, when night fell, he would make his way back to his tiny ramshackle abode made of discarded boards and rusty zinc.

Tonight would be different. He would be able to sleep peacefully with soft seats on which to lay down and a solid metal roof over his head. It was so much better than his old yard which most people would pass without even noticing as it blended into the dark trees so well. He had no intention of abandoning it completely as it was habitable in dry weather, though not so good in rainy or windy weather even with the multitude of black plastic bags strewn all over it. He still had no toilet. That was what the bush was for and he didn't really worry about where he washed or if he could wash at all.

There was no kitchen either, but he just needed dry wood and paper to start a fire and he could cook in one of many of the lidless pots he collected from the garbage dump. Usually he cooked turned cornmeal which was the cheapest staple to be found with the few dollars he managed to scrounge. When he succeeded in converting a tourist's day trip into a guilt trip he would buy chicken neck for the pot. Otherwise it would be cornmeal and callaloo or pak choi. Occasionally he would get piece of yam to cook with a few green bananas, a very rare treat with the cost of ground pro-duce these days. If he had no food he could always go to the charity kitchen and lay wait the arrival of the next generous patron. For now he was doing just fine.

The nice car was parked deep in the bushes, covered with dried banana leaves. It was meant to be his home, of that there was no doubt, because he had prayed to God every day to help him and now God was looking after him. Edible food and a solid roof over his head. A Subaru Outback no less. Life in Montego Bay was not so bad at the moment.

CHAPTER 14

Lester adjusted his hard hat as he stood watching the four workmen laying foundations for the playground on spare acres of Chinchillerz property. He did not need a hard hat, but the men were wearing them and he wanted to show that he was not a stuffed shirt. The playground was his idea, partly because he wanted to capture the primary and high school market by supplying their canteens with cold food products. He also loved the energy and vibrancy of little people.

He remembered his own high school days well and knew that the kids must be tired of eating patties with coco bread and bun with cheese every day. Lester was sure that a good percentage, particularly the weight-watching females and the sporty males, would welcome a healthy meal replacement drink and some iced desserts. He and Carter had sat with the product development team and agreed to start with three protein-infused smoothies: mango and carrot, wheat germ and pomegranate with honey, and the ever popular lemongrass and ginger. The next trial would be bissy, as there just had to be something delicious and healthy to made from the much heralded kola nut.

Carter had insisted there was no point in trying to stock schools with a full range of Chinchillerz products because many parents did not have spare money for extras. Lunch money and bus fares were the extent of parents' largesse, he had declared, and although Lester eventually conceded that his younger brother was right, he was not keen on the condescending tone Carter chose to adopt when it suited him. As if he, Lester, did not understand that parents could be short of money.

They had argued over this perceived slight said in front of the marketing executives, but laughed it off over a few drinks that same afternoon just as they did with any disputes that arose between them.

"Is two swing going to go hereso?" asked a workman.

His colleague looked at the area to which he was pointing. "No, man. A six suppose to go dereso, and two slide next to dem."

Lester sauntered over to the men. "Yes, six swings right here. I want a lot of space in between them, though. You know how kids are, they're going to be standing too close to the swinger no matter what signs you put up."

The workman nodded. "Yes, boss. Me understand."

"And remember, we're going to use the truck tyres round the storage area, guys. When they've been cleaned up, they'll make good seats."

"Dat will work well," another workman agreed. "Bwoy, is a nice big area de kids dem going get to play inna."

"Yes, man," said Lester proudly. "A seesaw and a roundabout coming as well, just need to clear the wharf. I want them to have a big climbing frame too and lay soft tarmac underneath so they can't hurt themselves."

"Dat suppose to well expensive, sir."

"Absolutely," Lester agreed.

He still needed to convince his parents to charge an entry fee for the playground. Ida and Terence wanted the local children to use it whenever they chose between 8 a.m. and 6 p.m. each day, as a way to give back to the community. They had rejected Lester's idea of paying an entrance fee, but he was not put off. He would bring forward his latest proposal soon and hope they saw sense. The new vision was to have children enter only if they could produce receipts for Chinchillerz products purchased at least seven days before entry. The marketing people would go for it and surely his parents could have no objection to that? After all, nothing in life was truly free. He made his way back to the main building, leaving the workmen to their project.

The men had spent a hard day toiling in the sun installing the metal framework for the children's swings. They rested for a half hour or so, eating barbecued chicken and rice, drinking rum chasers they brought in themselves, in between sipping chilled limeade generously provided by the company canteen.

"Come make we go get de tyre dem."

"Dem heavy you know."

"Me know man, come. You have de storeroom key?"

No-one had the key. One of the workmen marched wearily down to the security guard at the front gate. It was quite a distance to go and he was feeling decidedly tired by the time he obtained the key and made it back to the storeroom. Turning the key inside the lock of the concertina door, he beckoned to his colleagues who sauntered over and helped to push the sturdy door to one side. Three of them rolled the heavy tyres into the yard and prepared to wash them down.

"Bring de hose over here, no?"

"Come for it. Me tired man." The weary workman took off his cap and sat on a box in the storeroom gazing around him. "Me soon come."

"You nah come?" asked one of the men, sweat pouring from his face.

"You no hear me say me soon come, man? Under hereso nice and cool. Me need a five minute, man."

He saw no reason to rush back to the job, not least because his immediate supervisor was still out on the road and none of the Chin Ellis family was likely to reappear at this time of afternoon. Surveying his vast surroundings, he wondered what it would be like to work in a place like this and have access to healthy chilled food and drink around the clock. He stood and moved around the gigantic enclosure which appeared to hold at least twenty container loads full of products. The warehousemen and shelf stackers had mini-cranes as well as ladders to help them pile products up on high. Rows and rows of boxes of milk powder, desiccated coconut, brown sugar, flavourings and spices everywhere.

The workman felt his breath quicken. This might be his only opportunity and there was no time like the present. He walked quickly to the back of the storeroom and lifted a thick black tarpaulin covering up some smaller boxes. The labels suggested that the boxes contained milk powder and were due to be transported to Kingston in a week's time, although there was no delivery address.

He tore open a box, reasoning that there were thousands of boxes to be shifted before the staff got to these and noticed that one was open. They would blame one another for the theft, as by then the playground would be finished and he and the other workers would have long left. He regretted that he could not reverse his old car into this treasure trove and load it up with as much products as it could hold. Instead he would have to make do with taking as many packets as could be contained in his trouser pockets, socks and boots, until he could transfer them to his rucksack. As he left the warehouse, laden with stolen goods, he picked up a small box of vanilla spice and placed it under his cap.

For the next few hours the men scrubbed the tyres clean, bore holes in them, and expertly attached them to cables hanging from the steel frames. They tested their weight on each swing before moving on to the next one.

"Night soon come down, you know. A time we gwaan," said the thief.

"A true. A six o'clock me get up dis marning."

"Me gaan yah. Tomorrow."

The thief made light banter with his colleagues before walking up to his car. The engine spluttered as the vehicle shuddered, before finally giving an unhealthy cough. It departed, filling the air with a rush of stale grey fumes. His family would be pleased with the milk powder, and the vanilla flavouring would be an added bedtime treat. Peace would reign in his household tonight, thank Jah, and everyone would wake up happy.

CHAPTER 15

Thursday, 30 July, 8.10 a.m.

The children had ackee and saltfish with fried dumplings and peppermint tea for breakfast. Preddy had tried ganja tea on them before, but they didn't like it and didn't care that it was good for the blood. His mother swore that one dose had cured his asthma as a toddler, so he had been a fan practically his whole life.

Preddy was back over the stove, sipping his tea as he cooked. He enjoyed cooking and helping out at the charity kitchen one morning a week. He would cook his own pots at home and serve up the food in the well-maintained public grounds adjacent to the kitchen. His speciality was red peas soup cooked with chicken backs and feet, parts of the bird the middle-class usually rejected, but were cheap, nutritious and enhanced the flavour of a meal considerably. To this pot he would add carrots, thyme, red pepper, onions and season-ing salt. Most ground produce could be obtained cheaply if bought just before the food market closed in the evenings and he had recently managed to befriend a vendor who would drop off the produce at a nearby corner shop for the detective to collect at his convenience. The Styrofoam containers in which the meals were served were supplied free of charge by the larger supermarkets in town.

The crowd of homeless people was always there in the mornings eagerly awaiting the arrival of any benefactor. Even if there were only one or two indigents in sight when a vehicle pulled up, the situation would change within a few seconds. A new arrival had a magnetic effect and people would appear from the shadows, eager to eat and unwilling to form an orderly queue.

Preddy had long given up trying to enforce order in this situation and just tried to dispense the hefty food portions as quickly as possible. He enjoyed watching their faces light up as they held the steaming bowls to their lips unable to wait for the soup to cool. When time would not allow him to act as server he would cook the food and ask his domestic helper to attend on his behalf, dropping her and the food off outside the kitchen. At other times he would leave the food at home and ask her to transport it in a taxi.

Today he was loading up his teens with pots of rich food to take to the venue themselves. It was good for them to give back to society and realise that life was not all about the latest must-have electronic gadget. In recent years, he had tried to set aside more time for his offspring, who had lived with their mother since the break-up, but it was not uncommon for him to work twelve-hour days for several days in a row. He participated in their fundraising events and sports days whenever possible, even if it meant disappearing at half-time to make urgent calls and returning before the end of the game.

As much as he would have liked to accompany them today there were not enough hours in the day and he had to get back to business. He walked the children to the waiting taxi and made sure the containers were secure before waving them off.

"Don't eat out de food!" he shouted above the noise of the vehicle's engine.

"Nobody not eating out you food, Daddy!" replied Annalee cheekily. "Gwaan driver!"

As he re-entered his apartment Preddy received a phone call from a doctor at the local hospital. The medic remembered him from his days on the anti-narcotics squad and had recently heard his name mentioned in the news as the detective heading up the Chin Ellis case.

"We admitted a six-year-old girl suffering from a high temperature and agonising convulsions," said the doctor. "Her father drove her here and I saw him come running and screaming into the lobby with her."

Preddy waited, wondering why this was his concern.

The doctor continued, "I asked him what was wrong. He didn't answer. He just cried. Then the mother came in with her two other children, but nothing was wrong with them. I carried the little girl into the ward and asked her what was wrong and she said a knife was inside of her belly! I knew that wasn't true. Anyway I got a nurse to interview the parents and they told her that the child had a terrible stomach ache and gripe medicine didn't help her. They said she ate corned beef, callaloo and banana with a glass of milk, and that was all, no other substance had passed between her lips."

"And you say dat something did?" asked Preddy.

"Absolutely, detective," said the doctor. "I had the child sedated and then pumped her stomach to clear out the contents. They have been tested. No doubt in my mind that there are traces of cocaine in her system."

Preddy had not known what to expect, but it was not that. "I will pass on dis information to de anti-narcotics team and somebody will be wid you shortly, Doctor."

"Thank you," said the doctor. "I didn't know who to call, but because I heard the father say he has to go finish off his work at Chinchillerz, I thought of you."

Preddy flinched. "Actually, Doc, de narcotics guys have whole heap on deir plates. I'm on my way dere. How is she doing?"

"Well she's not completely out of the woods yet, but her temperature has decreased significantly and she has fallen into a deep sleep."

"Okay. Don't tell de parents anything. We soon come."

Preddy phoned Rabino and the two detectives arrived at the Cornwall Regional Hospital in Mount Salem within minutes of each other. Preddy knew that the weeping father was lying from the moment he opened his mouth as he was incapable of making eye contact at any point. The man tried to convince the detectives that the doctor was mistaken and there was no way his daughter had ingested any cocaine as everything she had eaten came from the supermarket. It was Rabino who had gently coaxed the now silent and stunned mother into speaking, reminding her that someone had nearly killed the child she had carried and nurtured for nine months. What was to stop the same thing happening to her other children and what if they died?

The mother sat holding the children on her knees to comfort herself rather than them. They could be no more than two and four-years-old and would not be aware that their sister was seriously ill. Their mother squeezed them tightly and told the detectives about the milk powder.

"Dat is de only drinks me see she drink and it no come from no supermarket," mumbled the distraught woman. "She a bother me say she want milk rather dan soda after her meal, and me send her go open de packet and mix it wid water herself." The woman caught her breath and Rabino rubbed her hand encouragingly. "Me hear she say it taste funny, but me no pay her no mind. Me busy wid dem other two little one, you know?" The mother began crying again, uncontrollably this time.

The father looked at Preddy through miserable eyes. "None a we never take de cup from her and try it so see what wrong," he said. "De cup no see-through, so me never see say it no look like milk."

It took quite a while for him to admit that it must have come from a batch of milk powder obtained from his job. It took even longer to admit he stole it from the Chinchillerz storeroom unknown to his supervisor or the business owners. He finally confessed that a dozen more packets were at his home, but some were the real thing as he and his wife had used one of them in their own cocoa tea.

"Me a no thief, you know!" the man cried. "A de Devil tempt me. A de Devil tell me say de Chiney dem rich and dem not going miss it, and me family poor and dem need it!"

Preddy felt some sympathy for the man, not because he bought into the idea of being poor and needy as an excuse, but because it had been a cruel lesson to learn and one which would stay with him for the rest of his life.

Strictly this was a matter for the anti-narcotics team, but there was no way Preddy could let go of this new aspect of the case. If he informed Superintendent Brownlow of this latest development, he would be ordered to back off and let the appropriate team deal with it. Somebody within the frozen-food empire was dealing in drugs, perhaps with the knowledge and consent of Carter and Lester Chin Ellis. Preddy wanted to see the evidence for himself and asked the father to take them to his home.

The detectives drove the contrite man back to his modest dwelling, a starter home in a small housing scheme. There they collected the suspect packages, placing them carefully into evidence bags. None of the packets were marked with the Chinchillerz logo and Preddy reminded himself that these products would have most likely been imported from another country, somewhere in South America most likely, and repackaged.

"You can read what write on it?" he asked Rabino, handing over the package.

The detective screwed up her eyes and peered at the tiny writing on the label. "No, sir. It's definitely not English or Spanish. It's too blurry though, I can't make it out."

"Are dese all de bags, sir?" Preddy asked the father.

The man silently opened the cupboard and removed the additional products, including the vanilla spice.

"Were dese hidden or boxed differently in de storeroom?" asked Preddy.

"A did whole heap a dem, inna one section to demself," he replied. "Cover up under tarpaulin inna box dat say delivery Kingston August 6. Me fix back de box good-good."

Rabino looked at her superior. "August 6, Independence Day."

"Me wish me never see dem things dere, Jah know!" the man wailed. "Me shoulda just do me work and go home. Me shoulda never go walk 'bout inna de people dem place."

Rabino said nothing, but she could not agree with him more. She hoped for his sake that his daughter did not turn out mentally or physically impaired when she did come to.

"We'll have to let narcotics know to come and get these, sir," she said.

"No, not yet," said Preddy quickly. "I will handle it."

His mind worked furiously. The goods were due to be moved in a few days. Raiding Chinchillerz and seizing the remaining products was not an option when they did not know who was moving them. Once the news made it into the public arena there was a danger the miscreants would cover their tracks and no-one could be charged. The child had not died, and there was no reason to believe the drug had got mixed up with legitimate ingredients stored elsewhere. He glanced at Rabino and wondered how he was going to ensure that this information stayed within the team. The less people that knew about it the better, but he could not carry out this investigation without the help of his detectives. He gathered the stolen goods and headed for the door.

"Take him back to de hospital for me, please," said Preddy. "I have an errand to run."

CHAPTER 16

Thursday, 30 July, 11.50 a.m.

The receptionist delivered a dazzling smile when she heard the buzzer and spotted Preddy waving at her. She pressed the button which allowed the heavy glass door to be pushed open then stood up straightening her floral jacket. Preddy strode through the entrance of the private laboratory and was immediately hit by the strong smell of perfume.

"Hello, Detective Preddy, how you doing?" She was a cute Black girl with short straightened hair brushed down firmly on her scalp, not a strand out of place.

"Not as good as you, Mish."

"You come to buy me lunch?" she asked.

"I did plan to ask Valerie if she want something to eat, but you can come too."

"She woulda box me down if me ever go put myself on your lunch date," she chuckled. "Make me call her for you."

"Do you think I could creep up on her, surprise her?"

"Okay, no problem." Her bright red fingernail pressed the intercom. "Can somebody open door two please, a delivery coming through. Gwaan down, Detective."

Preddy walked down the long wide corridor of the large single storey building, passing individual research facilities separated by glass partitions throughout. A white coated technician acknowledged the detective and held the door open as he entered. Valerie was in her cubicle and he watched her silently for a moment, noting her intense concentration as she bent over double examining something, glasses perched on the end of her nose, relaxed hair pulled away from her face held back with a rubber band. A photograph of her husband sat on her table and he wondered why it was still there. No pictures of his ex-wife were on display at his office whether he expected visitors or not. He tapped gently on the window and she remained oblivious at first, so he tapped again more forcefully this time and she looked up at him in surprise. She carefully set aside the object of interest before opening the door.

"Well, look here!" she said. "My personal Ray of sunshine."

"Hope I'm not disturbing you?" said Preddy.

"Of course not." She greeted him with a big kiss. "Stop talk foolishness. You know you can never disturb me."

"You can find time to eat lunch today, Val?"

"Mmm, not really, you know. Me short two people who gone on holiday and nuff work leave to do," she replied. "What's in de envelope?"

"I did want you to look at something, but if you busy it can wait till later."

"No Ray, is alright. What is it?"

Preddy drew a photograph out of the envelope and placed it in Valerie's hands. She fixed her glasses firmly on her nose.

"What dat look like to you?" asked Preddy.

"I don't know . . .bruised skin. You'll have to do better dan dat."

"It's de left side of Lester Chin Ellis's face. At least I think it's him. De photo was sent to me by someone wid a note saying de bruise was not caused by a fist."

"Ah, poor Mr Chin Ellis," Valerie nodded. "I should have known, now dat de case has become your mistress."

"Never," he said, wrapping his arm around her waist and squeezing her. "No way."

"Careful, you know. Dem soon start talk say you come here for woman and not to work."

She moved away from him and held the photograph under a desk lamp. "Why you don't ask de doctor what him think it is?"

"I don't even know who de doctor is and I can't go digging around or de lawyers will take issue wid me," he explained. "I can't take dat photo to de government forensics lab."

Valerie moved the photo under a magnifying glass. "You know it look more like de mark of an object fi true. A fist not going to do dat."

A rap on the door diverted her attention momentarily.

"Sorry, Valerie. A man from de beef farm down a Cascade want to know if de sample ready yet?"

"Tell him me soon come." She looked at Preddy regretfully. "Leave it wid me and I'll get it back to you later."

"As you wish, madam." He grabbed her hand and kissed it, bowing as he left the room.

* * *

Preddy was seated in his office at Pelican Walk that evening when his cell phone vibrated beside him.

"You decent?" Valerie asked.

"I'm at de station so my body is decent, my mind maybe not so much right now."

"Get your mind back on your work, Mr Detective," she laughed. "A business me deh pon."

Preddy sat forward in his chair. "What you have for me?"

"Dem must did use de bedsheet tie up something and lick him in him face," Valerie said. "It look to me like some tiny fibres on him face, but dem don't really look like facial hair."

"I'll have a look around de cell again, but I never noticed anything dem could use," said Preddy. "Unless one of de officers did take out de object long time."

"You believe dem woulda do dat?"

"Well, detainees not suppose to carry anything inna dem cell," he replied. "Officer can make mistake and don't search de man dem properly, and now a try cover up."

"Den Lester don't know what dem take lick him?"

"Him say dem punch him and him feel pain and him don't remember a thing, until him wake up inna him bed."

"So Lester is a liar?"

"Lester is a something, but I haven't quite worked out what yet."

"Well, I guess you can only look around and ask," she said. "Make sure you get dinner today, you know?"

"Yes, mam. Me soon gone home. You finish off your work?"

"Not all of it," she sighed, "but den dere is always tomorrow and tomorrow . . ."

"I know de rest!" he laughed. "Lock up de photo good for me till me see you."

"Talk to you tomorrow. Love you."

"Love you too."

Preddy locked his office door behind him and wandered downstairs to the cell that had remained empty and sealed since the altercation. He carefully removed the seal and used a key to open the heavy steel door. He surveyed the stark surroundings. The air within felt damp and the odour that clung to the discoloured walls was a mix of sweat, stale urine and flowery disinfectant.

All four inmates were brought into the cell during the course of Saturday night into Sunday morning. The desk officer, Wilson, should have witnessed the search of all of the men as it was his job to log their personal possessions. The duty officer, Nembhard, should have noticed any strange objects in the cell. Timmins and Franklin said they only carried out the arrest and never entered the cell, but they couldn't all be telling the truth. Wilson said he ran the fire drill to "keep people on their toes," but what if there was another reason?

Preddy tugged at the worn grey sheeting on the beds, straightening them out to see if anything was concealed and came up empty handed. Two bunk beds and a stained plastic bucket, nothing else. The iron bars on the windows were secure. He resealed the door and made his way back to his office.

"Detective Preddy," he said, after snatching his ringing phone from his desk.

"Detective, Ida Chin Ellis here."

Preddy had not spoken to the doyenne since his visit to Chinchillerz headquarters. "Yes, Miss Ida. I hope you are bearing up okay?"

"That girl, Carter's girlfriend, Zadie. Terence and I were talking about her. We haven't heard anything from her, not a word, but we remembered that she and Carter were quarrelling in his office." Her voice sounded strong and forthright, with an edge he had not noticed before.

"What were dey quarrelling about?"

"I don't really know. Carter said it wasn't anything, but she did slam his door so hard it sounded like a thunder clap," she replied. "We just decided to stay out of it since it's 'man and woman story.'"

"When was de argument?" Preddy began to scribble on his notepad.

"A few weeks ago now. That was the last time we saw her," Ida said. "I cannot believe that we don't even hear a word from that girl yet. She's Black and ungrateful you see!"

Preddy raised an eyebrow. Black people cursing Black people black was not a new phenomenon. Zadie was no darker than Ida. He wondered if Carter's death had brought out the worst in Ida or if she had acquired her superiority after marrying Terence. "Thank you for de information. We have been trying to speak to Miss Merton for a while now, but we cannot force her to come forward."

"How is the investigation going otherwise? You have any suspects?"

"We have some leads, but dere is nothing I can tell you at dis minute."

"What about that man you asked me about, the one behaving strangely at the funeral?"

"We are pursuing a few strong lines of inquiry at de moment," he assured her. "De case is top priority for us and we will do everything we can to bring de murderer to justice."

"I hope so. My son's death can't just go like it's nothing."

* * *

Ida hung up the phone wondering whether the police were really giving Carter's murder the attention it deserved or if they were treating him like any old naigger. They had barely acted to prevent Lester from being attacked, so why should she have confidence that they would put much effort into the murder case? That concern had led her to appoint her own private detective. The man was a shifty little creature who she disliked on sight, but came recommended by her lawyer and there was a need for independent eyes on the case. Terence knew nothing about the new hiring because when she first suggested it he chastised her and told her to let the police do their jobs. She forgave Terence because he was a man and men thought differently. He did not know what it was like to feel a child's heart beating inside of you and then to lose him.

Carter had always been by her side in the workplace. He was interested in learning the intricacies of the business, asking her questions about how the ingredients got from the farm to the factory and the logistics of deliveries. Lester, her loving, hardworking son, enjoyed sampling the foods and was very good at coming up with inventive flavours to develop, as well as new ways to market them. But he was more interested in the perks available within the business than how the business ran.

Yes, they were different, but they were both her beloved boys. Now that she had lost one and the other had suffered injury, her stomach was always twisted in knots and she found it almost impossible to eat. Every morning she awoke to the same tortured feelings. She wondered if there really was a possibility that Zadie had harmed her son in any way. If she did she would see to it that the girl suffered and suffered badly.

* * *

Zadie sat in her apartment staring at a picture of herself and Carter which was partially torn in two. It had been taken at Port Royal, the earthquake ridden town on the south-east coast that centuries ago had been classed as the wickedest place on earth. The couple had spent the day on a walking tour of the picturesque area admiring the historical buildings, the well-preserved fort, crumbling naval hospital, and many monuments of defence, before exploring the museums. That particular snapshot was taken after they emerged from the Royal Artillery Store, more popularly known as the Giddy House for its dizzying effect on the brain. There they had laughed and cuddled, trying to stare straight ahead while navigating sloping floors permanently set at a sharp gradient by the 1907 earthquake.

An eager local guide had shown them around the maritime community regaling them with scary tales of pirates, treasure, debauchery and murder. Without closing her eyes she could easily envision the British navy with their cannons and gunpowder at the ready to keep at bay any would-be invaders.

The photograph had reached this forlorn state two weeks ago after Carter had declared their relationship over. He unceremoniously broke up with her when he discovered that she had not been honest with him about her past. They had met in a gentlemen's club and he knew she was an exotic dancer and an extremely good one too. The first time he bought her a drink she was practically naked with only a G-string and strategically placed tassels to protect her modesty.

Lately, Carter had discovered that she once worked as an escort, which he angrily denounced as prostitution. They argued bitterly over the issue. How on earth did he think she could have afforded to leave home at seventeen? Where did he think her elaborate wardrobe and make-up came from? Whatever the American models were advertising was what she was buying and it didn't come cheap.

He refused to accept that on most occasions there was no physical contact with clients. Some paid for her to sit in their cars and talk to them for hours. The punters would talk about their marriages whether good or bad, about their children or lack of children, and about their jobs or friends. Others had paid for her to dress up in skimpy lingerie and parade in front of them in a hotel room. Her job was to do nothing but strut, spin and pose, and back and forth she went without any complaint.

Yes, she had slept with a few men who paid handsomely and were nice to her, and she always ensured that they used protection. She knew better than to admit to him that one or two had knocked her around. Hiding the bruises from friends and family had not been too difficult with her dark skin, and although she was not a fan of rouge she would apply it if needed to disguise the effects of a bad night's work.

What did her past life matter anyway, she had asked him. It was in the past and there was no reason to allow it to affect their relationship.

Zadie pressed the offending photo down into the over-flowing garbage bin and poured herself a large glass of wine. Being Carter's girlfriend sure had its privileges; riding in expensive cars, dining at sea on the yacht, getting into the best clubs free and being able to sample all sorts of delicious foods. Even now her freezer was full of sweet frozen Chinchillerz goods. Just thinking of their light mango cheesecake made her mouth water. She should have thrown them into the garbage too when he dumped her, but it would be a sin to dispose of food before it had passed its use-by date, however much it irritated her.

She had purposely avoided Carter's funeral as she was unsure whether her presence would be welcomed. Lester would not have minded, might even have been grateful for the support. If only she had met him first. Terence might have appreciated her too, but Miss Ida had a way of looking at her that made her feel unworthy. Part of her had felt the need to show respect for the dead as it would surely look cold-hearted if she didn't, but the idea of listening to glowing eulogies of an abuser held no appeal.

The first time he slapped her came as a massive shock and that was long before he had ever heard of her double life. On that occasion it was apparently because she needed to learn to mind her own business and stop trying to advise him. As if she should not care about what he shoved up his nose. She shook her head as the memories flooded back. As much as she had loved Carter Chin Ellis sometimes it had been very hard not to despise him.

The apartment was too silent so she turned on her radio and swayed slowly to the smooth rhythms that filtered through the air. It was time to dress up for a client she had performed a massage service on only once before. Obviously, it had pleased him. Now she needed to get the massage table ready and prepare the essential oils and towels. She was not up to providing any extras tonight and had already made that clear to him, but he seemed happy enough with the idea of a straight massage. She preferred these types of punters who did not want much. There was no red brick institution in the world that could produce graduates with comparable skills to hers.

She sashayed her way into the kitchen and opened the washing machine to check that her other essential item was there. Nestled within the drum of an unloaded stainless steel washing machine was a fully loaded stainless steel gun. Matching things looked so nice. She never used the machine which was purely a decorative appendage and looked satisfyingly expensive. The small pistol had been used just once. Only two people knew she had a gun and she intended to keep it that way. She closed the machine door and took another large sip of wine.

CHAPTER 17

Friday, 31 July, 1.52 p.m.

Preddy had convinced Rabino that the cocaine matter had to stay under wraps until the Independence Day movement. If everything went according to plan, someone would be charged with possession of and dealing in cocaine before the end of the holiday period, and depending on the real intended destination they might even add the charge of attempting to export cocaine.

Spence and Harris were told little, other than that Preddy had received a tip-off he believed to be good and they needed to watch Chinchillerz for vehicles departing on Independence Day which were likely to be carrying narcotics and had to be intercepted. The last thing he wanted was for word to get around that a sting was due to take place on the public holiday as the information was sure to reach Superintendent Brownlow.

"Will we get extra officers tae watch the place from dawn onwards, sir?" Harris asked, while they were convened in the evidence room.

"Er, it's unlikely," Preddy said, as he avoided eye contact by shuffling his papers. "We'll have to make do."

"Aye, but have ye asked, sir?" Harris pressed.

Preddy pressed his fingernails into the papers and kept his tone as level as possible. "We were not offered any more hands to deal wid phone calls because dere aren't any, and we certainly won't be offered any for surveillance."

"Maybe if ye say that the phone calls are getting out of hand or something?"

Rabino raised her perfectly groomed eyebrows in Harris' direction. Spence muttered something under her breath about "hard ears" and shook her head. Preddy forced a smile to his lips that was not reflected in his eyes. "Not going to happen," he quipped, and watched through the corner of his eye as Harris fell silent and finished off his own paperwork.

The team spent an exhausting morning going through the evidence and now were getting ready to head to a beach-side diner for a late lunch. There was still no sign of the suspect vehicle and the lack of this main lead was beginning to prey on Preddy's mind. A short break from Pelican Walk to get away from the photographs, notes and reports had to be a good thing.

Spence slipped her rubber sandals into a plastic bag, fully intending to kick them off at the beach and let her toes enjoy the warm sand. She was glad she had worn a skirt today as the temptation to let calming sea water cover her calves would be strong.

They sauntered down the stairs and into the front court-yard talking and joking while heading to their vehicles. They passed red and yellow hibiscus flowers which adorned the outer area of the courtyard, their deep green leaves standing out in stark contrast to the brown dried lawn. Luckily the plants did not need constant watering in order to survive as there had been no real rain for weeks. Watering the foliage in a time of drought was forbidden and so the desert-like appearance of the grounds had to be tolerated. The perennially green leafed mango tree was still heavily laden with delicious fruit and showed no obvious signs of depletion even though a few dozen had been picked, most of which were devoured by a grateful Glaswegian.

As they ambled toward their vehicles, Preddy's attention was diverted momentarily by the shadow of a person on the second floor.

"Go on ahead, I'll meet you dere," he said.

Harris looked at the detective curiously. "Everything okay, sir?"

"Sure. Soon come," he replied. "Order me a good-sized plate of brown stew fish and festival. Don't get any drinks for me yet."

Preddy spun around and quickly made his way back through the station entrance. It was nearly two o'clock in the afternoon and there was no reason why anyone should be near the room which contained evidence mainly related to the Chin Ellis family matters. Only his team of detectives and a secretary had access to the keys, yet he was sure he had spotted movement behind the blinds.

As he leapt up the first set of stairs he was greeted by a colleague he hadn't seen for a while who was making his descent.

"How's it going, Raythan man?"

"Ah, you know how it goes." Preddy smiled brightly while wincing inside.

"You have time for a drink?"

"Can't make it today, you know." Preddy resumed his sprint. "Catch you a next time though."

"Alright, me friend."

Preddy managed to avoid any further encounters as he covered the second flight of stairs. The evidence room was situated towards the end of a long hallway consisting of eight rooms, with only a janitors' storeroom and a small gym at the very end.

As he started down the hallway he saw a sweating Timmins walking towards him dressed in exercise vest, shorts and sneakers. The officer nodded at the detective and Preddy nodded back, his eyes following the man's departing form. He walked quickly to the evidence room and tried the door. A feeling of relief swept over him as it was still locked.

Peering through the shutters his eyes swept the room and determined that it was empty. He knocked on the janitors' door and, receiving no reply, opened it to find only bottles of cleaning tools and paper handtowels.

The door to the gym was slightly ajar. Although the officers referred to it as a gym, it was more of a weights room containing a good variety of dumbbells, kettle bells, exercise mats, fitness balls and one dilapidated cross trainer. Inside, an officer's uniform, black trousers with red seams, light blue short-sleeved shirt and flat black cap were hanging from a hook in the wall, with polished shoes arranged neatly beneath them.

Preddy closed the door and stood silently for a moment wondering if his eyes had been playing tricks on him. He really needed to shed the nightmares, get more sleep and drink more ganja tea. He walked slowly back along the corridor, stopping to listen at each door and peer into every room until he arrived at the top of the stairs. Perfect silence filled his ears and he was assured that no-one else was on the floor. He started his descent, picking up pace as he thought of the freshly cooked fish awaiting him.

* * *

Preddy placed the glass of ice-cold water in front of Harris and sat down beside him. He was a fan of this small cosy eatery designed to look cheap, although he could tell that a great deal of effort and money had been invested into making it appear that way. With bamboo walls painted in the colours of the Jamaican flag, perfectly thatched roof and ideal seaside setting, it was just the place to enjoy a snack and a chat.

The seats were recycled wooden kegs made comfortable by leatherette covered foam cushions. Harris liked this place too and thought the bars in Glasgow would benefit from seating like this. There was no danger of losing a chair leg since there were none, and drunken patrons could not pick up these heavy barrels, never mind throw them at anyone.

They had finished their lunch of fried snapper fish complemented with roast breadfruit and fresh cornbread, having arrived too late for any festivals. Diners needed to turn up for lunch much earlier if they wanted to enjoy the popular deep-fried sweet flour delicacy, the chef advised. The meal was washed down with blended carrot juice and ginger, and they had steered clear of work talk, discussing instead the perceived differences between the various Caribbean islands. Rabino and Spence had just headed off back to the station happily complaining of feeling overfed and needing to sleep off the after-effects of overindulgence.

Preddy was relieved that the foreigner appeared to be adapting well and enjoying the many delights the island had to offer. Although Harris had joined his team out of nowhere, he had made great efforts to settle in, sampling everything that was put before him, including the mannish water which a lot of tourists balked at. He seemed keen to be part of the team, even though at times he surely could not understand them when they descended into fast talking Patois, which usually happened when they were joking or arguing about something, or in the case of Spence, purposely trying to leave him flummoxed.

Nothing caused this white man to turn up his nose and he seemed genuinely interested in learning about his colleagues and their working lives. There had been no more attempts at playing the ginnal and no more displays of temper. Harris did have a tendency to forget that the Jamaican force was not as well-equipped as his own and he was not always keen on taking directions, but Preddy resolved not to hold these foibles against him. They were both very experienced detectives and if their positions were reversed Preddy knew he would not be keen on taking directions from Harris either.

"Come on, you've had time to think about it. You can tell me what you really think," said Preddy. "I won't tell a soul."

"Och, it's great, sir, really. But . . ."

"Go on. I promise not to be offended. Go ahead."

"Well, I find that if ye ask a Jamaican the time they dinnae really respond how I would expect. Ye know 'minutes tae five' they say, or 'minutes after six.' Well, what bloody time is it?"

Preddy laughed along with Harris while admitting to being guilty of this particular trait too. "For de majority of Jamaican's a few minutes is neither here nor dere you know."

"A few minutes? Seriously, the other day I got an appointment for the barbers at nine a.m. He turned up at five tae ten and couldnae understand ma annoyance. Didn't bother tae make an excuse or anything. It was just normal for him, I guess."

"On dat front, I'm pleased to say we are much better in de force. When you're off de job though if you get invited to a dinner or a party, don't bother to turn up on time. You'll be de only one dere for hours."

Harris nodded. "I believe ye. And another thing I've noticed is that all the young mothers seem tae carry their babies around in their arms. In all the time I've been here I've never seen a single pram or buggy. These girls must be much stronger than they look. Some of them are using only one arm tae hold the baby and the other tae hold an umbrella or cloth over the baby."

Preddy had never given the matter a moment's thought before, but now he realised that it was true. He had never been to Scotland, but he had been to London and to various states in North America and no-one carried their babies in their arms. Those without strollers had slings around their necks buttressed by straps around the waist. His own children had been the beneficiaries of car seats for travelling when they were young and he could not recall any instance where he or his wife had needed to walk for any length of time with the children in arms.

"You're right," he said eventually. "For some it will be poverty. For others, I'm going to guess dat it's because of lack of opportunity to purchase. No businessman is going risk importing expensive buggies if de market is too small. And wid our pavements de way dey are, well, I'm not so sure how good an investment it would be for de mothers."

Harris nodded silently and sipped his drink.

"Anything else bugging you? Excuse de pun."

Harris thought for a moment. "There are people selling things everywhere in the town centre in broad daylight. Food, clothes, CDs, knives, everything is spread out on the ground or hung up on the walls of legitimate businesses. Is it always like that?"

Preddy shrugged. "It's a bit messy. Sometimes officers seize de stuff, sometimes dey just move dem on. Higglers can be stubborn and determined as well as desperate. It's something I believe de parish council officers should take sole control of. We have more dan enough to do."

Harris drained his glass. "You've got bloody great water though, in the glass and in the sea."

"I won't argue wid dat."

"Okay, it's yer turn," said Harris.

"I'll pass."

"Och, come on!"

Preddy thought about the matter and turned to stare at his colleague. "I did want to ask you about your hair."

Harris grinned. "I'm sure that's supposed tae be ma line!"

"Ah, but I don't want to touch it though," Preddy smiled. "I just wondered how it is so red. Is it naturally like dat or you put something in it?"

"Aye, it's natural alright. I'm from good Celtic stock and all of us have ginger hair. I swear the Jamaican sun has made it even redder though."

There were many other questions that Preddy wanted to ask Harris, not least about how he had ended up in Jamaica, but he would save them for another time. He preferred to keep this encounter light-hearted and watch how the Glaswegian operated in full social mode. So far he had demonstrated no biases or prejudices and Preddy hoped that he would never come to regret accepting the foreigner on his team.

At that moment Preddy's phone rang. He exchanged a few words with the person on the line then hung up and stood. "We have an impatient visitor. Let's get back to de station."

The two detectives entered the Pelican Walk lobby a few minutes later. Preddy caught a glimpse inside the staff canteen and was slightly perturbed at the sight of Timmins, Franklin, Nembhard and Wilson all dining together. It would not do for the two arresting officers and the two duty officers to form a clique. Right now though, he had no time to think about them.

"Where is he?" asked Preddy.

"Him upstairs in room four," said the stand-in desk officer. "Him did down here a make up whole heap a noise! Dem put him upstairs and give him coffee to drink."

Lester Chin Ellis stood up angrily when the detectives entered the waiting room. "They told me to come and take my car this morning. See I've turned up now, it's late afternoon and they're telling me it's not ready!"

"I apologise, Mr Chin Ellis," said Preddy. "We have finished wid de car and it should have been brought back here by now."

"Let me just make a call and see where it is," said Harris, leaving the room.

"Sorry about dat," said Preddy. "How are you feeling?"

"Could be better," said Lester, appearing slightly calmer. "Everything is on top of me you know? I have to try and keep the family together. Everybody depending on me."

"I understand," said Preddy. There was something about this young man that he just did not like or trust. Lester Chin Ellis was all about Lester Chin Ellis. "We are doing all we can to get to de bottom of dis terrible tragedy."

"Thank you. Don't let this become a cold case, Detective. I know that plenty of murderers are out there and the police never get them."

"We will do our utmost best. You can count on dat."

Lester's phone rang and he retrieved it from his pocket. "I soon come, Mom. Yes, alright." He hung up and looked at Preddy. "See? Now Miss Ida is ringing me every minute to find out what I'm doing."

"I can only imagine what you and your parents are going through," He was still waiting to hear Lester ask him for details of the investigation or at least mention his brother by name.

Harris re-entered the room. "They're bringing the car round tae the front now, sir."

Preddy watched through the window as Lester left the building. He noticed Timmins walking under the archway entrance at the same time. A sense of disquiet overcame him as the two men appeared to acknowledge one another. The contact was brief lasting no more than a few seconds, but Preddy was furious and ran down the stairs.

"Officer Timmins! My office, now!"

Timmins looked up in surprise, but followed the detective up to his office. Preddy slammed the door and immediately swung around to face the nervous officer.

"What in God's name do you think you doing, man? What you talking to Chin Ellis about?"

"Take it easy, sir! He said, 'I remember you,'" the officer responded defensively. "I said, 'I remember you too.' Not a word more."

"Are you working against dis police force, officer?" Preddy put his face close to that of the shaken man. "You must know dat under no circumstances are you to have any contact wid Chin Ellis. He says hello, you ignore him. You see him on one side of de street, you go on de other. You understand me?"

"Yes, sir. I never really think 'bout it." Timmins held the detective's gaze.

"No, you never." Preddy finally allowed himself to take a seat. "You, Nembhard, Wilson, Franklin, none of you should have anything to say to Chin Ellis. I know de attorney told you dat."

"It just happened suddenly, sir, I didn't even know him was here. It won't happen again."

"You can leave."

Preddy did not want to think the worst of any of his officers, but he was gradually coming to the realisation that some on the squad might not be who they seemed. Yet again he would need to remind the officers of their responsibilities in relation to the case and he was tired of repeating things that should be second nature.

Timmins stood outside of the detective's door, took a deep breath and closed his eyes briefly. He reached for his flannel and dabbed at transparent baubles prickling on his forehead, then quickly walked away with fists clenched and a deep frown on his face. In his blind anger he nearly bumped into the burly superintendent and immediately offered his profuse apologies. It would be dangerous to have all the big men of Pelican Walk turn against him.

CHAPTER 18

Thursday, 6 August, 12.30 p.m.

The highway, roads and pavements were teeming with revellers as Preddy, accompanied by his two children, made the short trip to Sam Sharpe Square in the city centre for the final day of the six-day Independence festivities.

The annual celebrations always commenced at midnight on the 31st of July, with thanksgiving services in major town centres including a re-enactment of the reading of the Emancipation Declaration of 1838. It was a service Preddy usually tried to attend, but regrettably this year it had been out of the question. With too much on his mind he would not have been able to give the sombre gathering the attention it deserved, being an occasion when modern day descendants give thanks for the day the enslaved were granted freedom and could look towards a new beginning in their lives. The midnight event was followed in daylight hours by Emancipation observance services at churches and town halls where attendees were reminded of the huge sacrifices made by the national heroes to ensure freedom for future generations.

Most locals now referred to the holiday period as the Emancipendence season although the only two official holidays were the first and the sixth days of August. The second through the fifth of August were treated as normal business days or weekend days depending on where they fell during the week. Some workers regularly took advantage of the season and booked the whole week off to reflect on life in general and recharge their batteries. But on Independence Day the city was alive, celebrating that on 6th August 1962, Jamaica became a sovereign nation, independent from colonial Britain.

All four roads leading from the fountain in the centre of the historical cobbled square were cordoned off from traffic, leaving pleasure seekers free to traverse the area on foot. A large national flag atop the stately Montego Bay Cultural Centre fluctuated wildly in the warm breeze against a brilliant blue sky. The glorious sun smiled through, unencumbered by the thin clouds. For as far as the eye could see there were drapes of black, green and gold everywhere, even on the handcarts illegally encroaching on the square selling their aromatic wares. Tasty snacks, from boiled corn and peanut porridge to peeled sugar cane and sliced pineapple, were readily available. Men and women, boys and girls, old and young were bedecked in the national colours, with the Rastafarians adding a bold red to their ensemble. Preddy proudly displayed a Jamaican flag lapel pin on his official khaki suit.

The formal Independence Day proceedings began with the pomp and pageantry of a civic ceremony held under a huge marquee at which the mayor and several dignitaries were present. People who could not hold under the massive canopy sought refuge under giant umbrellas or under the sheltered patios of surrounding businesses, most of which were closed for the holiday. The custos of St James read the Governor General's message to the sizeable audience. Awards were handed out to outstanding residents of the parish including journalists, educators, medical practitioners, businessmen, community workers and farmers. Preddy spotted Spence and her husband Greg with their two little girls. She had taken up seats at the back to ensure a smooth get away if necessary. Harris was driving around the surrounding streets with a remit to pick her up if Chinchillerz was all go.

The JCF cadet band provided the musical entertainment. Preddy watched with pride as the young men and women put their considerable talents on display, although he had to disappear occasionally to take or make the odd phone call. Rabino and her boyfriend Clive were somewhere by the fountain, she said, although he had not yet picked them out in the crowd.

The detective was greeted warmly by the cheerful mayor bedecked in his ceremonial robe and chain, and he made time to mingle with other recognised heads of business including the minister for tourism who came over to congratulate Preddy for his work cleaning up the city.

Preddy planned to leave his youngsters to their own devices once they had dutifully sat through the civic function. A Speakers' Corner was organised in the grounds of the cultural centre, where amateur orators could read poetry and short stories to the appreciative crowds, but he had a feeling that his offspring would not attend. The youngsters were respectful, but their real interests lay elsewhere, and Roman had already expressed delight that a group of technicians were setting up a huge stage and had hoisted an enormous boom box onto it, even though the concert would not start until late afternoon.

Inevitably, Roman and Annalee would soon be on the hunt for burgers and French fries, while Preddy just wanted soul food, preferably served with a large helping of red pepper sauce. He had taken them to the local Chinchillerz once when they were very small and they had enjoyed the old-time chocolate tea flavoured ice cream, which was surprisingly good. Back then Chinchillerz lost out as being *the* place to be, due to the absence of cheap plastic toys that other fast food establishments were so fond of handing out. Having long grown out of such things, they were quite keen on Chinchillerz desserts and knowing his daughter's sweet tooth they were sure to end up inside a branch of the eponymous chain before nightfall.

They would then gravitate towards the loud, DJ-style music with the not-so-subtle lyrics which he often pretended not to hear. Being a father was not easy work, and being a disciplinarian when your children did not live with you permanently was a unique challenge, not least because the teenagers could pack their bags and head back to their mother if they disagreed with you. He was thankful that, so far, he had been spared the tantrums, nasty rows and door slamming.

It was nearly 2 p.m. when Preddy finally received the long-awaited call with news of movement at Chinchillerz headquarters. He discreetly alerted each member of the team. The teens each got a hug and more cash than was perhaps required, while he made them promise to stay together and return home by 9 p.m. at latest. That would probably get them home by 10 p.m., as they were one hundred percent Jamaican after all.

Driving towards the rendezvous position with Rabino, he prayed that the operation would be successful. It still rattled him that Harris had gone behind his back and spoken to Superintendent Brownlow requesting more officers for the Chin Ellis case. The superintendent seemed to believe that the requirement for extra bodies was to free the detectives who were being bogged down by telephone calls and time-wasting interviews. The issue of drugs and a stake-out had clearly not been mentioned, yet Preddy was still annoyed that the Scotsman had overstepped the mark. As the superintendent's announcement of more hands was made in front of the entire team, Preddy had no choice but to bite his tongue and thank his boss.

In the end it all worked out reasonably well as Preddy had put the three temporary officers on twenty-four hour surveillance duty of the Chinchillerz headquarters last night, with instructions to phone him if anyone was seen entering or leaving the storage area. They initially reported that a sign was attached to the main gate stating that it was closed for the public holiday, although the security guard was there and a handful of workers had arrived. The door to the storeroom was now open and a small van had been spotted reversing inside.

Top Road was monitored by Highway Patrol and there was no way that anyone could get past without the officers being alerted. Preddy had worked with these men before and knew he could trust them to act as a backup team. There was no need to tell them about the real point of the mission and so he didn't. He hoped the van did not take that particular route. Any mistakes on a chase along that steep thoroughfare could result in a treacherous drop for vehicles which broke through the safety barriers and went over the precipice. If the suspects took the low-lying Bottom Road the officers would have a much better chance of stopping them safely, and if they made it to the end of the Hip Strip they would come to a dead end after passing a small public beach and a university halls of residence. After that, ten feet high walls topped with barbed wire surrounding Sangster International Airport would ensure that neither man nor vehicle would pass through.

Preddy shrugged off his formal jacket to reveal a white T-shirt. He and Rabino sat in their unmarked car watching both roads carefully through binoculars. The strains of bass-heavy music floated from the square as the technicians tested their equipment, while the impatient partygoers remained blissfully oblivious to the police operation. The main section of mile long beach was still a heavily populated area even though plenty of locals were amassed in the city centre. Any form of physical confrontation here could be disastrous and Preddy hoped the Chinchillerz van would stop when accosted without the need for weapons to be drawn.

Harris and Spence were in their undercover vehicle further along Bottom Road, parked at the intersection with Top Road. Harris was dressed just like any other tourist in yellow short-sleeved shirt, patterned knee-length shorts and brown pumps, topped off with a straw hat. Spence was his polar opposite in smart blue skirt suit and strappy heels. The detectives each used their binoculars to spy the roads and crowded beach. The atmosphere was pulsating with the noisy colourful crowds shouting, cheering and blowing high-pitched whistles. A sole drummer beat out a catchy tattoo while the group of sun-worshippers around him bobbed their heads in unison and danced around.

Harris could not help tapping his feet. Anyone who did not get caught up in the magic of the beat must be a pretty unreachable person. He took in the media vans and sponsors tents before sweeping in the direction of the food kiosks where hungry queues were waiting to buy hotdogs, pizzas and jerked pork or chicken. The strong mixed smells of cooking oils and seasoned meats lay heavy in the air notwithstanding the salty sea breeze. He could see official cameramen with their huge lenses trained on a cordoned-off section of beach where workmen were laying a synthetic grass catwalk for an upcoming bikini fashion show. A live-stream beach party was also scheduled to take place on the Hip Strip that evening, and Harris calculated that any scene there would have a sizeable audience.

The Hip Strip was all about naked consumerism. Boutiques, jewellers and even a Harley Davidson store, nestled in between hotels and restaurants and gift shops. Craft shops selling huge wooden carvings that no tourists in their right mind would buy. Most were sold to the drunk or the high or those reluctant to disappoint desperate craftsmen. Harris fell into the latter category and was already wondering what he would do with his giant lignum vitae Rastaman head. Still, the lads at the station back home in Glasgow would no doubt love it.

Only one delivery vehicle had left Chinchillerz headquarters and was now making its way onto the main coastal road. Police officers with eyes on the premises advised the detectives to look out for a black transit van with lightly tinted windows containing a bareheaded male driver and his passenger who was wearing a red baseball cap. The hairs on the back of Preddy's neck stood up when he spotted the subject vehicle in the distance and he quickly radioed the information to Harris. As the target vehicle sped past him and towards the Hip Strip, Preddy put his foot on the gas and took off behind it with strobe lights flashing. Rabino drew her service weapon and sat with it poised in her lap.

The van driver gave no indication that he intended to stop and his vehicle narrowly managed to avoid a crash with at least one unsuspecting motorist as it raced along. The driver of a tour bus waiting to turn into the Walter Fletcher Beach car park sounded his horn in panic as the transit passed inches from his bumper and he cursed furiously at the disappearing van.

Harris could see the van approaching and pulled out ahead of it, tyres screeching from the sudden exertion. Both he and Spence leaned out of their respective windows waving their arms and indicating to the driver to stop. Harris gently eased down on the brakes, but the van driver swerved into the oncoming traffic and overtook him. The detective immediately increased his speed until his vehicle was back in front of the van, which was then forced by a large oncoming truck to fall in behind the leading car.

Preddy was almost on the transit's bumper when Rabino noticed the passenger bend down and appear to retrieve something from under his seat. She quickly leaned out and shot twice at the nearest rear tyre. The van suddenly turned off the road completely, surprising the detectives as it ploughed through the wire fence that separated the road from the beach. In doing so it knocked down thin concrete posts and carried off a trail of wire which had become entangled in the undercarriage. It was a miracle he had not taken out one of the many wooden JPS poles that lined the route providing electricity, which would have put an end to the blaring music. The panicked driver sped along the beach narrowly avoiding the palm trees, interspersed with candy vendors, coconut sellers and sunbathers who all scattered in fear.

The detectives turned their vehicles onto the beach in pursuit, with Preddy slightly in front of Harris. White sand particles sprayed up into the air like a magnificent glitter shower. A red and white Sandals catamaran full of barely dressed tourists sailed by. The tourists had no idea what the bedlam was about, but they waved Red Stripe bottles and whooped enthusiastically at the chase. Swimmers stood up in the water and watched the action on the shore. The queues at the food kiosks dispersed as some patrons ran closer to the beach to watch the pursuit, cheering loudly, many believing that it was sponsored entertainment.

The back tyre of the transit had deflated considerably and the vehicle started to slow down allowing Preddy to pull alongside the driver.

"Stop! Police!" he shouted.

The wheels of the transit eventually ground to a halt. Preddy and Rabino jumped out guns drawn. Harris and Spence pulled up immediately behind them.

"Come out with your hands on your head!" shouted Rabino.

The vehicle doors opened slowly and the men climbed out.

"What happen! Don't shoot!" screamed the driver who was sweating profusely.

"Put up your hands now!" demanded Spence, and the driver quickly obeyed.

Harris called out to the passenger. "Over here, where we can see ye! And dinnae make any move or ye will be sorry."

The passenger did as he was told, his eyes wide as he stared at the white man dangling a pair of handcuffs. "Wait, you a police?" he asked.

"A police fi true!" said the driver.

CHAPTER 19

Friday, 7 August, 9.45 a.m.

When Preddy heard that Superintendent Brownlow and Commissioner Davis were ready to see him he gulped down the last of his coffee, gathered his paperwork and made his way down the hallway. He would have preferred his special tea, but if they picked up the ganja odour it would start a whole other conversation he did not fancy having. The last time face to face interrogation with Commissioner Davis took place nearly a year ago. Ten months, exactly. The worst two-hour interview of his life.

Thankfully, the failed Norwood operation had been cleared by INDECOM within weeks. Preddy was back on active duty less than two months later, but he knew that pressure had been brought on the highest rung of authority to investigate and show the public that the police did not have free rein to kill civilians. The detective himself had not attempted to shirk from responsibility for the sting gone tragically wrong, but the police hierarchy refused to release Preddy's name or the names of any members of his team to the public.

Even a court procedure brought by a campaign justice group failed to get the names disclosed. The judge in the in camera case agreed with the national security minister that the names of the relevant police officers had to be kept secret in the interests of the island. His Honour accepted that their work was dangerous and their identities had to be protected so they could carry out undercover operations and infiltrate violent criminal groups without being detected. It was a national security decision and one that was in the public interest if the crime reduction targets were to be achieved.

The public, who were sick and tired of criminals literally getting away with murder, had overwhelmingly agreed with the court's decision much to the relief of the still smarting Police Commissioner. Over the following days, various names had been leaked to the public, including Preddy's, but the law enforcement authorities neither admitted nor denied the rumours.

Preddy took a deep breath and entered the interview room. His superiors barely acknowledged his greetings. He was now sat facing them in one of the very interview rooms in which he usually played interrogator. The blinds were up and the sun glinted in his eyes. The detective had no doubt that the room had been arranged this way to debilitate him, but he had rehearsed exactly how he would justify the Hip Strip chase. Valerie had assisted him with it as best she could, playing Devil's advocate, yet it remained to be seen whether they would accept the reasoning behind his actions. His eyes went from one to the other, wondering which man would attack first.

"Can you tell us why a woman took Ida Chin Ellis hostage this morning, Detective?" asked Superintendent Brownlow calmly. "On the poor lady's first day back at work too."

Preddy looked at the superintendent with raised eyebrows while his mind raced. "I have no idea, sir. Is de first I'm hearing about it."

"Oh, well maybe you can tell us about the cocaine poisoning that left her daughter in a coma?" asked Commissioner Davis, fixing the detective with a death stare. He was a solidly built, bald-headed man, with tiny eyes behind round glasses; the sort of person one might mistake for a pastor or Justice of the Peace, but Davis was way less forgiving.

Preddy felt as if the room was swimming around in front of him and he was glad to be sitting down, however uncomfortably. That the child was now in a coma was news to him. It had escaped his mind to enquire after her well-being and he had assumed she had recovered and gone home.

He now learned from his superiors that her mother had turned up at Chinchillerz telling the security guard that the bunch of flowers she carried were a sympathy gift for Miss Ida. The guard had contacted the businesswoman who had come down to the gate to collect it and as soon as the gate swung open the visitor had held a knife to the frightened woman's throat and dragged her back into the building.

As Preddy listened, the carefully planned responses to the questions he was not being asked became diluted in his memory and some evaporated all together. "It was my fault, sir. I kept the cocaine to myself while carrying out some investigations," he said. "I thought it would help with de overall investigation into de Chin Ellis matters."

"What Chin Ellis matters, Detective?" asked Superintendent Brownlow. "We didn't bring any drug charges against Lester. The only matters I know of that anyone should be investigating are the assault on Lester and the murder of Carter."

Preddy fell silent for a moment. "It was a mistake, sir. I thought I might find out if dere was a connection between a chain of events as I saw it. I will admit dat I didn't know what de connection was."

"So nobody knows about this cocaine business except you?" The superintendent was staring at Preddy with cold anger.

"Dat's right, sir," said Preddy.

"So, you were just working off your own hunch and no consultation with anyone else." The commissioner sounded like he was stating facts rather than asking a question, but Preddy could not resist a response.

"Dere was a time when dat would have won me praise not condemnation," he murmured quietly. "Initiative, I think it's called."

The superintendent bowed his head and put a hand to his brow. The commissioner's small eyes widened behind the glasses and the veins in his neck stood to attention. He scorched the detective with his look. "Tell me what your single-handed research has found out, Detective. You smashed up the Hip Strip, cleared all the beaches, frightened the tourists . . ."

Here we go again, thought Preddy, *the high command pretending that the tourists were poor delicate souls oblivious to the fact that police in paradise had to work*. He endured the commissioner's heated onslaught while realising that his carefully prepared reasoning had never stood a chance with this man anyway.

The commissioner was mad that Pelican Walk was in the news. Journalists usually had little to write about after a public holiday and Preddy had presented them with a gift for silly season. Having missed the printing presses the previous night, the overblown reports had so far only appeared online, yet already there were plenty of comments below the articles calling for the police to pay for damaged stalls and vehicles, and to take full responsibility for any repercussions on the summer tourist season.

No vehicles or stalls had been damaged to Preddy's knowledge, but why spoil a good story with the truth. He was pretty sure that with the noise of the afternoon's Independence entertainment the majority of people on the Hip Strip would not even have heard the two gunshots. The tourists were hardy souls who came to Jamaica for fun and excitement, not to sit in silence on deck chairs all day reading lurid magazines. A car chase would never cause them to abandon the island and in fact might encourage the younger ones to return more often. Never mind the scaremongering about Cuba opening up for tourism, Raúl was not going to let millennials run wild and free in his revolutionary garden.

As he sat listening to the tirade Preddy decided against reminding his superiors of the extreme pressure he was under. There were so many things that he wanted to mention. For instance, it was not easy to maintain the morale of his team, yet he did it every day of the week, year after year. Many a time he dipped into his own pocket to pay for food and drink, and encouraged his colleagues to exchange small talk to remember an existence away from the job. The most hardened of criminals had far better hardware and resources than the officers at Pelican Walk and everyone knew it. No matter which government was in power, the politicians could always be trusted to acquire brand new vehicles and award themselves generous allowances to run them while the police remained short of both vehicles and vehicle parts.

Great opportunities to catch criminals were squandered by the lack of people, equipment and tools which frustrated Preddy immensely, yet a foreigner appeared on board for a few weeks and suddenly more men could be found. It did not help either that Preddy had seen a photograph on the JCF website of a wine and cheese party held for a departing French ambassador at his spectacular residence at Tryall in the parish Hanover. In attendance were the superintendent and commissioner as expected, but in the background was the clearly identifiable ginger head of his newest team member. Harris had never mentioned it, and although the brief article was entirely focused on the ambassador's legacy, the detective did wonder why Harris had been singled out to attend the function since the high command never invited detectives to such events. He hoped that Spence and Rabino had not noticed the article as so far the team was devoid of any real tension. The strain between himself and Harris was a different matter.

Preddy took the verbal pounding well, and only a very observant person would have seen a twitch of his mouth when the commissioner made it clear that demotion was a distinct possibility and declared that he would consider removing him from the case entirely if no progress was made.

Preddy had never been removed from running a case in his life and had certainly never experienced the humiliation of demotion. His last promotion was six years ago and as far as he was concerned the only way was up. Whatever could he have been thinking? the Super wanted to know. Preddy knew what he had been thinking. That drug dealing was most likely being facilitated by persons unknown at Chinchillerz and they needed to be caught to protect the citizens of Jamaica in general, and the reputation of St James parish in particular. He was not to know that the cocaine infused products had not left the Chinchillerz warehouse at all or that the innocent transit driver and passenger thought they were being hijacked by armed robbers and had fled for their lives.

"I gave you men to answer phone leads, Detective," said the superintendent. "And now I'm hearing that you used them to spy on Chinchillerz headquarters."

"I thought dey were for use on de case in general. You didn't specifically say dey were for manning phone lines, sir."

"But this is to do with drugs," said the superintendent. "Why is it the first I am hearing about drugs?"

"I don't know what you and Detective Harris discussed, sir," said Preddy pointedly.

The superintendent looked at the commissioner who sat forward in his chair. "There are a lot of things you don't know Detective. Like who killed Carter Chin Ellis, which is what you need to find out."

"Yes, sir."

"Now, are there any other secrets you want to share with us?"

I can drink a whole pot of ganja tea and go a whole day without pissing, sir. "Not dat I can think of, sir."

"Well know this," said the commissioner. "None of us are indispensable, Detective. The mayor says he wants to see me, the security minister wants to talk to me, and the business people have started to make a noise. I don't even know what response we're going put out later. Tread carefully, Detective."

As Preddy stood, the superintendent said, "You ready to leave, Detective? Aren't you curious about the well-being of Miss Ida?"

"Yes, sir," said Preddy, quickly retaking his seat, "but I thought she must be okay since you didn't elaborate on it."

The commissioner looked annoyed. "Well, she was eventually released by her kidnapper. Whether she is okay or not is a different matter. I was informed that she looked considerably shaken by her ordeal and we took the precaution of escorting her to her doctor."

"I must apologise to her, sir. Is de doctor same place down Freeport she gone to?"

"No, the one at the medical centre in Rose Hall," said the superintendent. "And I hear that he is expensive too, so I hope she doesn't send us the bill for treatment."

"I will apologise, sir."

"I think you should stay away from her," said the commissioner thoughtfully. "Unless we have progress on the case to report, I think we should all stay away. Concentrate on the investigation."

"Yes, sir."

"Detective Preddy, I won't lie to you," said the commissioner. "If we had more manpower I would remove you just like that, today. The superintendent assures me that he doesn't have anybody else with as much experience to run the case, but I'm not so sure that we can't find someone — like Harris."

Preddy's stomach muscles tightened and his breath caught in his throat. "Sir, I will meet wid my team and get de case going in de right direction."

"Just see that you do," warned the commissioner. "You can leave now."

Preddy nodded at his superiors and left the interview room, unbuttoning the top of his shirt as he went. Harris? Over his dead body. Preddy made his way to the men's restroom, where he splashed cold water on his face and stared in the mirror, noting that specks of grey hair had begun to multiply. The door opened behind him and Officer Nembhard walked in. This was the last person that he wanted to see.

"Alright, Detective?"

"Yes, man. How you doing?" Preddy mumbled robotically.

"Me alright, sir. Me deh here a try keep it together, you know?"

"Dat's all we can do."

"How your case going? De Chiney murder? Everything alright so far?"

Preddy dried his hands on the coarse paper towel which once moistened felt less dangerous enough to apply to his face. He pulled himself up to his full height, dabbed at the remaining spots of water and threw the towel in the bin.

"Everything a gwaan well, man," he lied, and made his way out of the restroom.

* * *

The teenagers had come to meet their father at Pelican Walk and were sitting in his car waiting for him to chauffeur them home.

"Is dat your boss, Dad?" asked Roman peering at the white man who had climbed into the jeep next to their car and waved at them. "Bwoy, him hair red, eeh!"

Preddy's eyes followed his son's gaze. Annalee sprung to attention, momentarily discarding the messages she had been studying so intently on her phone and stared at the man too.

"No, dat is Detective Harris. Remember, I told you we had a secondee from Glasgow." Preddy took out his badge and polished it before replacing it in his breast pocket. "He is certainly not my boss."

"Oh, is him come from Scotland," said Annalee. "Him have kids?"

"Three, 'wee bairns' he calls dem, though I think dey are all high schoolers. He didn't bring dem to Jamaica though."

"You should bring him home and make him cook haggis for dinner," she suggested.

"Haggis?" asked Roman. "Wha' dat?"

Preddy looked at his daughter. "You know what haggis is?"

"Well no, but people in Scotland eat a lot of it like how we eat ackee and saltfish."

"Sheep heart, liver and lungs, dat is what haggis is," Preddy said.

"Me no want any of it," said Roman, wrinkling up his nose.

"Ugh! Me no want him come cook dat at all," said Annalee.

"If Harris can try mannish water, you can try haggis, don't?" Preddy said, while thinking that he himself would probably only try haggis for a dare and if the money was right.

"Dat is because you never make him look inside de pot and see de goat head in dere," said Roman. "If him ever see goat eyeball a look pon him, him run!"

Preddy started the engine and proceeded to reverse.

"We can say hello, Daddy?" asked Annalee.

"Sure," said Preddy through gritted teeth. He wound down the window and waved back at the detective. "Dese are my two problems!"

"Hello, wee problems!" said Harris.

"Hello, Detective Harris!" chorused the youths, waving cheerfully.

"Be good for ye dad, now. He's a hardworking man."

"We always good! Don't listen to what Daddy say!" Annalee grinned and waved again.

Preddy rolled up the window and made his way onto the main road. Harris had better listen to what he had to say. This was not a case that could be run by someone without connections to the locals and their customs, no matter what high-tech strategies were in use in Europe.

CHAPTER 20

Preddy stood under the porch of the Rose Hall medical centre, glad that it provided much needed shade from the sun's harsh rays. He was surprised that no-one responded to the sound of the buzzer, although he could see the two receptionists happily chatting away to each other. Maybe it was the plain clothes that they were ignoring, after all they did not know him. He took out his badge and pressed it against the window, using the other hand to hold down the buzzer. The door opened a few seconds later.

"Sorry, Officer," the woman said sheepishly. "Who you want to see?"

"Ida Chin Ellis's doctor."

"What is your name, sir?"

"Detective Preddy."

The woman looked at her colleague. "Call Doctor Sherman and tell him that a Detective Preddy wants to talk to him."

The law man took up a seat beside the door and admired the potted yellow orchids that had grown so tall they had to be secured to the walls. The aroma was clean and fresh.

153

Instrumental jazz music floated about the cool lobby, and he closed his eyes momentarily, allowing the calmness to seep through his veins. His vibrating phone disturbed his brief respite, but he quickly answered it for the caller was Detective Spence. Their conversation was short and as he hung up he experienced an adrenalin rush which enhanced the therapeutic effect of the ganja tea coursing through his veins. Soon he would have a car to inspect, a Subaru Outback.

"Detective Preddy? How can I help you?"

The detective looked up at the doctor, a pale-skinned man with a pointed nose who Preddy guessed was of Jewish heritage although he spoke with an infliction of Patois indicating that he had been exposed to Jamaicans for a good while.

"We can go somewhere quiet or we can talk right here, if you prefer?" said Preddy, tapping the orange envelope against the side of his knee. The doctor spotted the movement and his composure slipped momentarily.

"Er, why don't you come this way, Detective?"

Doctor Sherman led the detective along the hallway to a lift. As the door started to close the doctor said, "I guess that is what I think it is?"

"You guess right," replied Preddy.

A lady attempted to enter the lift and Preddy instinctively caught the door allowing her to get in. She smiled and nodded her thanks. The doctor again pressed the button for the fourth floor and placed a forefinger lightly against his lips shooting Preddy a warning look. The woman alighted in front of them on the fourth floor and walked in the opposite direction. Preddy was shown into an office with the doctor's name prominently displayed on a gold plated plaque affixed to the door. Preddy cast his eyes over the medical certificates adorning the walls and deduced that the doctor had done most of his training in Syria twenty years ago.

"How long have you been in Jamaica, Doctor Sherman?"

"Eight years now since I'm here. Citizenship granted long time ago." Doctor Sherman spoke with pride. "I'm not leaving. Even with all the foolishness that's going on here I still love it."

"Good, I think we need more people like you around. We need all de help we can get."

The doctor frowned. "I know I'm going to get myself into trouble now."

"No, you're not." Preddy took the photograph from the envelope and held it up. "Thank you. You obviously have a strong sense of morals."

Doctor Sherman did not respond immediately. He clasped his hands together, rested them on the desk in front of him and stared at the photograph.

"Lester came in here with his father, moaning and groaning like a child. Covered up under one big towel as if his face was hanging off or something. I was reluctant to even lift the towel. When I looked I saw part of his face bruised up and a tiny part of one of his teeth chipped. That was all. Big baby."

"Okay, so we know dis is not a fist." Preddy felt a certain warmth towards the doctor. He liked no-nonsense professionals. "Do you know what it is?"

"I have a theory," said Doctor Sherman. "I examined him close up and took some photographs. That sort of bruise is caused by blunt force trauma. Like when someone has been violently hit with an object or when the victim's head has come into contact with something hard. Maybe from some instrument used to hit him, or dropping on him from a great height, or from tripping or slipping."

"Do you know which one is more likely?"

The doctor stood up and walked over to a tall steel cabinet where he flicked through some files before taking one out. He returned to his desk and opened it, revealing even more photos of Lester taken from different angles.

"Well, all I can say, Detective, is that his face met with something hard."

"Could he have done it to himself?"

"It's possible, but I know that young man much better than you, Detective. He is vain. He comes here for a pimple.

There is no way he would hit himself or allow anybody else to hit him for that matter. No way. Trust me, he didn't see it coming."

"What do we have left, Doc?"

"He was taken by surprise or he tripped," said the doctor. "My guess is that this is a solid piece of metal, not a hammer which is too square. Something with heavy weight in it."

Preddy stared off into the distance for a few moments deep in thought. "Like a weightlifter's hex dumbbell? Would dat do it?"

"Yes, it could," said the doctor. "Why? The minister find money to buy exercise equipment for the inmates now?"

"No. We don't even have a proper gym for officers. Just a small room wid some weights, dumbbells and barbells, things like dat."

"So Lester found his way into the police gym while under arrest?"

Preddy shook his head. "Nobody gets special privileges. By all accounts he had a good few drinks dat night. I can believe dat someone hit him or he fell, but I'm trying to work out who and when." Preddy put the photos back into the file and handed them to the doctor. "I'll keep hold of de one you gave me."

Doctor Sherman folded his arms across his chest. "You mean the one you somehow got your hands on, Detective?"

"Yes, Doc," Preddy smiled. "Dat same one."

On the way back to Pelican Walk, Preddy gave more thought to what Doctor Sherman had said. Lester had removed a towel in order to have his injuries photographed by the doctor. The fibres that Valerie detected on Lester's photograph were likely from a towel, not from a covered object used to hit him. He wondered how an inmate or Lester could have got near to any weights. They were stored only in the gym although sometimes officers borrowed them and took them home for the weekend, usually to be brought back on Monday morning.

The detective swerved suddenly and pulled the car over onto the pavement, startling a newspaper vendor who had been walking towards the oncoming traffic waving his gossip rag at the motorists. The vendor was brave, there being two lanes of fast moving traffic to manoeuvre unless the lights were on red. He would skip to the opposite lane when the lights changed and try to convince those motorists that their day would not be complete without a *Star* newspaper. Every inch of his skin was covered up from the stripey socks and long-sleeved shirt, through to the coloured headscarf.

Preddy showed him a conciliatory palm and sat still deep in thought for a few minutes. A girl approached his window with a laden crate and struggled to heave it towards him. He shook his head at her. No box juice or soda sale today. A young man with a sponge and bucket quickly set about cleaning Preddy's windscreen, despite the detective's attempt to wave him away. Rather than produce his badge, Preddy rolled down the window and handed him a J$50 note. As much these traffic light workers irritated him, it was better that they annoy motorists in the day rather than terrorise them in their homes at night.

Back at the station he made a beeline for the makeshift gym which was completely empty and silent. The notebook on the counter top served as a register and held a record of the various officers who had borrowed weights and returned them. Preddy flicked the pages until he found the entry he had been searching for. Both Nembhard and Timmins had signed out for various weights on Saturday afternoon. There was no indication as to when they had been returned but a quick look around the gym proved they were all there. He lifted the heavy objects to his nose and realised that the usually tardy cleaner had recently wiped and polished them. Nembhard and Timmins, one or both of them knew something that they weren't telling. He closed the register, switched off the lights and made his way back outside the building.

At the rear of the station the other detectives had already gathered. They watched with great expectations as Marcus Darnay's Subaru was transported down the driveway on the back of a tow truck, and waited impatiently as the driver and his assistant carefully lowered the long sought after evidence to the ground in a far corner of the courtyard.

The police would never have known about the car but for the fact that a homeless man had returned from begging in the town centre the previous night and found the vehicle ablaze. He had flagged down a passing motorist to complain that his house had been set on fire and an unidentified man was seen running away. The firemen on site were suspicious of the cause of the fire and had alerted the traffic police who had done a follow-up on the car which by now was barely a shell.

Harris went directly to the vehicle's rear and studied the chassis. "Aye, those are bullet holes."

Spence bent down and looked closely. "Me never think Darnay woulda destroy him good vehicle," she said. "Me think him would maybe paint it, change de plate and give somebody to run robot."

"What does run robot mean?" asked Harris.

"A robot taxi is an illegal taxi," said Preddy. "Usually a private vehicle dat drivers use to run a public passenger service without a license."

Harris nodded knowingly. "Och, that would explain why we havenae heard from the driver who picked Carter up from Pelican Walk and took him tae the SUV. He's running a robot."

"Possibly, and with no tax and no insurance," said Rabino.

"Plenty of people do dat foolishness," added Spence. "And a so dem love kill off passenger wid dem bad driving, but de same passenger complain when you stop de car and tell dem to get out."

Rabino donned a pair of white gloves and carefully opened the charred trunk, pieces of which crumbled in her hands. "I'll get the crime scene officers to see if they can recover any bullets. We have a set to compare them to."

Preddy put his head through the rear passenger window which was now glass free. He scrutinised the remaining bits of soggy foam on the back seat.

"Darnay lucky him didn't get shot. See, dere is a hole in dis seat," he said, pointing. "And now we can't contact Darnay."

Although Preddy had been able to deter the press from releasing the make and model of car at the outset of the investigation he had not reckoned with the traffic police in this instance. They had alerted the media to the discovery of the car — to score well-needed points no doubt — without thinking of the consequences. The news folk did not play by the same rules as the police force and newsflashes had begun appearing in minutes. As a result Darnay's phone was now going straight to voicemail.

Superintendent Brownlow was informed of the latest development and sounded relieved that something was happening. Preddy knew his superior well and detected from his voice that all was not as it should be, although he decided not to push it. The man was probably still seething from the Hip Strip debacle.

CHAPTER 21

Monday, 10 August, 3.20 p.m.

The detectives resorted to keeping a close eye on Marcus Darnay's two paramours. With a common law wife and children at home, and a girlfriend who had given birth to his baby last year, he was sure to turn up. Preddy did not believe the claim that Darnay had gone to Miami to buy car parts. None of the airports had any record of him leaving the island, and US Customs had no evidence of him entering the country. Neither of his women was able to explain this anomaly and Preddy did not have time to waste with them.

Spence had been alerted by a neighbour that Darnay was at his girlfriend's home, which led her and Preddy to set off towards the woman's residence. Discreetly they parked their unmarked car a few doors away near to a primary school.

Spence noticed two small girls holding hands after getting off a packed minibus their crushed and crumpled green uniforms bearing witness to them having been squashed. They reminded her of her own two daughters. The detective quickly picked up pace and reached the children before they attempted to cross the busy road. She made eye contact with an approaching driver who immediately slowed down. She held their hands, one child on each side, and guided them across, then watched as the security guard let them through the school gate. The smaller of the two girls turned and waved at her shyly before dashing off up the drive behind her schoolmate.

Preddy smiled at Spence. "Mummy duty first."

"Always, sir. Always."

The apartment block had three storeys and at least thirty individual units. It was painted a garish shade of salmon that the hardware shop must have been glad to see the back of. They walked up two flights of stairs and Spence pointed to the door marked eighteen. As the detectives approached the front door of the flat, Preddy noted that there did not appear to be a second exit through which anyone could escape if they chose to run. The twenty-foot drop would be a bad idea. A young woman opened the door in response to Spence's knock.

"Yes, what happen?" she asked, bouncing her plump baby on her hip.

"Good morning, ma'am. Good morning, little man." Spence tickled the baby under his chin and he giggled. "My name is Detective Spence and dis is Detective Preddy. We're looking for dis man." Spence waved Darnay's photograph in front of the woman's face.

"Is my babyfather dat. Him not here." The woman glared at Spence.

"Where is he?" asked Spence.

"You no hear say him gone to foreign?" Her objection to the question was clear from her tone. "Me tell one a you dat yesterday when you a blow up me phone wid question."

"We have reason to believe dat a person matching dis description was seen entering your premises about an hour ago," said Preddy.

"A who tell you dat? Dem people round here fas' eeh!" She switched the child to her other hip.

"We can come inside and look?" asked Spence.

Before the woman could answer all three of them heard the sound of a creaking door inside the apartment.

"Who is here wid you?" asked Preddy.

"Is me and me baby alone deh here."

"Lady, if you are harbouring a criminal it going bad for you, you know," Preddy said.

"Me tell you say him not here!"

"You smell something, Detective?" asked Preddy.

Spence inhaled. "Yes, sir. It smell like weed."

Preddy pushed past the woman, followed promptly by his colleague.

The woman switched hips again and the baby wailed its annoyance. She patted his back. "A whe you a go? Come outta me place, man!"

Both detectives pulled out their guns and inspected the small apartment. Preddy looked at the closed bathroom door and caught Spence's eye. "Marcus Darnay, I advise you to come out now!" he shouted.

"Dem have gun, Leeroy. Come out and no bother make dem shoot up me place and kill off me pickney!" the woman screamed. "Me know 'bout dis policeman here and him love shoot!"

The door slowly opened and a frightened face looked out. The man immediately put both hands in the air while staring at the guns.

"Me tell you say him wasn't in here!" The woman's posture indicated that she was awaiting an apology.

"And is who dis?" asked Spence. "Come right out, sir!"

"Just a friend! Me no do nutten officer! Me just a visit!" The man quickly stepped out of the bathroom clad in long shorts, his chest bare.

Preddy replaced his weapon in its holster. The under-dressed man did share the same complexion as Darnay, but other than his short dreadlocks, bore little resemblance. His face was a completely different shape and he had a much slimmer build. The detective recognised him as a small time criminal, the type of coward who would wave a knife and snatch handbags or gold chains from unsuspecting female shoppers.

"A me friend. Me cyah have friend?" the woman asked defensively.

"Don't bother wid it, you know." Spence stared her down. "Dat weed dat you have burning will send both of you to jail, so no ask we no question. 'Bout friend . . .Darnay know you have friend?"

"After me and Marcus no deh again. Is not fi him business," she replied sullenly. The disgruntled baby struggled from her arms and reached out to the man, who took the boy and held him close. As Spence secured her gun she looked from the baby's face to the man's face.

"Oh, a so?" said Spence. "Well, when we speak to Darnay we will have to ask him 'bout dis male babysitter dat your son so obviously loves. Leeroy was it?"

"You no have to do dat, officer." The woman's tone suddenly took on a more conciliatory note. "Me not lying to you. Marcus gone weh."

"Children and second-hand smoke," said Preddy, shaking his head at the couple. "We'll show ourselves out."

On the way to the door he stopped and picked up the smoking spliffs together with the small bag of weed. Outside he scattered the herbs. He unrolled the joints and ground the potent content firmly under his feet. A shame to waste it, but they should have bought the green leaves and boiled them.

"You notice how de baby resemble him real daddy?" asked Spence, grinning as they walked back to the car.

"Me see it." Preddy cleared his throat and then said in a newsreader's voice, "Marcus Darnay was not located, but significant traces of infidelity were found on the premises."

"Pure jacket. God help de next generation. I wonder if Darnay would pay her a visit if he knew what was going on?" said Spence.

"Probably, but I wouldn't bet on her safety if he did," said Preddy. "He must have told her he's going away for a while though, for her to be so brazen wid de man, inna broad daylight."

"I agree, but he is here somewhere, sir. I just know it."

Preddy nodded. "And he'll make a mistake. We'll get him."

CHAPTER 22

Monday, 10 August, 7.30 p.m.

Preddy was at home with half an eye on a repeat of *Who Do You Think You Are?* and the other on fixing the microwave which had chosen an inappropriate time to give up the ghost. Guest celebrities of European heritage always enjoyed themselves the most, tracing their ancestors back to the year of nought and taking great delight in finding out that they were criminals, lawyers or both.

This particular interviewee was pleased to learn that her ancestors were imprisoned for refusing to mine coal. The detective felt pretty sure none of his ancestors would have been allowed to refuse to do anything and he wondered whether his own ancestry was even traceable. Enslaved people had their own names in Africa and any names assigned thereafter were mainly given to them by their masters. Each time a slaver traded a human being the new owner could change the name, and the detective was not confident about the veracity of any records that could be unearthed in his own case. Maybe when he was old and retired he could set about trying to find out the truth, though if the commissioner managed to pension him off early he might not need to wait until he got old to take on this challenge.

Preddy could not remember ever seeing any Chinese interviewees on the programme, but their ancestry, as far as settling in Jamaica was concerned, was well-documented. Most of them had first arrived in Jamaica in the nineteenth century, and finding the island to be much to their liking had never left. Terence Chin had come to Jamaica in the early 1980's, initially just to visit relatives, and he had taken a shine to the island too. It was impossible to enter a store or super-market in a built-up area and not see one or more Chinese people running the business, so prolific was their expansion.

"Dad, dere's a woman on here dat I think you want to see!"

Roman's voice took him away from his musings and Preddy put down the screwdriver. The microwave needed replacing anyway.

"Oh, as opposed to cats playing pianos and dogs driving cars?"

Preddy walked over to where his son lay on the floor with a half-eaten plate of jerked sausages and seasoned fries beside him. It was very rare that Roman ever viewed anything on his tablet that did not vanish as soon as his father appeared, so whatever this was it must be appropriate for parental viewing. Preddy flopped down on the floor, stretched out his long frame and stared at the small electronic screen.

"What do I need to see?"

"Wait one minute; it soon start, Dad."

Annalee pried herself from the couch and reclined on her father's back, peering around his neck at the tablet. Roman played the two-minute video watching his father's face from time to time. Preddy stared intently at the scene which fluctuated in clarity and zoomed in and out. Below the heading *Jamaican woman curses out police LOL!* he recog-nised the bustling background as Charles Gordon Market in downtown Montego Bay.

The market was a messy hive of activity where one could get anything from fresh fruits on their stems to ground produce clad in moist soil. You could even get ganja leaves if you knew who to go to and what to ask for. Most of the vendors did not stay within the confines of the market zone, instead they encroached on the pavement and car park, or even crossed a road crawling with delivery trucks to set up pitches which infringed the facing shops.

The angry woman did not appear to have her own stall anywhere. When the video started she was standing in front of a group of higglers, with her arms aloft, and then began pacing back and forth shouting her grievances in raucous Patois at anyone who would listen. She peppered her speech with lots of swear words that unfortunately Preddy's children knew too well, so any attempt to censure them would be futile. Annalee chuckled in his ear from time to time. Roman had already watched it, so did not react much. It annoyed Preddy when adults carried on like that in public, yet as the tape rolled on he began to think that he would probably be swearing too if he thought that his wrongly incarcerated son had been paid to beat Lester Chin Ellis.

The clip ended with the woman declaring, "'Bout dem have Major Organized Crime and Anti-Corruption team. All me hear 'bout pon TV and radio a MOCA, MOCA, MOCA. A shoulda JOCA it name. A pure joker inna dat deh place!"

The video had been shot that day and the detective could tell that it was genuine. So far it had racked up five hundred views. When it finished he asked Roman to replay it and they watched it again. Preddy shrugged Annalee from his back and she rolled off with a groan. He rubbed his son's head playfully as he rose from the floor.

"And dere I was thinking dat all you watch is football, cats and girls."

"Who, me?" Roman grinned.

"Finish eat you dinner," said Preddy. "And don't keep on de volume too loud, I need to go do some work."

166

"What you going do about de lady?"

"I don't know yet," he said truthfully. "Might go walk around in de market a morning."

The detective went into his study and closed the door. The bulk of his main work space was taken up by a long wooden desk covered in paper with three overflowing drawers beneath. A stainless steel lamp with an energy saving bulb provided bright lighting. His book shelves contained a set of non-fiction books mainly related to crime, investigations and evidence, as well as some statutes and cases on Jamaican law. A small white fridge stood in the corner containing a few bottles of energy drinks and meal supplement liquids for when he did not have time to move from his desk, let alone cook or eat a meal. And there was always plenty of ice which he would crunch if he didn't feel like drinking anything.

The children knew better than to enter this room at any time. Even if they knocked he would always walk to the door and open it to speak to them. Sometimes there was active case evidence lying around and he could not afford to let them see it, not least because some of it could be extremely gruesome. Neither of his kids should be exposed to photos of victims of rape, wounding or murder and he would protect their young eyes from it at all costs.

As much as he did not like the idea of taking work home, sometimes there just was no other way to get it done. At times it was more productive to do so as he had a standby generator at home and could cope with the power cuts inflicted by the Jamaica Public Service company. There were no generators at Pelican Walk and if the power company cut the power for "load shedding", as they called it, then the officers would have to light lamps and candles .It was not conducive to good policing and he sometimes wished that the government would level fines on the JPS for the inconvenience. It would never happen though, because various government offices owed millions of dollars in electricity fees and there really would be an economic crisis if the company decided to call in the government debts.

Utilities were always an issue. Even the water at the station was not a given and there were times when the water pressure was so low that barely a trickle emerged from the taps. The planned installation of a tank to catch rainwater would be a welcome addition to the station's resources, but that plan was first aired nearly two years ago. To this day, nothing had been done.

This must all be an eye-opener for Detective Harris. There was no way that electricity and water were ever an issue in Glasgow. They probably complained about a lack of coloured post-it notes and ball point pens. Preddy sighed, wishing that these were his kind of problems.

CHAPTER 23

Tuesday, 11 August, 7.05 a.m.

Preddy pulled into the busy market lane and crawled behind a stink garbage truck that hogged the road. The waste workers were in no hurry; they hopped off the back and sauntered to and from the refuse collection points. At times like this he was tempted to set the siren off, but forced himself to drum on the steering wheel instead. Besides, the truck did not look the sort that could be intimidated or bullied. It was marked *Seddon Atkinson* and gave the impression that it could take on an army tank and glide away unscathed.

Eventually it inched on its way, leaving a nasty stench in its wake. Preddy continued to his destination and climbed out of his car. The haphazard arrangements that he stepped into brought on a sense of frustration. This was a matter for the municipal police though and he had no intention of getting involved in cat and mouse games. Half of the vendors had no permits and should not be there. He knew from experience that those who operated legally in the market were incensed at having to pay fees to sell their wares while the people outside dodged the inspectors, paid nothing and got most of the foot traffic. Times were hard and everybody was a hustler, but sometimes an example had to be made to deter the would-be law breakers. Some vendors would have their goods seized and confiscated, others would escape with a warning and a few would have to appear in court.

It did not take Preddy long to find the woman from the video as she was recognisable on sight, although she appeared much calmer today. She sat at a spot just outside the market gates, her wooden cart full of fresh carrots, tomatoes, cabbages and onions, covered by a broad beach umbrella with plenty of holes.

She told Preddy of her difficulty in getting the press to listen to her, but she swore on the Bible that what her son told her was true. "All up a TV station me did go and dem send security fi me. Talk 'bout me a cause disturbance," she moaned. "Ah me pickney life me a defend, a no disturbance!"

Preddy watched the woman's animated face and arms that flew up and down as she spoke. She insisted that her son, Jerry Knight, was forced to hit Lester Chin Ellis. She repeated her tale that her son had been bailed out of jail by whom she did not know and had started buying expensive clothes, shoes and food. At first Jerry told her that he had obtained a day's work, but eventually, ground down by her nagging, he told what she believed to be the truth, that he had been paid to inflict the blows. Jerry had refused to tell her who paid him, but admitted he punched Lester twice in the face. Now her son had been charged with assault occasioning actual bodily harm, and had his case deferred until the end of September.

Preddy believed that she thought she was telling the truth, yet he knew Lester had not been punched. Jerry Knight would no doubt be able to answer the question, but there would be no opportunity to interrogate him without incurring the wrath of the police high command. As a matter of protocol, the moment the lawyers were placed on the case and all evidence was turned over to them he should not carry out any further investigations unless specifically asked to do so.

This was a matter which the lawyers might eventually be forced to address, but when? It was far more likely that the JCF would opt to settle the case without any in-depth investigation and the government would pay out millions in damages. Getting involved in this aspect of the case would endanger Preddy's already precariously balanced career, but he was convinced there was more to it than meets the eye when it came to Lester Chin Ellis and he was determined to find out what.

"I believe you, ma'am, I do," Preddy said. "Your son needs to talk to me."

The woman clutched her loose chest and smiled. "T'ank you, sah! Me going tell him fi call you."

"No," said Preddy quickly. "It better if you take me to him. You know where he is right now?"

"Him supposed to deh home," she replied. "Me leave him dere 'bout him a fry pancake. Pancake you know? All dem expensive thing pon supermarket shelf what we use to see and just walk past! A must only weevil a dem customer."

"Are you able to leave wid me, ma'am?"

She hesitated. "Bwoy, me have me things me a try sell off . . ."

"Well, you said nobody would listen to you and I am listening to you. I can't promise you dat I will have a next time to listen." Preddy gambled, and breathed a sigh of relief when the woman started to cover her goods with flattened cardboard boxes.

"Mikey, watch me things dem fi me, me soon come!"

Preddy drove the woman to her home in the Mount Salem district, less than two miles from the market. She pointed at a lane and he turned off the main road. The one room houses along the lane had rusty roofs secured with huge stones. Some houses showed signs of being extended, surrounded as they were by thin steel bars running vertically from the foundations. Clothes lay drying from the branches of nearby trees or spread out on bushes. Her tiny house was set on an open lot with a small unkempt garden and abandoned garden implements lying around exposed to the elements. An old bicycle leaned against the side of the building with an airless football tucked under it. She walked the detective to the rear of the premises and pushed the unlocked back door.

"Jerry, you in dere?"

"Yes, me deh yah, Mama. You come back soon eeh?"

"Somebody wah talk to you," she said, entering the kitchen with Preddy behind.

Her son was seated on a frayed two-seater sofa bed with a bottle of beer in one hand and a plate of pancakes in the other. He swung around from the TV in shock and his pancakes tumbled to the floor.

"A wha' dis?" Jerry asked, his eyes fixed on the bulge on Preddy's right side.

"A police, son. You need to talk to him."

"A wha' you go do, Mama! You mad or wha'?" he screeched. "You a go make dem kill me!"

"Nobody is going to do you anything if you tell de truth," said Preddy calmly. He looked at the man's mother. "Can you leave us alone for a few minutes please?"

The woman eyed Preddy with suspicion. "You nah do him nutten?"

"No, man. Me and him going talk. Dat is all," Preddy assured her.

The woman reluctantly retreated and the detective closed the backdoor behind her.

"Hello, Jerry," said Preddy. He retrieved the pancakes from the cracked tiles and replaced them in the plate. "It's a bit early for alcohol, but gwaan drink you beer, man."

"Hello, Officer." Jerry gulped a mouthful of the beer although he no longer tasted it. Something told him to do exactly what this man said.

"My instincts tell me dat you are not a bad guy, Jerry. Maybe a bit misguided, but not a bad guy."

"No, me no bad at all, Officer."

Preddy removed some shopping bags from a tired wicker chair and sat. "I believe your original statement. Remember when you said dat de policeman pull you from de bicycle and cause you to hurt your hand?"

172

"Yes, me 'member."

"Well, I believe you. I really do, but now I have a problem," said Preddy sitting forward in the chair and pointing around the cramped room. "My problem is all of dis."

"All of wha'?" Jerry squeezed the glass bottle without even realising it.

"Sneakers, sports bag, watch, de nice flat screen TV you watching and de food you eating. Sorry about dat by de way." Preddy said pointing at the now dusty pancakes. "You no have no job and de little things your mother selling at market didn't buy all dis."

"What she tell you?"

"Don't worry yourself about what she tell me. What do you have to tell me?"

Jerry looked glumly at his plate. The beer bottle was now empty so he could not even buy time by taking a swig.

"You ever hear about perjury?" asked Preddy. "Perjury is what you are going to commit in a few weeks and it is going to land you in jail."

"Me just come outta jail, and me never in dere fi nutten!" said Jerry earnestly. "Officer dem let me out and want me to go a court and me never did attack anybody!"

"You didn't box Chin Ellis? You sure you didn't hit him wid something?"

"Me never touch de Chiney bwoy!"

"So tell me what happened?"

Jerry fell silent again, and Preddy waited.

"Jerry, you alright in dere?" His mother's distant voice sounded concerned.

"Yes, Mama. Me alright!"

"Well?" pressed Preddy.

Jerry's shoulders slumped as he spoke. "Me wake up and see him like dat."

Preddy placed both hands to his temples and sighed. "Everybody wake up see him like dat. You wake up see him like dat and de two other inmate wake up and see him like dat. Everybody come see him like dat."

173

"Well, me wake same time him come in and him face stay so. De policeman who throw him in dere must know why him stay so."

Preddy stared at him. "He was put into de cell like dat?"

Jerry nodded. "Him never even inna my cell when dem bring him in. Me never did a sleep dat deh time, and me see when dem put him into one cell opposite me by himself. Me go lie down back and drop asleep must be for a good two hour. When me wake a de Chiney bwoy me see."

"Looking like dat, face bruised?"

"A it me a tell you, Officer! De door open and me turn roun' see him and me wonder how him look so," said Jerry. "Me just turn over back and start sleep again."

"Who give you money to say is you do him so?"

"De police bredda say me must collect it from one guy wha' sell cane juice down a bay. Me go down dere and him give me."

Preddy tried to remain composed, but his words came out in an urgent torrent. "What de policeman name?"

"Me no know him name." Jerry knitted his brow. "Him sorta tall, well maybe medium, and sorta slim to stocky."

"Well which one? Tall or medium? Slim or stocky?"

"Umm. Dem police guy all look alike to me."

"You would remember him if you see him?"

"Umm, me no sure."

Preddy fought to keep his frustration at bay. "De cane juice guy give you de money in an envelope or bag or something?"

"Yes, inna one big envelope."

"You still have it?"

"Yes, but no money no inna it now," said Jerry. "Me can take it give you."

"Dat's okay, just show me where it is." Preddy stood up and followed the slight man to the kitchen. The detective slid on latex gloves and picked up the crinkled white envelope sitting on the shelf. He placed it inside a transparent evidence bag and into his trouser pocket.

"You've been very helpful Jerry."

"Me no wah go back a jail," he mumbled miserably.

Preddy studied his forlorn features. The young man had barely reached the age of majority and was already trapped in a vicious cycle. "You sign any statement give lawyer?"

"No, me no sign nutten, Officer."

"Well, don't."

"Suppose dem gimme paper and tell me fi sign?"

"Your case is many weeks away and de lawyers are not dat efficient," said Preddy confidently.

"What going happen to me?" asked Jerry, with a slight shiver.

"I can't promise you what will happen. So far you haven't signed anything, and you haven't put hand on Bible and sworn to anything," Preddy answered, as he moved towards the door. "De taking of de money . . .well we'll have to see."

"Officer?"

"Yes, young man?"

"What you name?"

With two strides Preddy was beside the nervous man and put his hand on his shoulder. "My name is Detective Preddy," he said, squeezing Jerry's shoulder lightly. "Dis is an unofficial visit, understand me?"

"From Norwood?" Jerry's eyes widened and he gulped. "Yes, sah. Me understand!"

"Good." Preddy patted him on the back. "Now, I suggest you give de pancakes to de birds den get down to de market and help your mama."

CHAPTER 24

Tuesday, 11 August, 11.45 a.m.

A recent refurbishment had converted the building previously known as the civic centre into the Montego Bay Cultural Centre which housed a stunning museum and gallery. The once neglected site now stood as a proud addition to the downtown city landscape. Visitors came from near and far to admire the museum's artefacts, most of which were provided by the government while some were donated by wealthy, generous benefactors keen on establishing a major arts facility in the parish. Historical items of great significance to the island as well as modern paintings and sculptures occupied both floors of the two-storey structure. Tastefully arranged canvas posters hung from the walls outside informing the public of temporary exhibitions held inside.

"A what time now?" whispered Preddy.

"Him should be here in 'bout fifteen minutes, sir," replied Spence quietly, glancing at her watch.

"Him need to make haste. It cold in here."

"I hope him turn up. Him never sound too happy at all."

Preddy rubbed his hands together then crossed his arms to rub his shoulders. Even though he was wearing a long-sleeved shirt he could still feel the ice-cold breath of the air-conditioning unit numbing his shoulders.

Meeting in this area of the art gallery had certainly not been his idea. The exhibits apparently needed to be kept cool to protect their delicate fabric and prevent deterioration and decay. He wondered what effect the cold air had on the staff members who spent a good portion of the day indoors. Having been here before he knew that it was sensible to wear a sweater, but this meeting had been arranged at the last minute and it had completely escaped his mind to bring woolly protection.

He noticed that Spence did not appear to be feeling the cold, which was surprising for someone like her who complained about the low temperature when queuing up in businesses that liked to blast their long suffering customers with freezing cold air. On this occasion her attention was diverted by the extensive display of paintings and sculptures that occupied the dome-shaped interior. Plenty of sunlight came through the large fully sealed windows, but the heat of the sun lost out against the strength of the cold gusts. She examined the sculptures of the national heroes which were proudly displayed alongside the work of modern painters. The main exhibition focused on religion and spirituality although Preddy did not feel particularly religious or spiritual at that moment. In fact it was all he could do not to swear out loud.

"See him here, sir. Him early."

Preddy looked down the hallway and witnessed the approach of the well-dressed chief financial officer of Chinchillerz, Arroun Fisalam. The man glanced anxiously at the gallery attendant nearby and nodded politely before strolling past him and greeting the detectives.

"Shall we go this way?" he asked in a strong Indian accent, and indicated that the detectives follow him.

They walked down a stone staircase which Preddy assumed had been part of the original nineteenth-century court house which had once occupied the site. Fisalam used a large iron key to unlock the door to the small basement room and turned on the light. Warm air rushed out of the window-less chamber which held a few old benches and chairs, but was otherwise empty.

"You have your own room in dis place?" asked Preddy.

"No, no, my friend is the curator. I had to get special permission to use this room." His movements were apprehensive, as if he feared being thrown to the floor at any moment.

"Well at least it's warmer dan up dere," said Spence.

"So, you did notice," murmured Preddy.

Fisalam closed the door. "Sorry, I have business at the bank across the road. I just didn't want to be seen going into Pelican Walk police station, and at least this place is relatively safe from prying eyes."

"Thank you for coming to see us." Preddy sat down gingerly on a rickety-looking bench while Spence pulled out a chair. Fisalam was around fifty, although his face was deeply lined, like a sorrel petal dried out by heat. "I saw you watching us walking around at Chinchillerz and you were at de window when we left. I got de feeling dat maybe you had something to say?"

The finance man stood with his back pressed against the wooden door and looked from one detective to the other. He was glad that both were here, as he had heard disturbing things about the male officer. Fisalam removed his glasses and wiped his face with a flannel. "Not really, Detective." He ran a moist hand through his thin hair. "Don't you think I would have called you if I had something to tell you? Carter's murder is a terrible thing and that family means a lot to me."

"Why don't you tell us what de family means to you," said Spence, giving him a wide smile. "Dey seem really nice, Ida and Terence, quiet and humble people. Me like dem. And it looks like Lester really loves dem and looks after dem. Come take a seat and talk, man." She patted the chair next to her.

Fisalam's eyes brightened and he hesitantly moved over to claim his seat. Spence shook his hand clutching it for longer than was necessary and beamed at him. "I just love dat floor where you work, Arroun. It light and cool and spacious. You don't know how lucky you are to have such a comfortable place to work in. It nice, man!"

Fisalam smiled and his taut shoulders seemed to relax. "I can't complain. They look after everybody quite well, management and staff alike. Ida and Terence are strong business people, man. They don't let anything get in the way of the smooth running of the business."

"Bwoy, I would love to work somewhere where management united, you know," said Spence with a sigh. "Up at Pelican Walk is pure argument wid de boss man dem. You couldn't go tell dem dat you need water cooler and free drinks machine and all TV and pool table!"

"I certainly wouldn't dare," said Preddy.

"Well, the kids are the ones responsible for all that I guess. I say kids, I mean Carter and Lester."

"What were dey like together, Carter and Lester?" asked Spence.

Fisalam shrugged. "Like any two brothers really. They worked in harmony, they argued, they were back to making peace again." His eyes shifted to study the stone floor.

"What did dey argue 'bout?" asked Spence.

He rubbed his hands on the knees of his khaki trousers and said nothing.

"I know you love de family, Arroun," said Spence quietly. "Anything you can tell us dat might help to solve dis case will be greatly appreciated. Loyalty is a good thing, but it shouldn't get in de way of moral duty. Tell us what you know. Your name will never be mentioned."

His nervous eyes flicked over the detectives. "I didn't want to come here because I don't know anything. Really, I don't."

"You would be surprised at what people think dey don't know," pushed Spence.

The finance man took a deep breath. "At the time it bothered me, left me with a bad feeling, you know, then afterwards I thought no more about it."

"Go on," said Preddy.

"Lester was pretty mad one day, because he got the idea that his parents were planning to put Carter in charge of the financial operations."

"Dey told him dat?" asked Preddy, raising his eyebrows.

"He sort of deduced it. He had been suspicious for some time and asked me why Carter was always shadowing me. I just said 'because he asked to.' I didn't want to get involved, you see." He paused, recalling the incident. "Then one day after Carter finished shadowing me he went into Miss Ida's office, which is next to the drinks fountain. Lester went towards the drinks machine, but he didn't get any drinks. He was leaning up against the wall eavesdropping. A few minutes later Lester went running into his mother's office cursing and carrying on."

"Did he hear what Carter said?" asked Preddy.

"No idea."

"Well, what did Lester say?" asked Spence.

"It was hard to hear anything because Ida closed the door. I remember Terence went into the room shortly after. All I could see was Lester shouting and pointing. Carter had his palms up, you know, like he was telling him to calm down. He patted Lester on the back and Lester pushed him off and came back out furious. I mean his face was purple like the blood vessels were about to burst."

"When did dis happen?" asked Spence.

Fisalam tilted his head to the side and closed his eyes briefly. "About two months ago."

"What has de atmosphere been like since den?" asked Preddy.

"That is the thing. There was no real atmosphere as such, even on that day. Lester has always been like that. He can blow up and then switch back to being the most normal person in the space of five minutes. If I hadn't seen the alter-cation myself I wouldn't have believed one took place. For all I know they told Lester that he was mistaken. He and Carter were having lunch together in the canteen later the same day and playing video games."

"You did ask Miss Ida what happened?" asked Spence.

Fisalam nodded. "I did. She said 'nothing.' She hasn't even told me why Carter was breathing over my shoulder night and day. That lady keeps everything within the family. I wouldn't even bother to ask Terence about it, because if Ida's not talking, Terence will not talk either."

"So, do you think Lester could ever be mad enough to hurt Carter?" asked Preddy.

"Never." Fisalam shook his head vigorously. "Lester really loved Carter and Carter loved him too, Detective. That's why even though the memory of the altercation crossed my mind I didn't plan to mention it."

"Lester has a very good alibi anyway," said Preddy.

Fisalam nodded. "Yes, I understand that he was in jail at the time." He hesitated a split second before feeling brave enough to add, "Being assaulted."

Preddy decided to ignore the last bit. "Well, thank you for telling us. We prefer to follow all leads no matter how unlikely, and den discard dem as we go along."

"Dis might sound like a strange question, but does Lester have any money troubles?" asked Spence.

The finance man gave a hollow laugh. "Well, he doesn't have access to as much of the money as he would like, if that is what you mean. At one time he used to spend money like water, until Miss Ida put a stop to it. He gets a very good salary though, acting more like a product development manager, although he tries to get involved in everything."

"So he does have plenty of money?" she pressed. "His lawyer seems to be following up quite closely on a personal injury claim. Like he needs de money?"

"Lester cannot get his hands on what he calls 'petty cash' anymore," said Fisalam. "His idea of petty cash is not mine by the way. He has come to me before looking for money to buy a flat screen TV for his office when the one he has was only a year old. Two days later he was back wanting money to buy rims for his car. The car was new and didn't need any dressing up — or pimping as they now call it."

Spence said, "I guess him have an expensive lifestyle and image to maintain."

Fisalam nodded. "Quite so. Still, he didn't do anything to hurt his brother, Detective. You are looking at the wrong man." He stood and brushed off the seat of his trousers. "Now if you don't mind, I have to get into Scotia before the line stretches around the corner. They are so slow in that place."

Spence and Preddy rose in unison. "We'll have to continue our investigations. Thank you so much for your co-operation, Arroun," said Spence with another wide smile.

Preddy shook his hand. "Please call us if you think of anything else."

Preddy drove back to Pelican Walk deep in thought. Spence glanced across at her boss, noting his studious expression.

"So what do you make of Mr Fisalam?" she asked.

"He's a strange one. He clearly loves de family, but I sense he has some distrust for each of dem," explained Preddy. "For all we know Fisalam himself is involved. He did say Carter was always over his shoulder."

"I going look into him background, sir."

"Good idea."

"You going tell Super what him say?"

"No way," Preddy replied firmly. "If Super even thinks anybody is sniffing around Lester he will shut us down. He's in awe of dat family."

"So we just going leave it so?" asked Spence.

"What we really need to do is find dat shit, Marcus Darnay," said Preddy, tightening his grip on the steering wheel. "I'm pretty sure he can answer a lot of important questions." He glanced at her, taking his eyes of the road momentarily. "What are you doing dis afternoon?"

"Dat Zadie Merton leave a nasty message on Rabino phone, say she have nothing to talk to us 'bout," said Spence. "We going pay her a visit, try convince her to come in."

Preddy smiled. "You're a real charmer when you want to be. If anybody can convince her to talk, you can."

Spence grinned. "I do my best, sir."

"You know, maybe it wouldn't hurt to use some of dat charm on Detective Harris?"

"I going use something on him if him don't stop spray de damn place wid mosquito repellent," she laughed. "I will work wid him, sir, but I don't trust him and I don't want to be him friend."

"I hear you."

"Seriously, sir, him need him own office. You can't lend him yours?"

"What? And I move into de open-plan? No way."

"Thanks, sir."

"I didn't mean it like dat," said Preddy quickly. "If I give him my office I might as well give him my job."

"Fine." Her tone was surly. "Well, when him done poison we you will no have no team anyway."

Preddy frowned. "Look, I will talk to him if it's dat bad. I hadn't realised."

Spence chuckled and Preddy finally broke into a relieved grin. "You had me worried dere for a minute."

"I'm not saying don't worry 'bout him though, sir."

"How you mean?"

She shook her head. "Me and him working together and half de time me can't find him. Something is not right wid dat man and is not mosquito make him jumpy so."

* * *

Rabino and Spence walked into the dark dingy bar, cringing as annoyingly bad pop music assaulted their eardrums. As their eyes grew used to the poor light they surveyed the badly decorated surroundings. Red-painted walls, red carpet used to disguise a multitude of sins and chipped wooden stools that had seen better days. The scratched wooden bar top looked sticky as if it hadn't been wiped down all day and the detectives made sure not to stand too close to it. Sienna's Gentlemen's Club was a dive. The only thing that did look in relatively good condition was the wide stage with two steel poles secured firmly in the middle. The scantily clad girls that writhed away on them were the bait that attracted wealthy men to this hole.

"Can you imagine working in a place like this?" Rabino asked, screwing up her nose.

"No, but sometimes in dat damn hot office I feel like take off all me clothes!" said Spence. "Girl, you shoulda see inside a Chinchillerz. You woulda grudgeful gone to bed!"

Rabino smiled in the darkness, and moved the overhead tassels dangling near her face. Her eyes skimmed over the faces of the predominantly male clientele. She assumed that the few females present were friends of the dancers.

On stage, performers worked the poles in G-strings and tiny bras that covered nothing. The men sat as close to the stage as possible, admiring the lithe bodies, until they noticed the detectives and gradually started moving into the darkest enclaves.

"You think dem see we?" asked Spence with faux innocence.

"It's the jeans that did it," said Rabino. "We're way too overdressed for this place. Spotted in ten seconds."

A man who Rabino assumed was the owner sauntered over to them. "Ladies, what me do? You going drive away all me customers dem."

"We are not on duty and your customers have nothing to fear unless they are engaged in illegal activities," said Rabino politely. "We just came to have a drink and maybe talk to Zadie."

"Zadie? You mean Celeste? What she do?"

"Is just a chat we want. If she deh here we'll talk to her and leave. If not, maybe we'll just hang around until she come," said Spence.

"Wait deh," said the man in annoyance and disappeared behind the stage.

Spence eyed the baying punters with distaste. "Dese man come in like de two worthless puss at me yard. You know, like when you pick up a can of bully beef and dem see? You don't even need take off de opener."

Rabino grinned. Spence was forever moaning about the cats that her girls had brought home as kittens and whose presence she was apparently forced to tolerate. Strange then that she had given them nice names and bought them hair brushes. They probably slept purring on her bed.

A furious Zadie tottered over on her high heels, her face overdone in vivid lilac eyeshadow, red rouge and pink lipstick. She wore a long blonde wig that stretched to her waist, tiny silver shorts and an even tinier bra. On anyone else this get-up might have looked ridiculous, but Zadie was a stunning girl who could carry off anything with little effort. She reminded Rabino of Lil' Kim before all the bad surgery.

"You going make dem fire me! What you want?"

"We want you to come into de station and talk to us." said Spence. "You think is lap dance we want?"

"Ask what you want ask. Me no know nothing 'bout dat damn man," Zadie raged. "Him dash me weh. Me no know nothing 'bout him!"

"Miss Merton," said Spence, looking stonily at Zadie. "Dis is not a good environment for a chat. Believe me your boss would not appreciate it and neither would ours."

"Me can't come a no police station. You no see me a work?"

"After work is fine," said Spence. "What 'bout first thing in de morning? Just ring me when you're on de way."

"You going arrest me for something, Officer?" Zadie asked, shaking back her blonde mane.

"Why? You think we should?" asked Rabino, taking in Zadie's outfit from top to toe. "If so, you might want to bring your lawyer with you and change your clothes."

Zadie stared back at Rabino. "You think you better dan me because you can speak so? Is not your hair pon your head neither! No look pon me so! You not better dan me!"

Rabino moved closer to Zadie and leaned towards her triple-pierced ear. "Me way, way, better dan you, gyal," she whispered. Zadie took a step back, her mouth open and questioning although she did not utter a word.

Spence waived away a barmaid who was lingering nearby. "Thanks, but we not staying," she said. "You have our numbers, Zadie . . .sorry, Celeste. Tomorrow."

"See you tomorrow, Celeste," said Rabino. "Remember, wear something decent. No batty riders."

Zadie instinctively covered the name badge sewn onto her shorts, and muttered obscenities as she stared at the disappearing women. How dare these two flat-footed bitches come into her workplace and accost her like this?

"Your mouth need wash out, Celeste!" Spence threw over her shoulder and stepped out into the welcome sunlight.

"Celeste!" shouted a patron. "Come wine fi we no?"

"Make haste, girl!" said another man leering at her over his beer. "Me a pay good money fi see what you can do!"

Zadie forced a limp smile to her lips and looked at her eager audience. In the background she could see her newest most generous client, the man who visited her at home recently and liked the massage oils. She acknowledged him with a brief nod and took to the stage.

* * *

Ida Chin Ellis did not take the information well when the private detective reported his initial findings. She could not believe that a girl Carter had brought to the family home on more than one occasion was a common stripper and sometimes escort. Her son had introduced Zadie as a customer relations officer who worked at the convention centre and she believed him.

Now she learned that sometimes the girl spent all day and night writhing onstage in next to nothing, with drunken unfaithful men sticking dirty money into her underwear. On other days the girl gave one-to-one massages and to complete strangers too, though how Zadie could bear to touch the weaselly private detective was beyond Ida.

Where had Carter learned to appreciate a woman like this? Ida had always worshipped education and hard work and was a role model for her sons. Her first thought when she heard of Zadie's true occupation was that the deceitful woman had misled her innocent son, but the more she thought about it the more she realised it was not so. It would appear that Carter had not always been as honest with her as she had believed. Nothing got past Carter and it pained her to realise that he had any association with a woman who was bound to mix with countless undesirables and lowlifes that the city had to offer.

Even more painful for Ida was the knowledge that Lester must also have been aware of the situation because the brothers knew everything about each other. She fully intended to raise the matter with him when he arrived for the weekend. If only he had told her what was going on, maybe her youngest son would still be here today.

* * *

The restaurant chosen by Valerie was one of her favourites. With its high ceilings, spacious semi-dark interior and expert chefs, The Flamingo was popular with many locals, and Preddy had been looking forward to the dinner all day.

"What's de matter?" he asked.

"Nothing. Me not so hungry dat's all," she murmured. Her attention stayed on a small potted plant in the middle of the table, and she poked at its leaves.

Preddy ran his eyes over her, admiring her cream-coloured maxi dress. "Watching your waistline is unnecessary, it is spectacular you know."

She grinned and prodded him under the table with her toes.

"You drinking more wine?" He held up the bottle.

Valerie drained her glass and held it out. "Sure, why not?"

Preddy studied her for a moment before topping up her glass and beckoning to the hovering waiter. It was not like

Valerie to down glasses of white wine like that before she had even seen the starters. When the spicy chicken wings appeared, she barely glanced at them. He was sure that the arrival of the main meal would cheer her up and what a meal it was too; whole red snapper cooked in okra with sweet potatoes and her favourite coconut infused rice and peas. The detective waited until the waiter departed before reaching across and stroking his girlfriend's hand.

"Come on, I know you. Talk to me, no."

Valerie sighed. "It's nothing. Just life really. I am so tired of travelling back home on de weekend to my family, but I know Norman will never allow me to move David to Montego Bay."

"You ask him?"

"You crazy? I just got around to asking him about de divorce which went down pretty badly, although he did agree in de end."

"Maybe you could move out of de house, but stay in Kingston wid David for a while. Eventually your husband will get used to you both not being dere."

"Hmm, maybe." She fell silent again and used her fork to play around in the snapper.

Preddy decided to broach a subject that had been concerning him for some time. "You're still close to Norman, aren't you?"

"How you mean, Ray?"

"You still keep his photo," Preddy said carefully. "I noticed it on your desk in de lab."

Valerie shrugged. "It has always been dere. I've just never removed it. And anyway, if my son comes to de lab it helps him feel comfortable."

"And how do de razors help him?"

"What razors?" The fork froze on the snapper's head.

"De ones in your bathroom closet, Val," he said. "I noticed dem de other night."

Valerie put down her utensils, her eyes boring into him. "You tell me, Detective, what about de razors in my yard?"

"David's not shaving yet is he?" God, Preddy wished he was better at things like this. "I was just wondering dat's all."

"You know, for someone who has to interview people for a living you're taking a mighty long time to get to de point. Well, Detective?"

Her voice was icy. She tilted back her head and threw the whole glass of wine down her throat. "I guess it never crossed your mind dat dey might have been put dere for you? You're supposed to have a keen eye for detail. Surely you recognised dem as de same brand you use?"

Preddy's stomach twisted in knots and he cursed himself for his foolish thoughts. She was right. He did once have a packet of razors just like it in his own bathroom, although he had recently changed brands. He wanted the floor to swallow him up, but it wouldn't oblige so he made a grab for his own wine glass instead. He wished he could think of something calming and funny, but in his hour of need his wit deserted him. "I didn't think."

"You mean you overthought?" Her question remained unanswered. "I noticed you were running out de other day, and I bought dem for you." She spoke quietly and her shoulders slumped as if exhausted. "If you'd asked I would have told you to take dem wid you. I just forgot."

"I'm sorry." Preddy discovered a sudden interest in the décor of the room and moved his eyes all around it.

Valerie said nothing for a while as she watched him. "Tell me, who is it you think I'm sleeping wid, my husband or some other man?"

"You were right, I did too much thinking," It sounded lame, but at least he was agreeing with her and she couldn't be too mad about that. "My mind is all messed up, you know?"

"I'm really tired, Ray." She pushed back her chair and stood. "We can do dis another time, or not."

"Valerie, please wait!"

She dabbed her lips with a napkin, threw it on the table, picked up her purse and disappeared through the throng of diners.

CHAPTER 25

Wednesday, 12 August, 2.10 p.m.

Zadie Merton left Pelican Walk still fuming that the detectives had forced her to attend. How dare they waste her precious time with questions about that abusive man? If she was honest, it had not entirely been a waste of time. She revelled in the admiring gazes from drooling officers who watched her as she left, some of whom she recognised from their off-duty trips to the strip club. The females were obviously jealous of her fine shape and good looks while the males wished they could get her phone number and squire her around the town.

Zadie had made a point of dressing inappropriately in a tight silver minidress revealing a bold imprint of her thong, four-inch stiletto heels and expensive jewellery around her neck, arms and ankles. With their bad clothes, basic salaries and government benefits, the women could not compete with her, although Spence and Rabino seemed to think they were a cut above. Having licensed weapons simply gave them more leverage to bully citizens and could hardly make them attractive to any men.

The male detective leading the case was nowhere to be seen, which was a pity as she had planned to flutter her eyes at him and watch him crumble like the rest. The Norwood murder cop might have a reputation, but he was just a man after all. A white man was hanging around here too, she had learned, but he was not present either to witness what Jamaica's finest looked like. Zadie smiled wryly. The poor man came all the way from cold grey foreign probably expecting to find a few Miss World types. No such luck in Pelican Walk station.

Let the rest of them look, she thought as she placed her designer sunglasses firmly on her nose and sashayed under the archway and down the front path. They were all fools in this place and no amount of browbeating would get her to confess anything related to Carter Chin Ellis.

* * *

Lunchtime was over. The corridor was still as the two detectives moved silently towards the evidence room. This time Preddy was a hundred percent certain that he was not mistaken. Someone was checking up on the Chin Ellis evidence. Preddy gently turned the handle and opened the door. Harris reached in swiftly and flicked a switch. They stared at the shocked face of the intruder who blinked furiously as the sharp light assaulted his eyes. He straightened up and backed away from an open drawer. Preddy was in his face with two strides.

"What you doing in here, Officer? Speak, man!"

"Me just a check how things going!"

"Where you get key?"

Silence reigned as the officer looked from Preddy to Harris and back again. Harris closed the door behind him and stood against it with his arms folded. Preddy towered over the officer who tried to step backwards, but was stopped by a firm chair. Not for the first time the detective wondered how many Pelican Walk officers were intricately involved in this case.

"You know, I have never had to arrest an officer before and I can't say dat I am going to enjoy doing it, but I realise dere is a time for everything. Tampering wid evidence is a serious offence."

Timmins' eyes widened. "No, sir! Me never do anything to de evidence. Me woulda never do dat!"

"I want to know where you get key and what you doing in here!" demanded Preddy.

"Me borrow it from outa Odette draw when she gone a meeting."

Preddy cursed under his breath. The damn secretary was a sweet girl, but she did not think in the way that law enforcement representatives were trained to think. "And what exactly did you want to see in here? Talk no!"

"Now is the time tae speak, Officer Timmins," said Harris. "If we have tae cuff ye it'll be tae late."

Timmins's chest rose and fell repeatedly, his discomfort obvious to the two detectives. "Is just dat I noticed something earlier on and it was bothering me. A bracelet dat look like de one Carter did have on when we bring him in," he said. "Zadie Merton did have it on in here. Me never know her, so me ask 'bout her and hear say is Carter woman."

"Lots of people have his and her jewellery, Officer," said Harris. "Ye must know that."

"Me know, yes." Timmins looked sheepish. "Me never see any bracelet look like dat. It really look like de same one Carter did have and me say to meself 'suppose is de same one?' Me did just plan to watch de video of her interview."

Preddy felt his anger slowly dissipating, overtaken by adrenalin as his mind tried to work out the implication of what Timmins said. If Timmins was right, then Zadie had been in contact with Carter within the hour either immediately before or after his death. She had lied to the detectives. Preddy straightened up and gave Timmins breathing space.

"I wasn't here when she was interviewed," Preddy said, watching the officer's face. "You recognised it as Carter's bracelet?"

"How do ye know what bracelet Carter had on anyway?" asked Harris. "He didnae go through the booking process?"

"Carter reach over to try and stop us from arresting Lester and it fall off into de car. Me remember look pon it because it well shine. Him snatch it up and put it back pon him wrist."

"So if ye wanted tae take a look at the video why naw come tae one of the detectives with ye suspicions and let us run with it?" Harris asked. "Ye sure ye wasnae thinking 'Let's see what they have on me?'"

"No way! Me no have nothing to do wid any of dis!" Timmins was indignant. "Me couldn't go ask any question 'bout anything after dem done take me statement and tell me not to talk to anybody except de lawyer. Me never feel say it make sense to talk to lawyer until me see de bracelet up close."

Preddy cupped his hands together as if praying and raised them towards his pursed lips as he studied the nervous officer. "Detective Harris, rewind de video and let Officer Timmins see it."

Harris looked at his supervisor in alarm and hesitated momentarily. Preddy's eyes met his for a split second before the Scotsman grudgingly moved towards the recording equipment. He rewound the tape and pressed play before zooming in on Zadie's left wrist. Timmins moved slowly towards the screen and craned his neck to get a closer look.

"Well, what do you think?" asked Preddy.

Timmins' eyes remained fixed on Zadie's wrist. "It look jus' like it to me, sir. Serious ting."

"You sure?"

"Yes, sir."

Preddy walked towards the door and held it open. "Give me de key and leave. Right now."

"Ye letting him go?"

As the door closed behind Timmins, Preddy responded. "Are you questioning my judgment, Detective Harris?"

"But we dinnae know for sure why he was in here." Harris' face grew flushed.

"I believe him."

"He should be suspended or at least removed from the premises."

The look on Harris's face was one that Preddy had seen before, a look that would make a lesser man tremble, turn water into ice. One thing Preddy would not accept from any officer was insubordination and he would certainly not stand for it from a visitor, no matter his complexion.

"Well, Detective Harris," he said slowly. "I realise dat you have friends in high places, but wid respect, dat is not your call."

Harris appeared ready to say something, but bit his lip. An uncomfortable silence followed for a number of seconds while the two men studied each other.

"Aye, sir. Yer right."

"Now, how are we going to get hold of Zadie Merton's bracelet?"

* * *

Marcus Darnay was feeling decidedly skittish. He should have left the damn car where it was rather than risk trying to get rid of it, but he had been unable to sleep comfortably knowing that it was sitting in the bushes. His rash action had backfired. Now he was no longer free to walk the city streets in peace, although he had legitimate business to see to at the garage. His cousin was a nice lady, yet soon she would begin to question his sudden decision to come and visit her in St Ann after not being in communication for nearly two years. She had been told of trouble at home and had no idea he was avoiding the police.

Darnay liked the cool hills of Moneague and wished he had been able to visit under different circumstances and bring the family with him. It was a treat to sit under an abundant tangerine tree and eat as many succulent ripe fruits as his stomach could hold. His cousin had a small field of banana and plantain trees and he was promised a few hands of each to take back to the city with him.

194

Standing on the verandah of the large bungalow, he inhaled deeply, and savoured the smell of clean fresh air. Very little traffic ever passed by the property as it was set way back on a side road a good distance from the main road. An ideal place to rest and recuperate when you wanted to get away from it all. He sighed, knowing that he could not get away from his current reality for long. The children needed food and clothing and he needed to make money to support them. For the umpteenth time he wondered how he had stupidly allowed himself to be manipulated into this intolerable position.

CHAPTER 26

Thursday, 13 August, 3.30 p.m.

Preddy was writing notes on the whiteboard and Spence was fielding phone calls when Harris and Rabino entered the room. The Glaswegian's pale face had acquired an orangey pink colour which signalled to Preddy that he spent too long in the afternoon sun. He decided against giving Harris any advice about the dangerous effects of going without sunscreen. The white man was going to look quite strange in a few days when his burnt face would match his flaming hair.

Harris flopped down in his chair and spun it around to face his colleagues. He used a notebook to fan himself while Rabino sat beside him and adjusted the oscillating fan so that its effects were felt by both of them.

"We executed the search warrant on Zadie Merton's premises," said Harris. "Lovely place the young lass has got there."

"I'm sure she was glad you approved," said Preddy. "Did you have any trouble?"

"Not really, she didnae even look at the warrant," he replied. "Just gave Detective Rabino a really dirty look, then pretty much gave it up without much pressure. She was more annoyed that we interrupted her boiling her head."

"Huh?" said Spence.

"Steaming her hair," Rabino corrected him. "Her eyes were all red and puffy. I think she's one of those ladies that really does not like to be seen other than at her pristine best."

"Look at this," said Harris, as he took the evidence bag from his briefcase and held it up.

Preddy stared at the object in fascination. It was certainly a beautiful piece of gold jewellery and he could understand why it might be memorable to anyone who had seen it.

"We first checked with a few jewellers down at City Centre Plaza and they said it couldn't have been made in Jamaica," said Rabino.

"I phoned Ida Chin Ellis and she said Carter had his jewellery made in New York, as all the family do," said Harris. "I got hold of the jeweller and a right pompous twit he was. Talking about naw wanting tae disclose information like New York has some sort of jeweller-client confidentiality law. I convinced Mrs Chin Ellis tae get him tae talk."

"I'm glad we got her co-operation," said Preddy. "She never ask why you were interested?"

"Aye, she did," Harris replied. "Told her that it was very important and asked her tae trust me."

Preddy nodded, wondering whether Ida secretly trusted Harris to do a thorough job much more so than the rest of the team. Black people had a habit of placing way too much faith in white people despite the grim lessons of centuries of history.

"And get this, the jeweller said there is only one in the world," said Harris. "It was made especially for Carter and delivered tae him three weeks ago. Ye see that tiny number under there?"

He held a small magnifying glass over the bracelet and Preddy peered through it. "I see it."

"How did it get to Zadie and who else has had dere hands on it?" asked Spence. "Mr Darnay?"

"No visible prints on it," said Rabino. "She cleaned it up well. Seems she soaks her gold in ammonia and I can still smell the odour."

Preddy walked back to the whiteboard and tapped on Zadie's name. "Dis young lady's motive is possibly jealousy and anger at being cast aside. She seems to have received all sorts of gifts and money from Carter, but didn't receive de commitment she really desired, only a lot of ridicule, and if she is to be believed, abuse. Says she was working at Sienna's on Saturday night. We need to check her alibi and find out how she knows Marcus Darnay."

"She's one cold-hearted bitch to be swanning around in dat bracelet, like it's her trophy," Spence said.

"A woman scorned and all that," muttered Rabino. "She does have a nasty mouth though, so it wouldn't surprise me if she has an equally nasty temper."

Spence nodded. "As Chaka Demus say, 'a pretty face and bad character.'"

Harris stopped fanning and focused on Preddy. "We only have Officer Timmins' word that Carter had on the bracelet. He isnae an entirely reliable witness. Officer Franklin said he didnae see any bracelet."

"True, but I think I've read Timmins right," said Preddy, holding the man's gaze in an open challenge.

Harris frowned. "He could be sending us off on a wild goose chase, sir. It's a good way tae deflect attention from himself."

Preddy stared into the flared green eyes. "What we need to do is get dis piece of evidence in front of Marcus Darnay. Let him think his prints are on it. Wid dis and de car maybe we can get him to start talking."

Harris turned to his keyboard, but Preddy could tell from his body language that the Scotsman was not convinced. No doubt thinking all kinds of derogatory First World things about Jamaican detectives.

"Dat bullfrog Darnay still lying low, sir, but we will find him," said Spence.

"Who is Arroun Fisalam, sir?" asked Rabino, squinting at the whiteboard where the name appeared below Zadie

Merton's. Preddy had already placed a black line through the name of Kirk Grantham.

"Dat's what I was trying to find out. Seems clean as a whistle though," said Spence.

"He's de main finance man at Chinchillerz," Preddy explained. "Gave us a glimpse of de relationship between Carter and Lester. Looks like de two were very close, but dey argued quite often as well. Mr Fisalam is not a very talkative person, we had to drag de information out of him — or rather Detective Spence did. Apparently Lester got very upset at de suggestion Carter might be being groomed for de chief finance role. Seems like Lester is a Jekyll and Hyde person though, mad one minute, happy as Larry de next."

"You think Lester could have hired Darnay to murder his brother, then?" asked Rabino with a great deal of incredulity. "Can't see it, sir."

Preddy shrugged. "Zadie and Darnay, Lester and Darnay . . ."

"What no go so, nearly go so," quipped Spence.

"Sorry?" said Harris.

"Think of it as 'dere's no smoke without fire,'" offered Preddy.

"Och, I get ye."

"Lester could have asked Darnay to hire a gunman, or Zadie could," said Spence. "Darnay have alibi as well remember, he was at de Orchid Bar and plenty of witnesses swear to it."

"Drunk witnesses or at least alcohol impaired," added Rabino. "Some of them had been drinking around the clock."

"True," Spence nodded. "De bullets match dose found in Darnay's car."

"His car was definitely there," said Preddy. "Either de alibi witnesses are mistaken or Darnay loaned the Subaru to the gunman."

Harris looked across at the detectives. "So who is the light being shined on here? Seems more likely Fisalam would want tae have Carter murdered? Maybe he wasnae ready tae give up his finance role and hired Darnay himself."

"Wait." Rabino held up a well-manicured finger. "Let's not forget Carter was driving Lester's car so there's still a real chance that Lester was the actual target."

"He doesnae seem tae think he was a target at all. Denies he has any enemies or any links tae drugs," said Harris. "It's naw common for drug dealers tae go straight tae murder without issuing any threats anyway. They're more likely tae take warning action first, such as assault or property destruction. Going straight tae murder is stretching it a bit and they'd make sure tae get the right man." He paused suddenly as if remembering his position and quickly added, "but ye would know the clientele around here better than me."

"I think you're right." Preddy looked thoughtful. "Lester is now a murder suspect, but I don't want dat mentioned by anybody unless and until we have some real solid evidence against him. In de meantime, check Zadie's alibi. Either she or Lester is possibly guilty of aiding and abetting. Let's keep up de heat on Darnay, speak to his known friends, relatives and acquaintances. Darnay is de key to de murder and we have to bring him in."

Preddy lowered his voice as human shadows fell on the blinds. "And, of course, all eyes and ears should be kept open for four other persons within Pelican Walk whose names are not listed up here. We all understand de delicacy of de situation."

"Yes, sir," they chorused.

Preddy began to gather his papers. "I'll be in my office. I'll finish off my report and let de Super know where we are."

Harris's phone beeped and the Scotsman got to his feet. "Need tae say hello tae ma old mam before she goes tae bed," he announced. "It's pretty late in Glasgow."

Preddy watched him go as he walked briskly down the corridor with his phone planted to his ear and something in Harris's manner suggested to Preddy that the foreigner was not speaking to his old mam at all.

CHAPTER 27

Thursday, 13 August, 5.25 p.m.

As Preddy entered the conference room, there was no doubt in his mind that this meeting spelt trouble. Superintendent Brownlow sat opposite Preddy and did not smile when the detective walked in. The blinds were drawn and there was a pile of paper folders in front of him which Preddy recognised as personnel files. A feeling of numbness crept over him as the superintendent started to speak and he forgot about the report that he had planned to deliver to the boss. Here was the superintendent indicating that the rug was about to pulled out from under his feet.

Preddy learned that Commissioner Davis had placed his file into the category marked "recommended for retirement" and had submitted it for the attention of the national security minister. Preddy tried desperately to maintain self-control while listening to the voice of his superior officer. The superintendent swore he was in the detective's corner batting for him, but was himself under extreme pressure from the commissioner and even the mayor, both of whom were deeply troubled following the Hip Strip fiasco.

Preddy had known he was on dangerous ground although he had not accurately calculated how perilous it was. In fact, he imagined all rumblings of discontent had been quietly settled while the main investigation progressed, particularly now that the narcotics squad was running its own line of enquiries. He said as much to the superintendent.

"It all might have been done with," replied Superintendent Brownlow, "but you set fire to the mongoose tail, man."

"I'm not following, sir." Preddy felt the words coming from his lips, yet the hoarse voice did not sound like his own. He needed water, but there was no jug on the table.

"You were instructed, by Commissioner Davis no less, not to interfere with Ida Chin Ellis. Yet she says you were seen snooping around her doctor's office."

"I see," said Preddy weakly.

"Why did you go up there, man?"

"I had a theory, sir."

"About what exactly?" The superintendent stood up, hands folded behind his back. He began walking around the long table, but did not take his eyes from the detective. "Well?"

"It didn't pan out sir, it doesn't really matter."

"Hmm, well it certainly didn't pan out for you." The superintendent paused beside Preddy and looked somewhat deflated. "Why not stay under the radar? From the day of the Norwood raid you've been using up your nine lives like you have a death wish."

Not the Norwood raid again.

"Detective?"

"Sorry, sir? I didn't hear you."

Superintendent Brownlow's next words sounded as if they were echoing in a faraway place and the detective imagined he must have nodded off and ended up back in one of his nightmares. "Detective Sean Harris has been selected as your replacement. Harris is going to take over the investigation into the murder of Carter Chin Ellis."

"Harris?" Preddy whispered.

"This is not a demotion," the superintendent insisted, "only a temporary hiccup to get the case back on track. No-one will be informed that you're being considered for retirement. I deeply regret this outcome, but the commissioner demanded it be done and I could not persuade him otherwise."

"Super, tell me dis is not true."

Superintendent Brownlow reclaimed his seat and sat back, shoulders sagging. "I'm really sorry, Ray. Detective Harris has already been told and has accepted his new role. The commissioner says he's sure that you'll be able to work under him and take directions so that the case can follow a more . . .considered approach."

Preddy listened with clenched fists and wondered whether Harris had done anything to resist the commission at all. What did that sheltered foreigner know about running a murder investigation in Jamaica? The police high command had designated power to white men before and had given up after a few years. It was insulting to the constabulary in general that anyone should be flown in to take over, almost as if August 6th 1962 had never happened.

"So dis is all settled?" he asked, when he could breathe. "And I don't even get a chance to state my case?"

"Believe me, this is not what I wanted to see happen, but I don't have any choice in the matter. You have not been removed from the case."

"Although I guess somebody tried."

"I don't know who you mean, Ray. You know that I've always had your back."

"And when will de rest of my team be told about it, and by whom?"

"They are being told right now, by Detective Harris."

"You have got to be kidding me?" The weakness in his limbs disappeared just as suddenly as it appeared, replaced by a surge of rage. Preddy leapt to his feet and sent the chair crashing behind him. "Without even a conversation wid me first? Without me being present?"

"We thought it was the best way."

"Well, thank you, sir," said Preddy sarcastically. "I better go and find out what de rass is going on!"

"Don't do anything stupid, Detective!" called the superintendent to the detective's departing frame. "Detective Preddy!"

As Preddy strode along the corridor, he could now imagine a reality in which he was not a detective. The high command would strip him of his position completely, bowing to the pressure of external forces that sought to influence the island's law enforcement strategies. The parish of St James might be tough to police, but he was doing a thorough job and was well on the way to solving the murder of Carter Chin Ellis. The idea that he would throw in the towel at this stage was one that only a police commissioner, sitting in a New Kingston penthouse, could envision as a satisfactory state of affairs.

Preddy spotted the moving shapes inside the evidence room and turned the door handle which held firm. He banged on the door repeatedly in quick staccatos until he heard the sounds of it being unlocked from the inside.

"Wait, so you are filling in my . . .sorry, *your* team already?" said Preddy striding past the Scotsman. Preddy's face was specked with beads of sweat and his breath came quickly as he spoke.

The room fell still. Spence sat perched on a desk looking sullen, while Rabino stood beside a filing cabinet with a sheaf of papers in her hands looking extremely uncomfortable.

Preddy's eyes searched their faces before returning to the target of his wrath. "You couldn't wait? A you a de big man now and all a we going bow to you!"

Harris glared at Preddy. "Dinnae be an arsehole!"

"Wha' de fuck you say to me?" Preddy walked straight up to Harris and stood so close that their noses almost touched.

A secretary froze in the doorway clutching a tray of ice-cold lemonade and chocolate biscuits that the superintendent had organised in advance of him delivering the bad news. "Sir?"

"Get out!" barked Preddy. The woman quickly backed out spilling the drinks as she went.

"You too!" Preddy stared at Rabino and Spence. "Leave!"

Spence stared back. "But wait? A who you a talk . . ."

"Shut up, my girl," said Rabino quickly. She threw the papers back into the file and slammed the cabinet before grabbing Spence's arm. "Get your keys. Let's go follow up on Darnay."

"But I want . . ."

Ignoring the objections of her colleague, Rabino strong armed the irate Spence out and shuddered as Preddy kicked the door shut behind them.

"Yes now, backra," said Preddy. "Say all wha' you have to say to me!"

Harris narrowed his eyes. "Well since ye have given me an invitation. There'll be naw more cannabis smoking around here."

"What you say?"

"Ye heard me, alright. Ye must think I'm blind and have lost ma sense of smell. Every morning there's more mints flying through the air than there are bloody mosquitoes. Took me a while tae work out why naw one was offering me any."

In that moment Preddy wanted to hurt Harris. He wanted to squeeze his throat until the green eyes turned smoky grey. "You accusing me of something, you better have proof, backra."

Less than a foot separated the two men and neither would blink. "Ye smoke marijuana, or weed or ganja or hemp, whatever ye want to call it. That's what I'm accusing ye of."

Preddy could feel his gun rubbing into his side, reminding him that it was there. "Never in my entire life," he whispered. "Not a joint, not a spliff, not a cigarette, not a rollup, whatever you want to call it. Never."

"I know I smelled something."

"You rass deaf? I said never."

Harris blinked and looked confused. "Well, in that case, I'm sorry, Detective Preddy. Maybe I was mistaken."

"Maybe you don't want to make any more mistakes, Detective Harris."

A mist still clouded Preddy's brain, but it had thinned enough for him to realise that getting out of the room as quickly as possible was the best move. He continued to stare at Harris as he moved towards the door. "I'm sure you won't be needing me for anything."

"I think naw."

Preddy turned and opened the door.

"And Detective Preddy, please dinnae call me that again."

"Call you what?"

"Backra."

"No, massa."

* * *

It was now late evening and the sun had long gone down, although the temperature outside remained decidedly humid. The overhead fans were all on, as was the air conditioning and for once Preddy gave no thought to the electricity bill that would land on his mat. The apartment needed to be as cold as possible to keep his body temperature down. The detective was thankful he had not disposed of the stress tablets that the doctor prescribed months ago and he took a few to try and soothe his throbbing temples. Unable to face food, he had opted for bottles of cold coconut water, hoping it would settle his stomach and stop the bile encroaching on his throat.

Normally he would be sitting in his study with the door closed, but it had not been a normal day and so he took up a place at the dining table gaining some comfort from seeing his teenagers behaving like teenagers, oblivious to their father's dark mood. Davis, Brownlow and their redheaded puppet would not be the ruin of his family. If Valerie had been on speaking terms with him he would have called her, but she was not picking up or returning any calls.

When his laptop purred into life, he searched for information on the Chinchillerz empire and wondered whether it was possible that Lester would hire Darnay to harm his brother. Lester wanted money, hence the assault claim from which he clearly expected to profit, yet there was more than enough money and power in that family to go around and their empire was still growing. Lester would always be rich and powerful, whether Carter was dead or alive.

He thought about his own siblings, a brother in London and a sister in Rome. The idea of killing them for any reason was unimaginable to the detective, but he had met murderers and would-be murderers who disclosed reasons for murder that any right-minded person would consider completely illogical. Psychopaths were irrational people and it was clear from media reports that there were a good few of them running around unchecked on the island.

Annalee crept up and peered over his shoulder, studying the image of the young Chinese-Jamaican on the screen, whose face, along with that of his younger brother, could not be avoided even if one tried.

"He's cute, you know, Dad."

Preddy glanced sideways at his grinning daughter noting the teasing glint in her eye. Annalee was now fourteen and it seemed like only yesterday that he was helping her to ride a tricycle in a straight line. That was ten years ago. Gone were the thick plaits and coloured beads that danced when he threw her up into the air, replaced by the straight relaxed strands caught up in pony tails above each ear. Now the time that he had long dreaded had arrived, the time when she thought older boys, who up to two years ago had been slandered by her as a worthless species, were cute.

"I guess you could call him dat," he said grudgingly.

"Oh, Dad!" Annalee giggled. "'Bout you guess!"

She put her head on his shoulder and hugged his arm. "What happen to de man who attack him?"

"His trial is many weeks away," Preddy said, scrolling down the page so that the face disappeared from view. "Anyway, remember dat suspects are innocent until proven guilty."

"Him did look well guilty to me."

"You think violent people have a particular look, young lady? Dey don't, you know."

"Hmm, maybe not."

"No matter what dey look like people can do crazy things. Whether dey were born wid de predisposition or developed it because of de environment has never been clear in my mind. Sometimes it's a mixture of both. And sometimes an otherwise normal person just snaps and does something really bad and dat's it."

"You'll never snap, will you, Daddy?"

A vision of red hair above a sunburnt face flashed before Preddy's eyes and he swallowed.

"Of course not, Annalee."

Roman forced his attention away from the movie he was watching on TV. "What did happen wid the milk powder drugs from Chinchillerz? Dem find out who it belong to yet?"

"Not yet, narcotics are investigating," Preddy replied wearily. "But on a positive note de little girl who ingested it is doing fine and her doctor doesn't believe she'll suffer any adverse effects."

"Bwoy, some people well careless wid other people life, eeh?" Roman said.

"Very true, my son."

* * *

When Zadie arrived home it was nearly dawn. On the horizon she witnessed the shimmering orange glow of the sun as it slowly emerged from behind the hills. She drew thin curtains across the windows and then peeped through them, her hazel eyes alert to anything out of place. No strange people wandering around, no plain-clothed police officers, nothing except for a few cars going back and forth. It was still too early for most people to be up. The traffic would pick up when normal people started going to work and she was anything but normal people.

She kicked off her towering shoes and retreated to her spacious bedroom. It had been a long night's work and she was tired. A mass of discarded dresses strewn across the bed needed to be cleared away and she was not looking forward to the task. It had taken her about an hour to select a suitable outfit to wear to work and even longer to find a pair of shoes, mainly because she had such a wide choice of both. Slowly she dragged the dresses from the bed, returned them to their hangers and replaced them in the double wardrobe.

The movements felt mechanical as she did this every day for five to six days a week. Since Carter had unceremoniously dumped her, there had been less money coming in and she might soon need to work all seven days, until she found someone with cash whom she could publicly declare as her boyfriend. Another arrogant, demanding, rich man to treat her as his personal property and pay for the opportunity to be seen with her.

In the kitchen, she poured herself a glass of sweet white wine and gulped it down in one swift movement. Closing her eyes she relished the comforting warmth that coursed through her body. She bent low and peered at the gun through the glass front of the washing machine. The kitchen was not an ideal place to store a weapon, but the wardrobe would be the first place a police officer would look. At least that was where the officers went first in every movie she had ever watched. Those two idiots from Pelican Walk had come for her bracelet. What on earth could they possibly want with a bracelet? Good luck to them, she had plenty of other stunning jewellery.

CHAPTER 28

Friday, 14 August, 10.12 a.m.

Harris marched into the detectives' open-plan quarters and announced that Marcus Darnay had been sighted at his garage in Granville. Preddy's heart thumped in elation. His gut had told him that the suspect had never left the island, and gone were his misgivings that Darnay might have been murdered by his hirer, and disposed of. Darnay was alive and this time the detective felt sure it was not a false sighting.

Preddy crunched loudly on a mint and writhed in his seat as he watched Harris standing at his desk fiddling with something. Preddy curled his hands and stabbed his nails into his palms. "You might want to go right now before he disappears again, Detective Harris," he finally offered through clenched teeth.

"Aye, and I would like ye tae come with me, Detective Preddy." Harris picked up his car keys and held them out towards Preddy.

"Sure," said Preddy. He leapt up and walked past his new boss, ignoring the outstretched keys.

"Two bulls, one pen," mumbled Rabino, and shook her head as she watched Harris follow behind Preddy.

"Sir, you need any backup?" called Spence, quickly getting to her feet.

"Yes, dat would . . ."

"Naw, we can . . ."

The voices came simultaneously and Spence looked from one man to the other. Preddy held up an apologetic hand towards her. "Sorry, I thought you were talking to me."

The two men disappeared and Spence sank back into her seat.

"I was," she whispered.

Harris drove while Preddy sat in the passenger seat, giving directions when necessary. They travelled mainly in uncomfortable silence through winding streets heading to the outskirts of the city. Their pockets of stilted conversation did not extend beyond whether they would need to take Darnay by force or whether he would come quietly. The detectives determined that they were equipped for the worst of the two eventualities.

The houses became smaller and the unofficial garbage heaps grew more noticeable the further they went, discarded old fridges a repeated feature of the landscape. Political slogans were painted in orange or green along the sides of the culverts and scrawled on signs hanging from trees. Even though it was morning, many working-age young men were leaning up against ramshackle shops waiting for their lives to begin.

The detectives headed closer towards the Granville community on rugged roads. Each time Harris ran into a pothole Preddy wished he had accepted the keys. Jamaican drivers crossed lanes to the wrong side of the road to avoid craters, but not Harris. The jeep was built for these roads, yet the effect was still jolting. Preddy wondered if Harris could not see the holes or if he just could not judge their depth. This was neither the time nor place to give the foreigner a lecture, but Preddy badly wanted to point out that the JCF could not afford new vehicles. He winced as the bumper narrowly missed a goat which chose the wrong moment to decide that the grass was greener on the other side. There was even less money in the force's kitty to compensate farmers for their crushed livestock.

Darnay was bent over double attending to a young child at his feet when the black jeep screeched to a halt on his secluded forecourt. As the detectives ran towards him he stood upright and insolently looked Harris up and down.

"So, wha' de rass you fah, colonizer? You no know say your time done long time?"

"Mr Darnay," Harris smiled as if greeting a long lost friend although well aware he had been insulted. "It's a pleasure tae finally meet ye."

Two customers emerged from inside the garage to see what the commotion was about. A mechanic remained inside tinkering with a broken down vehicle. In a nearby car sat a young woman who Preddy recognised as Darnay's common law wife. A woman who days earlier had promised to notify the detectives if she ever saw or heard from their subject of interest.

"Cute baby," Preddy said, stroking the head of the tiny boy playing with his rattle, a boy who actually looked like Darnay. "Not much of a place for an infant though, Mr Darnay."

Preddy picked up the fallen rattle from which the sticky tape had begun to strip and noted that it was heavier than it appeared. No toy was really childproof, no matter what the manufacturer said. He pasted it down firmly again and shook the object in front of the child's animated face.

"My bwoy pickney is my business. Wha' you want?" Darnay swooped down and picked up his son, before snatching the toy from Preddy.

"Now dat is not a nice way to greet us, is it, Mr Darnay? We have a few questions to ask you. You've been very evasive for de past few days."

"You no see me have work to do?" the wanted man blustered, and clutched the child as if it was armour.

"Like what?" Harris enquired. "Ye tell me what work can be more important than assisting the law?"

"Me say wha' you want, Officer Whitebwoy?"

"I can live with Officer Whiteman, Mr Darnay, but it's actually Detective Harris."

"We came to give you de good news dat your car has been found," said Preddy. "But I guess you heard 'bout it already?"

Darnay looked sullen. "Me no hear nutten."

"Oh, so you just disappeared because you felt like a few days' holiday?" asked Preddy.

"Jamaica no free country?" Darnay directed his disdain at Harris. "Since 1834 Black man can go wherever we want whenever we want. Member dat."

"Aye, and today ye want tae come tae the station for questioning. I have a short fuse that's getting sunburnt. Remember that."

"De station a no place fi me," said Darnay, moistening his lips. "Me have people to see and business to run."

"We came here tae arrest ye, Mr Darnay. Now ye have a choice, ye can come quietly or naw." Harris patted his pocket which revealed the outline of handcuffs.

Darnay's eyes followed this movement nervously. "Damn police always a harass people, man! Why you can't leave man alone?"

Preddy shook his head at him. "Because you refuse to change your life, Mr Darnay."

"You no need worry yourself 'bout my life. My life is right here, inna my hand."

"You need to put down your life before you drop him, and come wid us," said Preddy.

"Me don't do nutten wrong," insisted Darnay. "From time to time me make a bad choice, but . . ."

"Bad choice?" Preddy interrupted. "Bad choice is getting a permanent tattoo of a baby's name and birth date."

Darnay frowned. "Say wha'?"

"A man is dead. You can go stand up in front of jury and tell dem 'bout you 'bad choice.'"

Darnay glared at Preddy. "Alright, me will come."

"We dinnae have a nursery at the station though," said Harris.

"Me a go give my bwoy to him mama. See her park over deh so."

"Go ahead, sir." Harris moved aside and allowed Darnay to pass with his son.

Darnay walked in front of the detectives who remained at a respectful distance allowing him to say goodbye in private. He handed the little boy through the drivers' window. The woman opened the car door and stepped out with the child, clearly arguing with her partner.

"Seems a wee bit annoyed that he's given up on his babysitting duties so early," said Harris.

"Particularly as he hasn't been a hands-on father recently," agreed Preddy.

In a flash Darnay leapt onto a motorbike, gunned the engine and sped away from the forecourt leaving the angry woman and screaming child behind. A customer stared after his departing motorbike in astonishment.

"A whe de bumboclaat you a go wid me bike!"

"Och, here we go!" shouted Harris sprinting back to the police jeep, followed closely by Preddy.

Harris set off at pace behind Darnay with blue lights flashing and siren screaming. A gas tanker in front of their vehicle prevented the detectives from getting a clear view of the motorbike. Harris sounded the horn wildly, but the eighteen-wheeler was too big and too heavy to nip out of the way.

Darnay veered off onto a side road while Harris, driving too fast to stop, flew past on the main road. Preddy slammed the dashboard in exasperation and then unholstered his gun. Harris cursed as his jeep travelled on for at least thirty metres before it slowed enough for him to do a safe U-turn. He followed the side road knowing that the fugitive was at least a full minute ahead. Harris hesitated at an intersection. A phone card vendor gesticulated wildly, pointing out the way to go. The detective put his foot down again and followed the man's directions.

A far away hump in the road made it impossible to see what lay ahead of it. As Harris approached it he came upon a cloud of dust and applied the brakes sharply as a cluster of driftwood shops suddenly appeared in view. The stolen motorbike lay upside down where the collision had bent a lamppost, dislodging the Western Union sign which now hung precariously overhead. Darnay was nowhere to be seen. A crowd of people were huddled over something in the road, screaming and shouting.

The detectives ran towards the group with guns drawn and ordered them to get back. As the people moved away an old man became visible. One of his legs was bent in an unnatural position beneath him and his badly twisted bicycle wheel told its own tale. Harris shouted out to phone for an ambulance while he crouched down and tried to make the groaning man comfortable.

Preddy looked up and realised that a second group of people, mainly young men, were shouting and whacking away at something in the grass verge. By the time he got there Darnay was recognisable only by the light blue shirt and white shorts he had been wearing earlier, both of which had new red streaks.

The detective fired his gun once into the air. The crowd bent low and quickly melted back from the bloody fugitive. One of the assailants dropped a stick and fled. Darnay's face was covered in blood which drained from his neck and pooled onto his chest. It was easy to tell which side of his body he had landed on, as the skin hung loose from that arm and leg exposing red flesh beneath. Preddy was unsure which of the other injuries were caused by Darnay's encounter with the gravel and which had been caused by the incensed vigilantes. The fugitive groaned, but did not speak and Preddy was just glad he had survived.

An ambulance eventually arrived on the scene, carefully negotiating the uneven roadway, and was followed by a local police car. Preddy spoke briefly to the two responding police officers. The paramedics loaded the injured old man into the ambulance first, accompanied by a middle-aged woman who clutched his hand and mumbled prayers through her tears. Darnay's bloodied body was lifted in next and a paramedic climbed in with him, escorted by a police officer under request from Preddy. He had a lot of questions to ask Darnay and the time for playing games was long over.

"If he tries to run shoot him in de good leg," Preddy said.

"Yes, sir."

He watched as the ambulance pulled away and then approached Harris, who was busy rummaging around near the overturned bike. "What we have here?" asked Preddy.

"A smartphone with a damaged screen and Darnay's young bairn's rattle," said Harris holding one item in each hand. "It's held together pretty well considering."

"Hmm, let me see dat toy."

* * *

Preddy sat in the evidence room by himself surveying the many piles of information gathered on the case. The largest batch of notepapers sat in a manila folder and related to calls made just after the ten-million-dollar reward was announced by the Chin Ellis family. The extra officers assigned to help with the overflow had managed to go through most of them, thanks to the help of the rest of the team, but nothing of significance popped up. Strange how every citizen suddenly knew something when there were ten million reasons why they should. The job was hard enough without idle distractions.

He was disappointed that the doctors refused them permission to interview the injured Darnay who was now under armed guard at Cornwall Regional Hospital. What he really needed was for someone to admit seeing Darnay in the vicinity of Carter's house, or better yet to have found the murder weapon. The suspect needed to have pressure heaped on him from a great height.

As Preddy picked up a folder, a piece of coloured paper fluttered to the floor and he bent to retrieve it. On it was written a man's name and phone number. No date to indicate when the message had been taken, but he recognised Spence's handwriting. A second later she walked into the room with a thunderous look on her face.

"Have you spoken to dis guy yet?" he asked.

Spence put down her files and approached the detective screwing up her eyes to see from a distance.

"Mr Delmere?" said Preddy.

"Oh, dat's de paper I've been looking for all morning, bartender at Sienna's," she said, reaching for the note. "You know how much time I waste wid people pon phone today? Look like some a dem just love attention. Even dis morning me interview one girl who don't know nothing, but she asking me all kinda question. Me tired ah dem!" Spence kissed her teeth loudly.

Preddy knew the warning signs well when it came to stress. Spence was a hardworking woman who did not suffer fools gladly, but even the best detectives occasionally experienced burn out.

"I tell you what," said Preddy. "I'm just going to finish dis page den I'll go down and get some drinks. Phone calling is thirsty work."

"You can say dat again, sir." She reached for the phone and dialled Mr Delmere's number.

"Oh really," Spence said into the phone. She clicked her fingers to get Preddy's attention. He swung round in his chair and looked at her as she gave him the thumbs up. "And when was dat?" Spence asked.

"What happen?" mouthed Preddy, impatient for her to get to the end of this one-sided conversation.

"Thank you for dat, Mr Delmere."

"Is what happen?" asked Preddy, before Spence had even returned the phone to its cradle.

"Zadie Merton. She left de strip club early on Sunday morning, probably around one a.m. Seems she forgot to mention it."

"Zadie and Darnay," murmured Preddy.

"She cried off work saying she had a migraine and needed to get away from de stage lights," Spence continued. "We need to find out what she has to say 'bout dat."

"No wonder she was so reluctant to come forward," said Preddy.

"I know say dat girl well lie!" Spence narrowed her eyes. "Now dis me want to hear 'bout from Zadie broad mouth."

"She really likes you too, I hear," said Preddy, smiling as he got to his feet. "Soon come."

He walked downstairs to the canteen and leaned over the counter trying to see inside of a frosted-glass cooler that was full of bottled drinks — sodas, flavoured-water and juice. The lady sitting behind the counter rose when she noticed him.

"Give me de juice, please, one bottle of each." Preddy took the refreshments and headed back up towards the evidence room, passing Timmins on the way. The men nodded at each other.

"Alright, sir?" said Timmins.

"How you do?" said Preddy without stopping.

Timmins scowled. He wanted to ask Preddy if there was any news on the bracelet, but it was clear that the detective did not think he was worth the time of day, even after he had given the team such a good lead.

When Preddy returned to the evidence room Rabino had appeared and he rued the fact that he would now have to give up his own drink. Rabino looked up at him.

"Oh, thank you, sir," she said. "Is the pineapple mine?"

Preddy smiled and waved the bottles in the air. "I'll let Spence take her pick I think."

Spence looked up and flopped backwards in her chair dramatically. "You save me life! Give her it, me love de mango."

"Is Harris around anywhere?" asked Preddy. "If I go back downstairs I guess I need to find a drink for him too."

"Him say him is de boss." Spence cut her eyes at the empty chair. "Make him buy him own drinks."

Preddy would not be drawn. "Is just drinks, ah no nothing."

"Saw him earlier, but that man is well shady sometimes," said Rabino. "I don't know where he's gone now."

"Maybe him find another wine and cheese party to go cock up," suggested Spence. "Look like him well love dem things deh."

* * *

Night had begun to fall when Preddy exited the rear of Pelican Walk station. Silver stars blinked faintly in the sky as it rapidly changed from light blue to dark blue. He made his way to the car park where sat police issue jeeps as well as private cars belonging to officers, interspersed with vehicles belonging to members of the public seized for some traffic offence. Most were towed for having no insurance although some were taken for having bald tyres. It was noticeable that the working police cars sitting alongside the seized cars had equally defective tyres.

For once he wished that the car park was not so well lit. Usually, when the bulbs blew they would stay unchanged for months. Coincidentally, all four were replaced the day before the arrival of one Sean Harris. A group of officers exited the building and nodded at him as they headed for their vehicles. When they left Preddy sidled in between the vehicles and began searching for his target. He stopped beside a white jeep, checked the registration plate and tried each of the doors. They were securely locked. The detective cupped his hands and peered through the rear side window.

Behind him the station door opened and he crouched down pretending to tie his shoelace, waiting for the person to pass. When the silence resumed he turned his attention back to the window. He ran his fingertips along the top of the window seal and pushed against it. After some effort it began to slide down. Once a sizeable space had been created, Preddy used both hands to push it down firmly. He then leaned in and used his flashlight to examine the interior.

"Detective Preddy."

Preddy leapt back so abruptly he hit his head on the window frame. He steadied himself and stared at the officer.

"Officer Timmins." It was hard to appear unfazed when standing there with a flashlight, but the detective did his best. He fumbled for the off switch and resisted the urge to rub his pulsating head.

"You looking for something in particular, Detective?"

"Making sure de vehicles are secure, Officer."

"Vehicles? But a one car me see you a look inna." Timmins folded his arms across his chest. "And a long time you a look pon it too. Me see you from upstairs."

At the sound of the back door opening again Preddy looked beyond Timmins' shoulders and identified the departing shape. Footsteps crunched loud on the gravel as the body came nearer. Preddy bent double, lunged at Timmins and dragged him towards another car.

"Down, quick!"

Timmins obeyed. He could not see the cause of the danger, but in this line of work he had learned to duck without asking questions when told do so. The two men stayed hidden behind the car. Timmins pulled out his service weapon and held it to his side. Preddy signalled him not to move.

The footsteps halted outside of the white jeep and the detective watched as the man's boots ground out a cigarette. He knew those boots well and had often seen them attached to a tall, bow-legged body.

The car door opened and closed, the headlights went on. It took an age for the engine to start and Preddy held his breath praying that the driver would not notice the open rear window. Slowly the vehicle pulled away. Preddy waited until the sound of its engine was distant, before standing up and offering a hand to the dishevelled Timmins.

"A wha' de rass a gwaan, sir," the officer asked, breathing heavily. "A couldn't Nembhard we a hide from?"

"Actually . . ." Preddy sighed and contemplated what to say.

"What him do?" asked Timmins.

"Before I answer dat, I have one question to ask you," Preddy said. "And I don't want to hear no nonsense, just yes or no."

"Gwaan ask."

"I know you've heard dis question before. De night you and Franklin picked up Carter and Lester, dem did ask for your name?"

Timmins felt his legs wobble and was thankful that Preddy's flashlight was off. He had lied about this previously and now Preddy was practically forcing him to lie again. The crickets on the dry lawn chirped loudly in an aggressive manner, taunting him. Even the car horns, tooting on the main road, suddenly seemed much nearer. All this noise when he needed to think and think quickly.

"Be very careful, Officer. Remember is just me and you here." Preddy said darkly as if reading his mind. "I don't have no listening device or recorder."

Timmins thought about where his struggling career could possibly go after this. Preddy would deem him untrustworthy and might even force him to transfer. Those damn Chin Ellis brothers were so cocky and entitled that he had taken an instant disliking to them. If only he had just answered the question and given up his name instead of breaching protocol and putting his career in jeopardy. He was not even sure why he had chosen to lie to the detective in the first place, except that the mention of murder had caught him off-guard. Lying was never his thing. He pushed the thought of his career reaching a premature end from his mind.

"Yes, dem did ask we," Timmins said, hanging his head. "We never tell dem."

Preddy exhaled silently and leaned back against a car. He savoured the cool evening air as he admired the bright array of stars that winked at him from on high. The detective had always believed this element of Lester's tale.

"Come wid me," said Preddy.

CHAPTER 29

Friday, 14 August, 2.02 p.m.

Zadie dusted the display cabinets, carefully removing the more valuable ornaments to buff and replace them. She hated housework and still held onto her dream of becoming a wealthy kept woman, renouncing the need to do any menial labour. A dream she had come so close to achieving. The idea of having a domestic helper appealed to her vision of grandeur. Carter had sent her a cleaning woman from time to time, but she was not keen on strangers touching her possessions and she had so many expensive trinkets that it might take a while to work out if something was missing.

One woman had made off with a pair of gladiator sandals that could not possibly fit over her fat ankles. The thieving woman had taken them from beside the front door where Zadie had placed them with the intention of dropping them off at the Salvation Army. If she had stolen one of the many boxed pairs in the shoe closet the theft would never have come to light. When Zadie demanded their return the woman had turned nasty and threatened to beat her. Not being a fighter Zadie had backed off, but she was now much warier of the characters that crossed her threshold.

As she pulled out a vase a folded water-stained document fell to the tiled floor. It puzzled her for a moment until recognition dawned on her. Of course, this was the paper the Pelican Walk officers thrust at her after turning up unannounced, boorishly demanding entry and refusing to give her time to finish her hair or get dressed. They had gone straight to her dressing table, removed one of her many bracelets and left within a few minutes. The white man was cute in a strange way although she was not a fan of red hair on any man. Black, brown or auburn were fine, but red and blonde were not manly colours. As for that long-weaved woman, just because she could twang like somebody reading BBC news did not make her queen of St James. If the policewoman had hung around longer Zadie would have given her an object lesson in how to dress femininely. Flat black shoes were definitely out, jeans had never been in, and long-sleeved blouses were for church. Many a time Zadie had limped in agony all day on stilettos rather than swop for kitten heels or flat shoes. Flip flops were a travesty of foot fashion and only good for beaches or indoors when not expecting visitors.

She sat on the arm of her sofa, straightened out the crinkled document and started to read. Her unlined face gradually descended into a deep frown. The paper fluttered from her fingers to the ground as she sat stock still, staring without seeing. Eventually she got to her feet and walked in a trance-like state towards her kitchen. She opened the washing machine.

Zadie had never been a fan of guns, but this one was a gift and she had not wanted to cause offence by refusing to accept it. Although still a teenager, her apartment was full of gifts given to her by so many admirers that she had trouble remembering exactly who gave her what, but she would never forget where the gun came from.

Her mother had always encouraged her to study hard and try to "make something" of herself, so that she could buy whatever she needed. Her father had just mumbled that she would never starve, but she should always have pride and not be a doormat. She wondered what life would have been like had she listened to her mother and taken the route to higher learning. Maybe it would have been nice to have business cards with *Zadie Merton, Ophthalmologist* or *Zadie Merton, Chemical Engineer*. Business cards were for professional people and she certainly could not order any as *Zadie Merton, Exotic Dancer*, not that anyone knew her by that name anyway as to them she was just Celeste. No surname. She was yet to meet a man who wanted to educate a beautiful woman, and that could only be because said woman would then pursue a career and be less likely to accede to the wants of a man.

Slowly Zadie slipped off her indoor clothes and headed to the bathroom. She had been fooling herself all along and now he had made a fool of her too. For a few minutes she stood in front of the elongated bathroom mirror and for the first time since she was twelve years old she did not like her reflection. The tears coursed down her face as she slid to the floor naked and sat doubled up with her chin on her knees. It was an age before she unfurled, stood up straight and wiped her face. Her thoughts were much clearer than they had been in years and she knew that by nightfall her life would have changed forever.

She slid into a sleeveless yellow cotton dress that floated out from the hips and fell way below the knees. The dress was ideal for Caribbean weather as it allowed breeze to billow through while protecting the wearer's modesty. It emphasised her dark skin and her enviable figure, but she rarely wore it because it was way too long for her fine legs. She applied colourless lip balm to her fully formed lips and smacked them together. The eye pencil and mascara usually applied three or four times a day were not given any consideration. Her hair would have benefitted from a few brush stokes, but that would have taken up valuable time and she no longer had any to waste.

She opened her closet and ran her eyes over her vast shoe collection feeling a sense of distaste at the multitudes of high-heeled strappy shoes. The unloved flats were few in number and it took her the briefest of moments to slide a pair onto her slender feet. Flats must be good for running. She placed the gun carefully inside her handbag and gave a quick glance around the apartment that she would never see again. She closed the door behind her.

* * *

The canteen was reasonably quiet when Officer Timmins entered. Three other officers were present, but he was interested in dining with only one. He purchased a bottle of pineapple juice and a soy patty, and pulled out a chair opposite the targeted officer.

"Wha' happen, man?" said Timmins.

Nembhard chewed on his seasoned fries. "Everything good you know, bredda."

"You no hear say dem find Darnay car and ah examine it?"

"Eeh-eeh?" Nembhard's voice was cool and unruffled. "Den me no hear say it well burn up?"

"Yes, man." Timmins nodded. "It not in a good state at all. Dem can't find no fingerprint nor nothing like dat. Dem find a bullet in de backseat though, so dem can do nuff wid dat."

Nembhard placed his fork carefully onto his plate. "Bullet inna de backseat?"

"One man a Red Hills did shoot up de car and de bullet inna Darnay car match de man gun." Timmins explained. "Darnay well careless, man. A jail him a go as sure as night follow day."

"Dem have to ketch him first." Nembhard wiped his lips and got to his feet.

"How you mean?" Timmins raised an eyebrow. "You no hear say him sick up a hospital? Him not going nowhere for now."

"Oh. Dat is good news." Nembhard picked up a toothpick and stuck it in his teeth. "Later."

225

Timmins glanced at Nembhard's unfinished fries. The man was a big eater who never left a crumb for an ant. As he watched his colleague's departing figure he wondered whether Preddy could possibly be right.

* * *

Back in the detectives open floor, the team tried to maintain a degree of optimism while waiting for the chance to interview Marcus Darnay, but patience was just about ready to pack up and leave. Rabino was on the phone making yet another of her hourly calls to Cornwall Regional Hospital. The doctors continued to stonewall all attempts to speak to the patient until he was out of danger which they reckoned could be at least another day or two.

"Yes," said Rabino to the person on the other end.

"Yes?" Harris pricked up his ears and looked over his monitor at her. It was not a positive sounding yes, but it was better than all the "no's" she had been uttering.

Rabino shook her head, making a slashing movement across her throat. Preddy watched her with a sinking heart. *Please God, do not let Marcus Darnay be dead*, he thought, as Rabino put down the phone.

"He can't speak, sir. His voice has gone, temporarily, the doctor thinks." She stretched across her desk and picked up a bag of mints. The plastic crackled as she unwrapped one and placed it into her mouth.

"You should offer one of dose to Detective Harris," said Preddy with a smirk.

"Oh sorry, do you want a mint, sir?" Her hand was poised to throw one at Harris, but he frowned and shook his head while giving Preddy a death stare.

"See me here," said Spence, hands ready to catch a sweet.

Preddy turned his attention back to his screen. Harris did the same, staring blankly at it.

"Damn," muttered Harris after a few minutes. He repeatedly rapped his fingers on the desk.

Preddy rocked back in his chair and studied the white man's sunburnt face. "He can write, right?"

"Hmm?"

"Marcus Darnay cannot speak, but he can write."

Harris stopped drumming and realisation dawned on him. "Right." He scooped up his car keys and beckoned to Preddy to follow. "Let's go."

As they entered the hospital the sight of weary people in reception caught Preddy's attention. It had not been so bad the last time he was here, but now the air-conditioning unit had clearly malfunctioned leaving the building feeling unbearably hot. The place was quiet and stifling without that cooling comforting mechanical hum in the background.

The silence was short-lived. Someone, a recipient of bad news, began to wail and flail on the ground. Preddy thought it was a woman, but as he got closer he realised that the howls came from a man.

A mother who had been breastfeeding her child sat motionless, apparently unaware that the baby had long ceased feeding and her full breast was lying unused on his cheek. A few patients turned to stare at the official-looking white man and his colleague as they entered the lobby, but most ignored them and remained lost in their own personal misery.

The detectives followed the receptionist's directions and made their way via the lift to Darnay's ward. A policeman stood guard outside the en-suite room where Darnay lay still, dressed in a white hospital gown. The cuts and bruises did not appear to be so bad now that his face was clean. His left arm and leg were covered with absorbent bandages. On his right arm silver handcuffs glimmered in the slim bead of sunlight that penetrated the half-drawn blinds above his bed.

"Marcus Darnay, we meet again." Preddy pointed at the bad leg. "Dat look painful."

Darnay glared at him through swollen eyes and Preddy smiled brightly at the detainee. "You never seem happy to see me anymore. I could develop a complex, you know. Sorry I couldn't bring de natural lady wid me to cheer you up."

"Just Officer Whiteman again, I'm afraid." Harris picked up a medical chart from the end of the bed. "Marcus Adyemi Darnay. Adyemi. Nice. Fractured left ulna . . ."

"A whe' you a call-up call-up me name so fah?" he croaked angrily. "You no have nutten fi do?"

"Och, so ye can speak!" exclaimed Harris. "Fancy that."

Preddy sat heavily on the bed. He wriggled around in a show of making himself comfortable and pretended not to notice Darnay wince with each movement.

"Well yes, we do have plenty to do," said Preddy. "Every road we go down leads us straight back to you. But de doctors don't want you to try talk, so we going try spare your voice."

"I was going tae ask ye tae write, but both of yer arms look a bit fragile," said Harris. "I'm going tae ask ye a series of questions. Nod once for yes. If the answer is naw just keep still, okay?"

"Paper," whispered Darnay.

"So, you happy to write?" said Preddy. "Fine."

Preddy put his head outside the room and beckoned to the police guard for the key. He returned to the bedside and released the suspect's hand from his shackles. Darnay instantly tried to pry the gun from the detective's holster. Preddy held on to his weapon firmly and used his weight to body slam Darnay's chest, pinning him against the hard mattress. The invalid cried out in pain and swore loudly. Harris pointed his weapon at Darnay's temple and the desperate man gave up his futile struggle.

"Understand something, man," warned Preddy as he straightened up. "If you make another stupid move I going shoot you. Not in de leg and not in de arm. De coroner will come get you."

"Dinnae let that happen, Mr Darnay," added Harris.

Darnay gazed longingly at the window, while Preddy followed his gaze. "If you even made it dere is a five-storey fall for you, and if you survive you'll be coming here month after month through de door marked *wheelchair access only*."

"He's naw going tae try anything, are ye, Mr Darnay?"

"Me nah go nowhere," Darnay conceded faintly.

"First we're going tae talk about the Subaru, then we're going tae talk about Zadie Merton," said Harris. "A bullet in yer car matches those taken from a man who shot at ye on the night of Carter's murder. Did ye kill Carter?"

Preddy handed Darnay pen and paper which he clasped and held close to his face concentrating intently as he moved the pen carefully over the page. When he handed it back to the detective Preddy crumpled it and threw it in the corner narrowly missing a nurse entering the cubicle. The detective received a reproachful look as she picked up the paper. She unfurled it to reveal a drawing of an oblong with stick legs and something resembling a snout at one end and a curly tail at the other.

The nurse shook her head at Darnay and retreated from the room with what appeared to be his medication. Although Darnay was in great pain he forced himself not to beg the nurse to return.

"Officer, gwaan 'bout you business," he mumbled. "Me done tell you say dem thief me car."

"You are our business," said Preddy. "And you're going to answer de questions."

Darnay stirred and cleared his throat, eyeing Harris. "Kingfish done long time you know, yet you still deh here a take up space. Why? Who you ketch? You no serve no purpose now."

Harris was amused by this, having recognised the reference to the crime team led by an English crime fighting chief years ago. He accepted that all white officers would probably be connected to Operation Kingfish by the public at large for the foreseeable future.

"Ma purpose will soon become apparent tae ye, Mr Darnay."

"I heard dat you and your family all got granted visas, to de land of de Mounties of all places." Preddy said. "Congratulations. Well done."

Darnay went perfectly still and this time the pain really did set in. His temples pulsated and his eyes blinked rapidly.

Preddy was pleased that he finally had Darnay's undivided attention.

"So, you're getting your woman and kids out of de way next month, all nicely set up in Vancouver? Just in time for back to school eh? And den you're going to join dem under a different name," said Preddy, handing Darnay another piece of plain paper. "Is dat de plan?"

"One nice big happy family," said Harris. "I love those. And ye can choose any colour picket fence ye want, doesnae have tae be a white one."

Darnay placed the pen and paper on his chest and gripped the side of the bed with his bandaged hand. His eyes began to brim with water.

"Dere is still a chance dem can make it," said Preddy wistfully. "You now . . . well, you going have to do time. How much I don't know."

"We'll see what can be done for ye if ye co-operate," said Harris. "If somebody paid ye tae do this ye need tae tell us now."

"Me never do a damn thing," mumbled Darnay.

"What no go so, nearly go so," said Harris in pitch perfect Patois.

"But wait." Darnay's eyes grew round and for a split second he forgot his pain. "Dis white bredda no easy! Me never do it, me ah talk de truth!"

Preddy's lips tugged into an involuntary smile. Jumping from white boy to white brother, completely bypassing white man, was a considerable social leap for Harris, whether he appreciated it or not. Preddy reached into his inside pocket and took out an object which he held up by the window pretending to study it.

"You know, my kids had rattles when dey were babies. Never dis loud and never dis heavy. I'm guessing dat de nice baby of yours took dis rattle home and your wife's fingerprints will be all over it. Am I right?" said Preddy. "Maybe even on de bullets inside too? What do you think de Canadian

230

authorities will say if she gets charged with illegal possession of ammunition?"

"If the murder weapon's at her house ye might want tae tell us all about it."

Darnay closed his eyes and thought about the grand plans of which only he and his main woman should have been aware. They must have interrogated her and had obviously frightened her into revealing their plans. He would have been a new person in a new land of opportunities and would have started his own bakery in Vancouver, giving the deprived Canadian-Jamaicans some of the tasty treats they missed from back home. The patties, meatloaves, coco bread, cornbread, sugar buns, spice buns, grapefruit soda and ginger beer, he could see them all on the black, green and gold shelves displayed on banana leaves. His children would go to good private schools and benefit from a First World education. They would learn to twang in English like the best of them and probably learn French too.

Even that outside baby son would be filed for eventually, once Darnay had settled. In his mind's eye he proudly watched the children graduating from high school in pristine gowns, throwing black caps into the air, clutching that scroll of paper that he never managed to get his own hands on. Paper that would give them a chance to start solid careers, gain great advantages in life and make the most of opportunities that had eluded him in his youth.

"Wake up, Mr Darnay," said Preddy, prodding at the patient's good toe. "Physical evidence does not change. It does not disappear. It tells it like it is. Give your family a chance for a life, Mr Darnay."

Darnay eyes remained closed, but he was listening and he knew that the next words that came out of his mouth could send him to jail for a long, long time.

Preddy's phone rang and he listened to the voice on the other end while looking at Harris. "Let's give Mr Darnay a minute more to think about what he wants to do," he said, and they exited the room.

CHAPTER 30

Friday, 14 August, 3.12 p.m.

The concierge acknowledged Zadie with a bow and a smile as she entered the five-star hotel. She walked down the red carpeted corridor, tracing steps taken on previous visits to the premises. Ornate chandeliers hung from high ceilings and two large well-stocked aquariums provided live distraction for the elite clientele. One contained baby turtles which peeped around the submerged stones and swam beneath the water. The other contained a mixture of small and large colourful fish and plants existing in perfect harmony. She did not bother to greet either of the receptionists who were busy booking in new visitors, and they barely glanced at her.

Sometimes the door was left ajar, but this time it was firmly closed, as he was not expecting her. She looked up and down the hallway. She pressed her face against the door and knocked on it, listening for movement. As she waited impatiently she remembered that the opulent suite took up a good portion of the west wing and he could be anywhere within. Her knocking was more urgent this time and finally she heard his voice.

"Is that room service?"

"Zadie."

"Soon come, baby! Soon come! Just finished in the shower."

After what felt like many minutes yet could not have been more than one, the door swung open.

"Zadie, what's happened sweetie? Come in, come in."

Zadie accepted the invitation and the half-naked man found himself staring into ice-cold eyes on a face that was unadorned although still clearly beautiful. It was not just the missing make-up that made her seem vastly different. Her red eyes, stained puffy cheeks and unkempt hair were evidence that she had been curled up crying. He walked towards the mini bar and stooped to check the contents.

"You're well in need of a drink, baby. Talk to me."

"You piece of Chiney shit!"

"Whoa! Jesus Christ, Zadie!" Lester spun around, clutching the bath towel around his waist. "What did I do?"

"What did you do?" she repeated. Her voice rasped as if sandpaper was trapped in her throat. "You make dem kill Carter, no true?"

"No, Zadie! You mad, woman! Why would you ever think a thing like that?"

"Think it? Me know it!"

"No, baby, you're wrong!"

"You see what is missing?" Her eyes blazed as she waved her slight wrist in the air. "Hmm, answer no? Look at me arm."

Lester stared at the angry woman and could not imagine what she was referring to. "I don't understand, baby."

"Where you get de bracelet, you shit?"

"Bracelet?" Gradually, realisation set in and his heart began to palpitate. "I bought it in New York weeks ago. Bought it just for you!"

"Liar!" Zadie's voice wobbled as she spoke. "Carter did buy it. De police say so!"

"What police? They made a mistake!"

She opened her handbag and quickly removed the small pistol, watching as Lester's eyes widened and he began to retreat. He tucked the towel firmly onto his waist and raised both palms in front of his chest.

"Pelican Walk police," she said, advancing on him. "De warrant says dat Carter had it on dat night. You get somebody to murder Carter. Your owna bredda!"

"No Zadie, I swear to you! It never happened!"

"No? Dere is no other bracelet exactly like dis pon de planet and you a tell me 'no'?" she blazed. "Why you lie so, Lester? You lie and wicked."

"Zadie, listen to me." Lester continued to move backwards and suddenly found his back against a large mahogany chest of drawers. The expansive room now felt as if it was shrinking by the second, becoming a tomb. "The police made a mistake, baby, I swear!"

"You never give me dis gun for protection did you? You give it to me after me tell you say if Carter lick me again I going do him something," she said breathlessly, pausing to level the gun at him.

"No! Your work dangerous, baby. I wanted to make sure you could fend off aggressive men!"

"You hoped I'd use it to kill him, eeh? Do your dirty work for you? Answer me!"

"You're wrong! Why in God's name would I kill my brother?"

"A dat me a wait on you to tell me, but looks like you not going do dat!"

Zadie blinked away her tears and swiped at her eyes with her forearm. Lester picked up a large vase and threw it in her direction. As it hit the wall beside her there was an explosion that sounded like a loud clap of thunder. The gun flashed and fell from her fingers. The bullet flew into the chest of drawers, splintering the tough wood on its way and Lester recoiled as a splinter skimmed his shoulder. As Zadie reached down for the weapon Lester moved forward swiftly and kicked it away. He pushed Zadie violently against the wall hitting her head. Her knees gave way beneath her and she slumped to the floor.

Lester retrieved the weapon and threw it into a travel bag before discarding the damp towel. It took him only a few minutes to dress and throw his remaining belongings into the bag before making for the door. He stepped over Zadie as she lay still watching him through glazed eyes, her breath coming in shallow gasps. As the door closed behind him she raised her aching head slightly, eyes searching the floor for her handbag. She tried to reach for it but, feeling too weak to move, she lowered her face on the cool tile again.

* * *

The hospital lobby was sparsely occupied when the police officer arrived to change shifts with the guard on the fifth floor. He avoided the lift as the loud pinging noise when the doors opened might attract unwanted attention. Several flights of stairs later he observed the on-duty guard standing at the end of the ward, far from Marcus Darnay's room, engrossed in conversation with a pretty nurse. The officer crept to the door and gently opened it.

"So, dis is where dem have you?" he whispered.

Darnay's eyes flew open and he stared at the approaching figure in alarm. He tried to move his good arm, forgetting momentarily that it was shackled to the bed.

"What you going talk say?" demanded Nembhard. He leaned down and pointed cold steel towards the patient's face.

"Officer Nembhard, welcome." Harris stepped from inside of the en-suite bathroom, with Preddy behind him.

Nembhard jerked back and spun around, replacing the weapon in its holster as he tried to regain his composure.

"So ye come tae say hello tae our guest?" said Harris.

For a few seconds Nembhard said nothing, but his hands were visibly shaking. "A no nutten if me come see him. Me just interested to see him cause me hear 'bout him," he finally ventured.

"You show your interest by sticking a gun in him face?" said Preddy. "What possible interest could you have in him?"

"You never see me trouble him." Nembhard held his body bamboo straight and tilted his chin up.

"Naw, ye were just showing him how well ye polish yer muzzle," said Harris.

"Don't none a you try kill me," wheezed Darnay in panic. "Nurse!"

Preddy gave him an unsympathetic look. "Nobody not shooting you, shut up you mouth."

"I tell ye what, Officer Nembhard," said Harris. "Ye can go back tae the station. We'll get the answer tae the question ye just asked him and then we'll come and tell ye all about it."

"I'm sure we won't be long," added Preddy. "Just make sure you don't go too far."

Nembhard hesitated. His eyes moved rapidly from Preddy to Harris and back again, before fixing on Darnay.

"Go on, out with ye!" demanded Harris. "Now!"

As Nembhard retreated a nurse entered with some medicine for the patient. She propped Darnay up and made him swallow the medication. She glanced suspiciously at the detectives as she checked the bandages. "You alright, Mr Darnay?" she asked.

Darnay nodded. "Yes, mam."

Preddy closed the door behind her. He read the statutory caution to Darnay who wearily acknowledged that he understood and was speaking of his own free will and did not need a lawyer. The detective then started recording the conversation on his phone.

"How do ye know the officer that just left the room?" asked Harris.

Darnay frowned as he lay as still as he could. "Me don't even know is who dat."

"You don't know Officer Nembhard?" Preddy moved closer so that he could see into Darnay's eyes. "Den how him know you?"

"Bwoy, me can't tell you dat, Officer. Believe me, me no know him."

"How did ye come tae know Zadie Merton?" asked Harris.

"Zadie Merton? Look here, me hear you call dat name already and me no know her. Me no know dem people wha you asking me 'bout." Darnay was indignant. "Me think you did want ask me 'bout Lester."

Preddy and Harris exchanged surprised glances.

"Me no know Zadie Merton and me never really know Carter neither. A one time Lester call me to go try help fix Carter engine, but me and Carter never exchange two word."

"You tell so much lie I don't know what to believe," said an exasperated Preddy.

"Officer, is not lie me telling you now."

"So you do know Lester?" said Preddy. "De man you once swore blind you didn't know, and who say him don't know you?"

Darnay rolled his head slightly to face the wall so that he did not have to bear the detective's penetrating stare. "Me meet him first when me did a do lottery scam," he explained. "Me not even know how him track me down, but him ketch me."

The damned lottery. When Preddy first became aware of this new technology-based crime his initial reaction was that it would never catch on, but the scammers proved him wrong. "You were trying to steal money from him?"

"No boss. Me get a foreign number and ring it and scam one old woman. All twice a day me ring her and a try reel her in. Florida she deh and me never know who dat woman was. A did Lester auntie to rass! A thirty thousand US dollar me get outta her," Darnay recalled, with something that sounded suspiciously like pride. "Lester come into de internet café a cuss claat and tell me say a jail me a go. Me say to myself, dis a big-big man what have power and Jah know me tired a jail!"

Preddy looked at Harris. "You following dis?"

"Aye, this miserable coward picked an old woman's pocket in Florida and dinnae fancy more jail time."

Darnay lapsed into silence and decided to study the off-white walls which contained nothing but the scrawl of crayons and some unidentifiable stains. Not even a tropical picture or an inspirational quote plaque to lift his spirits.

"Speak up, Mr Darnay. Tell us about Lester. Now isnae the time for ye tae go all shy."

"Me help Lester wid likkle thing from time to time, you know? When him want some weed me always get it for him. And nuff time him don't pay me too, not one red cent. All sometime you don't know how me want do him something bad, but me know say dem would hang me before dem make me get away wid box down a Chiney man."

"So, you supply him wid drugs whenever him need it," said Preddy. "We found a quantity of drugs in his car de night Carter was murdered. Cocaine. Is you supply dem?"

"Me don't know anything 'bout dat," said Darnay quickly. "A herb me know 'bout and me no know what him do wid it after me give him. Me and him no hang out a smoke nutten." Darnay felt and heard his bowels churn loudly. "Me no feel so well, Officer," he grumbled.

"Aye, murder will do that tae ye," said Harris. "It's a right shitty business."

"Me no done tell you say me no murder nobody! If me did murder nobody me woulda never come back a Mo Bay. Me woulda never set foot nowhere inna St James!"

Preddy walked around the bed and stood blocking Darnay's line of vision. "You get de chance to tell what you know and you still not saying much. You surely going down for murder."

"A mus' Lester do it, man," whispered Darnay. "A him."

"What? Speak up," said Harris.

"A Lester borrow me car Saturday night. Believe me Officer, a Orchid Bar me did deh fi true. Him phone me two time. One time to ask me if me deh a Orchid and few minutes later to tell me to come outside. Me frighten fi see him dress up inna black, look like thief and a hide away under bush!"

Preddy inhaled deeply. Finally they were getting somewhere. "Talk."

"Him borrow me car key and take de car and gone. Me go back into de bar. Me have nuff eyewitness, boss, me a tell you! Me never leave dat bar till 'bout six Sunday morning,

By dat time de car park up under one tree inna de Orchid car park. Me couldn't believe it when me see de bullet hole in deh! Quick-quick me carry it go garage and me try take out de bullet dem. Afterwards me panic and drive it go a one woodland go hide. Me nah tell you no lie!"

Harris understood enough Patois to appreciate Darnay's disclosure. He looked at Preddy. "Do we believe Mr Darnay?"

"A de truth me a tell you, Kingfish!"

"Yes, we believe him," said Preddy.

Although Preddy knew he had finally heard the truth he also knew there was no way Lester could have got out of Pelican Walk station and back without help from an officer and all signs pointed to Nembhard.

"You did see anyone wid Lester?"

"Is Lester one me see out deh. It did still sorta dark and me did hear one car engine a run, but me never see de driver good."

"Give us a minute," said Preddy and beckoned to Harris. The detectives left the room. They stood outside the closed door occasionally peeping through the glass to check on the suspect. Darnay lay back on the pillow, eyes closed.

"Nembhard was dere. He thought he was seen by Darnay, but he wasn't," said Preddy.

"Aye, one of our own is involved in a murder. Fuck!" Harris shook his head.

"Nembhard used his own vehicle and drove Lester from Pelican Walk to de Orchid Bar. Lester took the Subaru and drove to Red Hills, shot Carter and drove back to de bar. Nembhard waited, picked him up and sneaked him back into de station," said Preddy.

Harris frowned. "And then an inmate beat Lester up? Something is missing. Lester disturbed the man's beauty sleep?"

"I have a different theory about dat injury, but let me work on it."

The phone in Harris' pocket rang and he snatched it up immediately, strolling away from Preddy, who stood thinking about Darnay's tale. The man was telling the truth. There was just enough time for Lester to have made it from the station to Red Hills and back to the cell again in time to be notified of his brother's murder.

"Spence and Rabino have got Zadie and she's telling quite a tale, about Lester," Harris said. "I told Rabino we'd soon finish up here and get back."

Preddy nodded as he opened Darnay's door and the two detectives re-entered.

"So, we will find proof on your phone dat Lester called you?" said Preddy. "Give me him number."

"De phone up at me yard pon one shelf," said Darnay. "Me did think 'bout get rid of it, but is a new Galaxy smart-phone, man, de latest. Me no know what Lester do wid fi him phone, me no dash weh my own."

"We picked up a broken phone nearby where ye fell off yer motorbike," said Harris. "Who does it belong tae?"

"A mine dat too," replied Darnay. "Dat is not de latest version and dat is de number me woman call me on. Me girlfriend use de other number."

Harris shook his head, unimpressed by Darnay's over-complicated love life. Preddy walked away from the bed towards the window where he peered down into the car park. An ambulance pulled up, siren wailing, and yet another deceased soul was wheeled on a gurney shrouded in white cloth from head to toe.

Preddy turned back to Darnay and folded his arms. "Tell me something, why were you at Carter's funeral?"

"To see if me coulda spot a killer," said Darnay quietly. "Me couldn't believe dat bad-breed Chiney bwoy could a kill him likkle bredda. Me look at him pon TV and can't see it. Me did want to look at him up close."

"And did ye see what ye expected tae see?" asked Harris.

"De man cold!" Darnay gave an involuntary shudder and yelped in pain. "Him pretend like him no see me, but him see me. Him cry and him eye red, but when you look into dem you no see nutten! Me a tell you him take me car and go kill him owna bredda!"

Harris stared at him. "And ye didn't think that ye could report it?"

Darnay forced his painful head around to look at Harris. "Report it? No, star! I know say no matter what I tell police dem going link me wid de murder and say is me and him do it, although me no know nutten 'bout it. Report? You must mad!"

"And now look where ye are, still linked tae the murder," said Harris. "Surely ye have heard about aiding and abetting? That includes failing tae report matters when questioned."

"Me never get anything from Lester, you know." Darnay appeared broken. He turned his swollen eyes towards Preddy. "Dat man just mess up me life. Me never have no involvement inna no murder. Him borrow me good-good car and bring it back full a hole."

"So you just removed de bullets and said nothing?" said Preddy incredulously. "You never call Lester and ask him about it?"

"No way! Inna my mind me say de police not going find out say is Lester do it, because him suppose to inna lock-up. Dem soon pass it off as an unsolved murder," he explained. "Afterwards me get nervous and go set fire to it and check say it done now. No car, no link to me. A dat me get wrong."

Preddy did not doubt that the case could so easily have become an unsolved murder. Now he could tie Lester to Darnay and to the car, but only with Darnay's word. Any defence lawyer worth his salt could show that Darnay was a thoroughly unreliable witness.

"A what a go happen to me now, Officer?"

"For now ye need to stay here and get better," said Harris.

"We'll see what can be done after dat," said Preddy noncommittally. "I'm warning you though, do not attempt to get in contact wid Lester Chin Ellis under any circumstances."

"Not even inna me dream, boss!"

CHAPTER 31

Friday, 14 August, 4.23 p.m.

When she finally managed to call the emergency number, Zadie had specifically asked for Detective Spence. By the time Spence and Rabino arrived at the hotel she was laying on a sofa in the lobby being attended to by the on-site nurse. As Spence sat down beside her, Zadie instantly sat up crying hysterically and put her head on the detective's shoulder. Spence was uncomfortable, but did not pull away. Instead, she allowed the distraught woman to weep unchecked as she told her story while the detective's sleeve soaked up the tears.

Zadie confirmed that Lester had at least two phones and she could contact him on either one when she needed to. Rabino had tried to telephone Lester and listened in vain to the continuous irritating ringing before each call finally disconnected.

"So you really mean you did a carry on wid you boyfriend bredda?" Spence could not help but ask the question that had been bothering her for the last few minutes.

Zadie dabbed at her nose with tissue while pulling a handful more from the box. "Me did well love Carter, but sometime him coulda wicked," she moaned. "Lester did love Carter too. Me can't believe him coulda do dis!"

"He clearly didn't love Carter enough to leave his woman alone," said Rabino. "Doesn't sound like brotherly love to me."

"You never know Carter," said Zadie quietly. "Sometime him bully me, and him don't listen to me when me tell him must stop fool wid cocaine. Him tell me say me too fas'. Lester was just a casual thing at first, because him did nice to me."

"The cocaine at Chinchillerz belonged to Carter?" asked Rabino.

Zadie nodded and blew her nose. "Yes. I don't know where him get it from, but him always carry it to Kingston go party and share wid him friend dem. And if him not going dere, him send it inna delivery van. Me ask him what him going do if police ever catch him. Him say him will give dem a big money and it done."

"If he ever knew how close he came to killing an innocent young girl . . ." said Rabino. "A child swallowed that cocaine."

"Him did wicked sometimes, but him woulda never want to do dat," replied Zadie, surprising herself by her need to defend him. Even in death he maintained a hold over her.

"When we ask Lester if him know you as Carter girlfriend him never even want to acknowledge you," said Spence, watching her closely. Without all the make-up and bravado Zadie looked just like what she was, a naive nineteen-year-old girl.

Zadie allowed herself a tense smile. "Dat sound like Lester."

"Guess him couldn't say 'yes is Carter girlfriend and my sometime chick too.'"

"When Carter dash me weh Lester tell Carter say him is a fool, but him couldn't mad tell Carter anything 'bout me and him," sniffed Zadie. "Since Carter dead is only one time me see Lester until today. Him give me de bracelet and tell me dat me must give it a few months for everything to quiet down before me and him could talk again."

Spence shook her head. "Dat man don't have no heart."

Zadie shivered and rubbed her upper arms. Rabino took off her thin linen jacket and placed it around Zadie's shoulders. "We'll get him, young lady. Don't worry."

* * *

Preddy looked up from his paperwork when Rabino and Spence got back to Pelican Walk. He got up out of Rabino's chair and grabbed a spare one nearby.

"You took a while," he said. "Everything okay wid Zadie?"

"Yes, sir, her father came for her," explained Spence. She grinned broadly. "Speaking of fathers, we went on a diversion to see Darnay. Since he eventually gave you de information we needed we decided to return de favour."

Harris swivelled his chair around, a deep frown etched in his forehead. "What favour exactly?"

After slicing her new boss with a look, Spence turned to Rabino and said, "Let me be Darnay, and you be me."

"Er, no." Rabino gulped from a bottle of cold water. "You be you, mad woman. I'll be Darnay."

"Chuh! Alright."

Rabino slouched into a seat, kicked off her shoes and put her trousered legs on the desk, eyes closed. Spence walked towards her holding out her black linen jacket. "Mr Darnay, look what I brought for you. You forgot your jacket."

Rabino barely raised her lashes as she mimicked Darnay. "Ah no my jacket dat, natural lady."

"Ah no your jacket?" Spence studied the fabric with exaggerated thoroughness.

"Me never have on no jacket."

"You sure ah no your jacket?" Spence held it up in the air and waved it as if to straighten out the creases.

Darnay eyed her. "Den me no must know what me wear?"

"Sorry, my mistake. I coulda swear ah your little jacket dis." Spence made a show of neatly folding the garment.

244

"Alright sir, I'll have to find out who de jacket belong to. Try to sleep peacefully." She could barely get the final words out in her effort not to laugh.

Rabino exploded into a fit of giggles. Preddy joined in the laughter. Harris watched, amused by both the amateur performance and the subsequent hilarity. "Okay. I didnae get what that was about."

"He thinks a baby boy is his," said Preddy. "Not de boy we saw at de garage, another younger boy. It's a Jamaican thing. We say Darnay got a 'jacket.'"

Harris absorbed this information with a frown. "So if someone comes here tae report a stolen jacket they're really talking about child abduction?"

"No," Spence chuckled and wiped her eyes. "Mind you don't make people box you down fi insult dem."

"What would you say in your country?" asked Rabino.

Harris shrugged. "That he's an unlucky sod?"

"A child deserves to know their real father." Rabino sat upright and straightened her clothes. "Saves Darnay a lot of money and heartache in the long run too."

"If he gets it," said Harris, before remembering Preddy's interrogation of Darnay. "Och, so that's what the tattoo business was about?"

Preddy nodded. "Darnay isn't entirely stupid. When de medication wears off he'll put two and two together."

"We were hoping to find Lester hiding in him hospital room, but no luck," said Spence. "You hear anything else yet, sir?"

"Not a thing," replied Preddy, before he could stop himself.

Harris shot Preddy a look. "Naw. The media are reporting that there's been an incident at the Empire Hotel involving Lester Chin Ellis and we want tae speak to him in regard tae our enquiries. No information has come in since."

Preddy stared at his notepad without really seeing the words. He badly wished that Zadie Merton had phoned them first before going to confront Lester. It was not hard to understand how anger and outrage led to her doing so, but vigilantism was not to be encouraged under any circumstances. Now their person of interest had morphed into their prime suspect and gone to ground. His parents adamantly denied all knowledge of his whereabouts. His villa at Sandy Bay was under heavy surveillance, yet so far, nothing. Preddy had placed phone calls to every person he could think of, but there were no sightings of the man at all.

The detective had theorised at length about Nembhard's role in the murder and had drawn the conclusion that Lester's injuries were caused purely by chance. No-one inside or outside of the station had hit him with anything. Nembhard had placed the gym weights on the rear passenger foot-well of his jeep which bore the evidence in the form of shallow indentations as he always carried them there. An intoxicated Lester had either stumbled into the vehicle and made contact with the weights, or he had lain flat on the back seat and fallen onto them during the ride. Lester's face had been covered with a balaclava so he might not have been able to see properly. The microscopic hairs that Valerie had detected in the photograph were fibres from the hood and not from a towel. But the detective was not yet ready to share his theory with the team and certainly not with his new leader.

Preddy retrieved the reports provided by Officers Wilson and Nembhard and ran through them yet again. He then reviewed their disciplinary records. Nembhard should not even be on the force, but he had successfully appealed a decision to dismiss him for being absent without permission on various occasions. There was a definite pattern with this officer. Hard evidence was needed to nail Nembhard this time, but nail him he would. Preddy walked across the room towards Harris, pulled out another chair and handed him Nembhard's report.

"What are we looking at?" asked Harris.

"When Nembhard was asked why he didn't call a doctor he said Lester didn't need one. Textbook stuff, if someone is injured you get a doctor or take dem to hospital. What you don't do is reach a conclusion dat dey are okay."

"Agreed."

"Nembhard said he took de injured Lester from his cell at around 4.30 a.m. as he needed to separate him from de inmates. Wilson did not see Lester at all after he was booked in, so we only have Nembhard's word for it dat dis is what happened. Nembhard was not seen again until 5:25 a.m., so even if we believe him dere are at least fifty-five minutes unaccounted for where he was unseen. He was out driving Lester."

"Seems like Officer Timmins was mistaken and we do offer a chauffeur service after all," mumbled Harris.

"The city is not so big and the roads were almost empty at dawn. That's plenty of time to commit the crime," said Rabino. "Lindon Nembhard. I can't believe the man could have helped Lester."

"And him still wandering around here too," said Spence. "A gwaan like."

"I can have him arrested," said Harris.

"I don't think dat is a good idea," interjected Preddy, adding as a painful afterthought, "sir."

"Och, and why's that?" Harris tapped his pen repeatedly against his desk while focusing on the detective.

Spence sat upright and stared at her new boss. Rabino glanced towards Preddy. If they could harness the ice in the air there would be no need for the oscillating fans.

"Circumstantial evidence does not work well wid juries in dis country," replied Preddy. "If we arrest him on what we have we're going to regret it, trust me."

"A true," muttered Spence. "We no have no murder weapon. All we have is Darnay and him never see Nembhard."

Somebody did have the goods on Nembhard. If it came to it Preddy would call on Jerry Knight to identify Nembhard, although he was determined to keep the mis-guided young man and his hardworking mother out of it if possible.

"Nembhard is no fool," said Preddy. "He has been on de force long enough to know how to play a game of cat and mouse. Once he finds out Darnay cannot identify him it will be a much harder game for us."

"That's right, sir," said Rabino. "Nembhard has been up against the brass more than once before. We'll soon hear about victimisation."

"He practically stuck a gun in Darnay's mouth," said Harris.

"And if he had pulled de trigger we would have him," Preddy retorted.

Harris took a deep breath and got to his feet. "I'll think about it. I'm popping down tae the front desk. Call me if there are any sightings of Lester."

* * *

Darnay's common law wife called Pelican Walk repeatedly, ranting about the police holding onto her sick man for nothing. The nuisance calls ended when an infuriated Spence returned one of them and informed the woman that if she still wanted to make it to Vancouver she should not phone again. Spence had also given the woman directions on where to find Darnay's smartphone and suggested that she might want to bring it in. Less than an hour later the phone was with the policewoman. Spence identified the phone number Darnay claimed belonged to Lester, which differed from the numbers Zadie had given them. It came as no surprise that the phone rang unanswered.

Preddy was having better luck as he had received the phone call he had been waiting for. After a painstaking search among overgrown bushes and sharp brambles, Timmins had found a discarded black hood in the extensive grounds of the Orchid Bar. No gun. It would now be a matter of collecting Lester's DNA and he felt sure that it would be a perfect match.

"Thank you for trusting me, sir," said Timmins, his voice sounding hesitant down the phone line.

"I know you never shoot dat dog," Preddy replied.

248

"What dog, sir?"

"Carter dog."

* * *

The team was assembled in the conference room making phone calls to Lester's known haunts, of which there were many within and outside of St James. Harris was waiting for Superintendent Brownlow to finish his meeting to give him the latest news and Preddy was feeling aggrieved that he was not the one awaiting the superintendent's availability. Harris could not have done this without him and would now, no doubt, pretend that he had been instrumental in getting to this point.

Preddy was not about to let that happen because, as Rabino had correctly assessed, he was not a man given to being humble, worse still in the presence of a foreigner. He would read any report Harris produced and demand to be allowed to include his own comments where the men differed in their recollection of events. Nobody was going to retire him off without a fight. There would be no joining the expats and returnees in the cool hills of Mandeville to await death.

"Detective, are ye ready tae go?" Harris got to his feet and started gathering his notes.

Preddy was startled out of his musing and said nothing. Harris could surely not be speaking to him, although he was looking straight at him.

"The Super is ready tae hear us. He's got the commissioner with him as well."

"Umm, yes," Preddy replied, stumbling as he pushed back his chair. He grabbed a stack of papers. "Can I suggest you invite dem to de evidence room, Detective? It will make things easier to explain."

"Aye, I can do that." Harris headed for the door.

"I wonder which one a dem going hit de other first," said Spence as they left.

Rabino said, "The commissioner isn't going to let anybody raise their voice in his meeting, much less raise fists. He'll throw the two of them out."

A table and chairs were arranged for Harris and Preddy in front of Commissioner Davis and Superintendent Brownlow. A jug of iced water and four glasses were in the middle. The commissioner had never been in the evidence room before and he took his time sauntering around and inspecting the local maps, whiteboard full of comments, and well-fingered mugshots stuck to the walls by drawing pins.

"Speak, gentlemen," demanded the commissioner. He sank into a seat and looked directly at Harris.

Harris waved his hand in Preddy's direction. "I've asked Detective Preddy tae fill ye in."

Commissioner Davis scowled. "Oh, I thought you were leading the investigation?"

"I am, sir. That's why I can ask ma colleague tae do the honours," said Harris, maintaining the commissioner's gaze.

The superintendent coughed and looked at Preddy. "Go on, Detective."

Preddy stood up and moved to the whiteboard. "The Chin Ellis brothers were arrested at 2.08 a.m. and brought to the station, arriving at 2.23 a.m. The arresting officers Timmins and Franklin released Carter at around 4.06 a.m. Dere's at least a ten mile radius in which all dis happened."

Preddy pressed coloured pins into the blown-up map of the parish of St James as he spoke, highlighting the distance between Pelican Walk station and Carter's Red Hills home. He also identified the side road where Carter had collected Lester's car and used another pin to indicate the Orchid Bar.

"Minutes later Nembhard takes Lester out of his cell to an unknown location. Wilson was not as alert as he should have been, but I don't think he was involved. I think Lester changed his clothes and Nembhard gave him back his phone. He called Darnay. He knew dat Darnay hung out at de Orchid every Saturday night and he wanted to make sure he was dere. Nembhard has a white jeep. He drove Lester out of de station and straight to de Orchid in his jeep. Lester called Darnay again from de car park and gets him to bring de Subaru keys outside. Lester takes de Subaru and goes after Carter."

"So we are sure Darnay didn't do it?" asked the commissioner, looking distinctly uncomfortable.

"Darnay has a solid alibi. He was drinking all night inside the bar, sir," Harris said.

"What does the CCTV show?"

"At Pelican Walk?" asked Harris. "Sir, as I'm sure the superintendent will explain, our CCTV cameras arenae . . . fully functional. There is naw CCTV at the Orchid."

The superintendent grimaced. "We have no good film from that particular camera. What we do have is very grainy."

Preddy put another pin at the murder scene. "Lester shoots his brother, takes his bracelet, jumps back into the Subaru and narrowly avoids being shot. He drives back to de Orchid, throws away de hood and leaves de car for Darnay. Nembhard picks Lester up and smuggles him back into Pelican Walk, straight through de back door before dawn. Lester changes clothes again. Wilson would not have seen dem if he was at de front of de building. He didn't see Nembhard for nearly an hour."

"What is our evidence?" asked the superintendent. "Marcus Darnay could be lying."

"He could be sir, but I really don't believe he is. I think he loaned de car to Lester because Lester has a hold over him. He threatened to turn him in as a lottery scammer and Darnay is planning a whole new life abroad. Darnay only knew about de murder when he saw de news on TV on Sunday evening," said Preddy.

"Hmm, well he would say that," said the superintendent.

Harris looked at the superintendent. "Nembhard did draw his weapon on Darnay in the hospital and he didnae sound like he just wanted tae say hi. We had tae intercept him quickly."

"Darnay has been given a second chance for his family. I think he's telling de truth. We do not have de murder weapon, but we do have de shell casings and bullets which match de eyewitness gun." Preddy cleared his throat. "Officer Timmins has located what I believe to be de hood Lester wore to carry out de murder."

Harris frowned and tried to catch Preddy's eye, but the detective studiously avoided his gaze.

"We have his DNA sample?" asked the commissioner.

"No, sir," said Preddy. "De evidence will be kept in secure custody until we do."

The commissioner rubbed his sweating palms together. "Where is Officer Nembhard now?"

"He's still on duty, sir. He's aware we're very interested in him," said Harris.

"So how did Lester get assaulted in Nembhard's custody if the two of them were working together?" asked the superintendent.

"Dat one had me confused for a while, sir." Preddy pulled out the photograph of Lester's bruise from among his documents and placed it on the desk in front of the superintendent. "De young guy who's charged with assault, Jerry Knight, said he didn't touch Lester and I believe him."

The commissioner glanced over at the photograph. "What is this?"

"Lester's face. I think Lester fell and hit his face on some weights dat Nembhard had in de back of his vehicle. Nobody hit him wid anything and even his own doctor says dat it is not a fist mark."

Harris reached over the desk and spun the photograph around. He pushed the photograph back again and his face began to take on the colour of an otaheite apple as he stared at Preddy. Harris picked up the jug and poured himself a long glass of cold water.

"And you agree with this theory, Detective?" asked the commissioner, addressing Harris.

The Scotsman fixed unblinking eyes on Preddy. He held a paperclip in one hand, turning it over and over between pale thumb and forefinger, before slowly bending it out of shape and snapping it in two. As the seconds ticked by the commissioner grew impatient.

"Detective Harris?"

Harris's steely green eyes pierced Preddy's steady brown ones. "Aye. Absolutely, sir."

The commissioner looked triumphant. "Good work, detectives. I'll arrange the warrant. You go bring in our suspect. Alive."

Harris allowed Preddy to precede him as they left the evidence room. Preddy headed towards his own office, aware that Harris was on his heels. Preddy's neck felt warm and he loosened his collar. It did cross his mind that if the fire-breathing foreigner picked up a heavy object along the way there would be no opportunity to duck and dive all Matrix, in Keanu's style.

"Ye kept that photograph hidden and I cannae think why," said Harris as he slammed Preddy's door, rattling the framed awards. "What's with ye? We're supposed tae be a team."

"I don't even know where it came from. Just appeared on my desk," said Preddy evenly, as he walked around the desk towards his chair. The white man's face had taken a strange colour and Preddy wondered if he should offer him a seat. "I'm glad dey didn't ask me anything about it."

"And ye dinnae think the rest of us needed tae hear about yer bloody theory before the brass did?"

He would not offer the foreigner a seat. "I only just worked it out in my own mind."

"Like fuck ye did! All information out in the open, remember? This is what got ye intae this mess in the first place, keeping everything close tae yer chest as if ye dinnae trust the rest of us. Ye did it with the Chinchillerz drugs investigation that ye made yer own personal private investigation and ye did it again today! Och, 'here's a photo' and 'there's a hood' and 'there's the weights' like these just cropped up."

Preddy wished he had never sucked on any mints today and could have sent the essence of cannabidiol his aggressor's way. He leaned back wearing a fake contrite expression. "You're right, sorry. I didn't initially see any link between Lester's assault and Carter's murder or I'd have told de team."

"Och, really? Bullshit! Ye think I havenae realised that while ye were telling all of us tae stay clear of Timmins, Nembhard, Wilson, Franklin, ye were busy working with Timmins? Timmins found the hood!"

"I only used Timmins when I knew he wasn't involved in de murder."

"And ye knew that how exactly?"

Preddy shrugged. "My gut told me, and it was right."

"Is there anything else ye think yer gut needs tae tell me?"

It loves ganja tea, the stronger the better. "No, nothing Detective Harris."

"Good, because I swear tae God, Detective Preddy, next time I will throw ye under the bus." He swung open the door and stormed out without bothering to close it.

"I believe you will," mumbled Preddy.

As Preddy drove home listening to instrumental reggae music he could not resist making a phone call. Annalee had often warned him about distracted driving despite the fact that she herself often created the distraction. His daughter was right, but as he had explained, the nature of his job meant that sometimes it just couldn't be helped. Emergencies could cause inappropriate behaviour, endangering motorists and pedestrians alike. This was no emergency call, yet his weary heart thought otherwise.

"Hey you," he said nervously.

"Hey."

"I've missed hearing your voice. Tired of de answer machine." Silence filled the air while he waited, listening to the engine purr. His fingernails pierced the steering wheel. "Sorry I was stupid."

"I'm sorry you were stupid too," Valerie said, but he could tell from her voice that she had softened.

"I love you, you know, woman?"

"Good thing, because I love you too."

"My case has really blown up," said Preddy feeling more comfortable now. "And I've had one hell of a day."

"You want to talk about it?"

"Yes and no."

"You know you keep too much to yourself, Ray," she said and he heard the frustration in her voice. "You alone can't solve all de crime in St James. Sometimes you have to think about delegation, or dat brain of yours will forever be overworked and thinking up all sorts of bad things about de innocent people around you. By all accounts you have a good team. You should use dem."

"You know somebody said pretty much de same thing to me earlier. Not as nicely though."

"Oh, who?"

"A white man wid a red head and a bad temper. Him have balls though. Not many people would dare come into my office come talk to me so."

"Well, if him can get some sense into you, Ray, I'm on his side," she said. "You sure you don't want to talk about it?"

"I can't and it's not over yet," he said regretfully. "I have one hour to change, grab some nightgear and den back out again."

"Well, be very careful," she said. "And I know you not stupid."

255

CHAPTER 32

Friday, 14 August, 10.04 p.m.

Preddy and Harris entered the Doubloons, having convinced the security guard that he could either let them through or spend an all-inclusive night at Pelican Walk police station. The chastened man was not allowed to inform the Chin Ellis family of the detectives' arrival. No time for niceties when a murderer was on the loose, particularly when the suspect was a man of means.

Ida opened the door to Preddy's incessant ringing and banging. She was dressed in a long yellow nightgown, her greying hair in tiny curlers. Harris stood beside his colleague, his keen eyes surveying the house and grounds for any signs of movement. Terence was at the top of the stairs clad in pyjamas, bending and peering over the banister.

"Where is he?" asked Preddy. He handed her the warrant as he stepped into the grand hallway, gun drawn and pointed at the floor.

"Wait, something was wrong with the phone line? What didn't you hear?" she snapped.

"Parents lie for children all de time," said Preddy, "you wouldn't be de first."

"You're here to hurt my son, aren't you?" Ida clutched the neck of her nightgown. "Answer me, Detective Preddy!"

"Miss Ida, your son is unpredictable. We're tired of searching for him. We need to talk to him. Right now."

Her look was scathing. "So, you're just going shoot him and tell the world he shot first."

"I have no intention of shooting him," said Preddy as calmly as possible. "My interest is to speak to him about matters dat he can shed some light on."

"Where is he, ma'am?" asked Harris.

She glared at him. "I already told you, he's not here! It's just me and my husband."

"Ye won't mind if we look around then will ye?"

"Go look!" she said with a sweep of her arm.

"Mr Chin Ellis, if yer son is up there now is the time tae tell us," said Harris looking up at the anxious man.

"He's not here! You don't hear?" Terence barked, gripping the banister so hard that his knuckles turned white. "What's wrong with police in this country?"

Preddy concentrated on Ida. "He in de beach house?"

She gave him a sullen look. "How would I know? He comes and goes as he pleases. He's my son."

"Ma'am, ye need tae let us look in there," said Harris. "If he comes quietly there'll naw be any problems."

Miss Ida snatched up a set of keys from a rack by the door and strode past the detectives into the humid night air. They followed behind her as she marched down to the beach house.

"Lester! Lester, you in there?" his mother called.

"Lester! Police!" shouted Preddy, taking up a position to the far side of the door. He beckoned to Ida to open it, which she tried to do while fumbling with the key. Her shaking fingers were unable to fit it into the lock. Harris gently removed it from her hands and opened the door, using his foot to push it as far back as it could go.

"Lester, this is Detective Harris with Detective Preddy!" he shouted, then looked at Ida. "Turn on the light."

As the lights went on it was clear that whoever had been in the apartment had left in a hurry. Papers and books were scattered everywhere and clothes strewn over the bed and floor.

The detectives searched the building from corner to corner, but the search proved fruitless. Preddy used his phone to dial Lester's number. Seconds later the target phone began to ring and was located under a T-shirt on the floor in front of him. Ida watched nervously as Preddy pressed a few keys on the unearthed phone, lighting up the various numbers dialled, and then signalled to Harris.

"Darnay's number. We've got it."

"Where is he?" asked Harris patiently, as the three left the beach house. "Miss Ida, listen tae me. We have good reason tae believe that Lester was involved in Carter's murder. If we're wrong, then he can defend himself."

"You people must be smoking something strong in that station!" said Ida.

"Apparently naw," murmured Harris.

Her eyes penetrated Preddy. "Lester loved Carter, just like the rest of us!"

"Den he can tell us all about it himself," said Preddy. "Look, we know he was here earlier."

"I don't know where he is, Detective. How many times do I have to repeat myself?"

"We'll just take a look around his room," said Preddy, walking back towards the house.

They rummaged through Lester's bedroom, hoping to find the murder weapon or even ammunition. Preddy surveyed the huge room and tried to work out if anything was missing since his last visit.

Ida walked towards the bookshelf and took up a framed photograph, staring at the image of her beloved family. There she was sitting beside her two gorgeous sons at age ten and twelve, with her loving husband, all smiles. Carter was missing a tooth, but still looking his usual cheeky self. Lester was making rabbits ears over his brother's head while

Terence hugged the two of them closely. Never would she have guessed that ten years later she would be in this terrible position with one angel gone for ever, and the other being hunted down like an animal by the police.

"Miss Ida, please. It better if we find Lester dan any other officers," Preddy pleaded. "Whatever you may think of me, I swear to you dat I will not shoot without provocation."

"We will treat your son fairly, I promise," added Harris.

"The gardener's old car is missing," she murmured. "He may have taken it. It's a red Honda Civic."

"Where would Lester be headed?" asked Harris.

Ida shrugged wearily. "There is an apartment in Bluefields Bay."

Preddy frowned. "Bluefields Bay, Westmoreland? I thought he lived at Sandy Bay?"

"I leased the Bluefields apartment a few months ago, because the boys love that side of the south coast. He likes to go down there."

Preddy fought hard not to show his anger. "You should have told us dis before."

"He's my son."

Ida described the property and the detectives raced down the stairs, striding purposefully towards their jeep. Outside, she stood in the night air, twisting damp hands together while watching them speed away. For a long time she stared at the dark mounds of the hills above, which now reminded her of tombstones, and prayed that her son was safe. Eventually she made her way to the kitchen and poured herself a glass of chilled water. Drinking late at night would do nothing to help her sleep, but there was little chance of falling asleep tonight. Lester did love Carter with all his heart, she knew that. Everybody knew it, except the blasted police.

It was true that the two had not seen eye to eye over numerous things, but that was nothing new. They were close brothers and that was what close brothers did; they fought and argued, made up and laughed. She did not know what to make of the drugs seized from Chinchillerz that the police suspected belonged to one or both of her sons. Young people experimented at will, yet she could not believe that either son would get involved in drug dealing. They had more than enough money. Her heart fluttered suddenly. Carter had enough money because he knew how to manage it and she had placed no restrictions on him. Lester did not know how to manage money and was recently restrained by a credit limit, although he had seemed quite content and there was no visible change in his lifestyle.

She brushed away the cloudy thoughts. Someone must be framing her sons. Neither of them were drug dealers or drug users and Lester was certainly no murderer. He would soon give himself up so that they could question him and realise their terrible mistake. She vowed to call another news conference in the morning and appeal to Lester to hand himself in, that was, if the police had not tracked him down first.

Through the kitchen window she peered into the murky night, and saw a slim shadow moving in the distance. She thought it must be a trick of the light and the low-hanging palm trees. If only she had not left her glasses upstairs. As her eyes became more accustomed to the moonlight it became clear that it was indeed the shape of a person. She could not tell whether it was a male or female, but the shape was certainly shorter than Lester. Seconds later she heard an unmistakeable purring sound. Ida turned and ran to the bottom of the stairs.

"Terence! Terence! Quick! Lord God! Somebody's stealing the chopper!" Her breath caught in her throat as she ran back to the window and watched it wobble and lift off. Whoever was flying was going to die a painful death as the gas was practically on empty.

* * *

Police in the adjoining parishes of Hanover and Westmoreland were on the lookout for the suspect's latest mode of transport and officers from nearby Savanna la Mar had agreed to make their way to Bluefields Bay. As Preddy sped along the main road, Harris took a phone call from Rabino.

"Talk tae me."

"The car has been spotted close to Buddles Mountain near Bluefields, sir. Sav police have been told."

"Okay, meet us there, Detective," Harris lowered the phone and looked over at Preddy. "Where's Buddles Mountain?"

"More dan an hour away."

Preddy hogged the middle of the highway, dodging potholes and ignoring the obscene gestures of angry motorists. They journeyed at a furious pace, eventually leaving St James and entering the parish of Westmoreland heading in a south-westerly direction towards the shimmering coastal waters of Bluefields Bay.

There were few lampposts in Bluefields Bay, the moon providing the sole lighting. Fishermen's boats lay upturned like huge beached whales on the sand. Houses were few and far between and all were dark as to be expected in an area where most people rose hours before the sun did, even the well-heeled who just wanted to sip coffee and watch the boats set sail.

A row of headlights illuminated the local police who were guarding the red car which lay in the banking with the keys in the ignition and engine still running. Preddy and Harris pulled up beside it, followed by Spence and Rabino in their jeep. Both front doors of the abandoned vehicle were wide open. The glove compartment was also open and empty, and on the floor were a few scattered documents.

Preddy shone his flashlight at the surrounding bush and discovered what appeared to be a trail. He looked up at the mighty black monoliths in front of him, dark and forbidding, not the sort of place he fancied exploring in the middle of the night. No wonder the local officers had made no move to venture up into the unknown. Many areas of Jamaica were just like this; green, rocky and cavernous, mainly unexplored, places where undiscovered insects and supposedly extinct creatures could dwell in peace.

"Well, Detective Harris, we going in or not?" he asked.

Harris followed his gaze and inhaled deeply. "Aye, I guess we are."

"We might be able to get some canine help," said Preddy taking out his phone. "Lester does not like dogs."

After making a call Preddy adjusted his bullet proof vest and checked that his gun was properly loaded and securely holstered, while Harris rummaged around in the back of the jeep.

"I dinnae suppose anyone's got night vision goggles?" he asked.

"Night vision goggles?" Spence repeated as she holstered up, her scathing glance lost in the dark. "We have jeep, gas, gun and bullet. You can stay deh." She adjusted her own vest, strode past him and headed toward the mountain. "Night vision goggles."

Preddy said nothing, but could not prevent an involuntary smile from crossing his lips and for a brief moment was grateful for the cover of darkness. They turned up the narrow bramble-covered track that appeared to have been created by goats rather than by humans. Under the thick lining of his rubber lug soles he could feel the sharp stones.

As they walked they shouted into the silence of the night.

"Police! Lester, give it up!"

"Lester Chin Ellis!"

"Don't make dis hard, Lester!"

"Lester!"

CHAPTER 33

Friday, 14 August, 11.51 p.m.

The hackles rose on the frightened young man's neck. Although he had considered the prospect of them finding out he was in Bluefields, he had not bet on them arriving so quickly. He had barely changed clothes before the flashing blue lights came tearing down the coastline. Now it seemed as if even the pitch blackness would not put them off following him up the mountain.

He crouched down closer to the cold ground and looking up saw a steep track barely visible by the light from the moon and almost obscured by the heavy overhanging trees. As he crawled his way up to higher ground he cursed silently at the thick foliage that interrupted his passage and scratched his torso. His no longer white expensive cotton shirt was partly in threads and his designer jeans were now scuffed more than was fashionable. The heavy denim restricted the movement of his tired legs.

His parents had taught him never to wear torn clothes no matter what work he was doing or where he was going and he had followed that sensible advice his entire life. Still, they would never have imagined him crawling on his hands and knees in the dark and hiding from the police. He tried not to concentrate on the eerie desolation and intense blackness that appeared all around him. The rocks and caves hid who knew what and he could not bear to contemplate running into any form of wild creature. Yet what awaited him below was far more devastating and the reasonable comforts he enjoyed were now at risk.

He continued his climb upwards and vowed not to look backwards again. Having teetered precariously over one ledge and experienced the accompanying feeling of nausea he would not make the mistake of repeating the move.

At first when he heard the dogs he thought it was just his imagination. The odd dog could always be heard idly barking, but this sounded like a dozen or more. Every sound was exacerbated in the blackness, even his own breath, so he could not be sure whether his imagination was playing tricks. The crickets sounded overgrown and he envisioned them the size of small bullfrogs. Something brushed past him minutes ago, but it must have been an alarmed mongoose as it was way too large to be a rat. Owls watched him. He could hear their gentle cooing and see their eyes wide and studious, missing nothing.

As he reached a flat piece of rock he forced himself to peer through the trees behind him and in the distance could see dancing torches. The officers still seemed a good way away, although the intense barking now sounded much nearer and he knew that he was not imagining things.

The hunted man's feet began to feel cold. He looked down and realised that he was up to his ankles in water. Although he could not see ahead of him he could hear the water rushing and he shuffled as quickly as he could towards the sound. A tiny waterfall not more than three feet tall was nearby and he quickly crept behind it, feeling the ice-cold water pour down his neck and envelop his back and legs. He felt a twinge in his spine and realised he could not crouch like this for too long, and so he slid into the murky depths of the water, dragging a long stick of dried bamboo with him.

The fugitive stayed beneath the water, eyes closed against the tiny organisms that bounced against his face. He gulped in air through the bamboo while trying to keep his body as still as possible. This spring was too small to hold crocodiles or the like, but who knew what else was keeping him company under there. He had no idea how much time had passed. What felt like hours must have been minutes. The barking of rabid dogs which had previously seemed so close now appeared to be fading away and he wondered if this was just wishful thinking on his part or the effect of water in his ears.

The voices, both male and female, which had called out so aggressively were now muffled. If his body had not been so cold it would have appreciated the feeling of relief that passed through it, but as it was, his bones just felt stiff and painful. He forced his eyes open and through the haze of the water could clearly make out the shining moon.

Everywhere around him had fallen silent, except for the waterfall whose gentle trickle stood out in the stillness. He breathed a prayer of thanks to the God whose voice he tried to avoid hearing six days a week. He would give it a couple more minutes, just to be safe.

CHAPTER 34

Friday, 14 August, 11.58 p.m.

Harris eased himself on top of a steep rock, breathing effort-lessly. Rock climbing was one of his favourite hobbies, and a trip to the Blue Mountains was on his list of things to do before his Caribbean posting was over. Having mastered Ben Nevis more than once, Jamaican mountains would be a breeze, a beautiful, botanically rich one. He walked slowly over to where a large shape lay moving in a small hollow formed by a mass of great stones. As he approached the shape, it appeared to press itself closer to the ground as if hoping to be absorbed into it.

"Lester!" he shouted and nearly fell over backwards as the wild hog that had been warily observing the intrusion jumped to its feet grunting and fled from the unwelcome trespassers. The Scotsman was grateful that the animal's blunt ivory tusks had not managed to graze him. Spence grinned in the darkness as she held out a hand and helped steady him on his feet, before continuing the arduous trek.

A few strides later Spence stopped abruptly and whis-pered something to Preddy who came to a halt by her side. Rabino noticed and clicked her fingers to get Harris' attention.

He returned to join them and the four stood silently for some time staring at the wave ripples in a waterhole.

Spence took aim and threw a rock towards the spot which sent a piece of bamboo flying across the water. Almost immediately a head breached the surface spluttering for air.

"You know say you never hear 'bout Jamaicans a dead from hypothermia?" said Spence.

"Not on the island anyway. For the ones abroad it's a different thing," said Rabino.

"Dat's because most Jamaicans are not stupid." Preddy shone his unyielding flashlight in the direction of the fugitive. "We do not swim fully-clothed in mountain springs at midnight where de temperatures reach minus figures."

"And we don't walk for miles in soaking wet clothes," added Spence. "Inna strong breeze."

"We certainly don't do that." Rabino agreed.

"This is one odd Jamaican, I guess," Harris concluded.

The suspect dragged himself to the end of the spring and hauled his aching body out of the water. He lay sprawled on his face in the weeds, arms outspread above his head, with legs straight. Rabino knelt on his back and dragged both arms down behind his waist.

"And don't try anything." Preddy stretched his handcuffs to Rabino who quickly attached them and dragged the man to his feet.

"Lester Chin Ellis, you're under arrest for . . ."

Preddy shone his torch in the man's face, seeing for the first time the haunted features that bore no resemblance to the prime suspect. He was brown-skinned like Lester, but that was about it. His eyes were very round and very wide.

"A whe'de rass!" Preddy exclaimed. "Who you?"

"Misser Chin gardener, Officer! Do no shoot me!"

"Fuck," said Harris, and placed his hands on his hips.

Preddy walked up close to the shaking man. "Where Lester gone?"

"Me no know, sir! Him say him not staying inna Jamaica!"

"Oh, hell," mumbled Rabino.

"Shit!" said Spence.

Preddy closed his eyes briefly and it suddenly hit him. Aviation glasses. The pair of aviation glasses in Lester's room were missing second time around. "Him going to de aerodrome!" he said, turning abruptly to start the descent. "Him have another car?"

"Me see him get inna one, yes, but me couldn't tell you what type. It too dark," the gardener said.

"Walk up!" said Spence, prodding the shivering man in the back with her hardware. He shuffled off quickly in the direction of the others, still handcuffed, and risked a glance over his shoulder.

"Ma'am, me can get one dry shirt or something when we reach a road? Me hear wha' you say 'bout hypothermia and me no want get it!"

Spence poked him roughly. "Move you claat!"

CHAPTER 35

Saturday, 15 August, 12.50 a.m.

Lester abandoned the newly stolen car and waited in the dense bushes surrounding the aerodrome. It had not taken him long to drive the smooth roadway from Bluefields to Negril as traffic had thinned out considerably. The car's owner was probably in bed asleep and it would be a long time before the theft was reported. Lester had bought time, although how much he did not know. He needed to get into the aerodrome and away from the island. There was only one certainty: his destination would not be an overflowing Jamaican prison. Spending a few hours in a jail cell was bad enough and he was not planning on a do-over.

He lay flat on his stomach, eyes closed, chest palpitating. His mind ran on Carter as it did one hundred times a day delivering the same sharp pang of pain. Carter would be the first to chastise him for running from the police and then he would come up with something inventive to thwart the officers' efforts. Dear Carter. Both annoying and helpful, cautious and risk-inclined.

Lester loved his brother and he hated him too. Everything was about Carter nowadays. All of his life Lester had been told to look after his little brother, even when his little brother was blatantly wrong or determined to do something downright foolhardy. As they grew older he had watched as his parents, particularly Miss Ida, tended to rely more on Carter when it came to business advice. To add insult to injury they were secretly grooming Carter to take over as chief financial officer which would have been unacceptable in anyone else's book. That hallowed position belonged to the eldest son, not the youngest. His birthright was not something to be discussed and debated.

Having accosted them, he had been told that he "needed more time to learn to respect money." *Learn to respect money?* Lester sneered. He respected the hell out of money and was in touch with it on a regular basis, using as much of it as he could to buy toys and weed for himself, as well as presents for girls. Girls like Zadie. What was the point of being filthy rich and not spending the money enjoying yourself?

With Carter at the helm, access to that easy money would dry up totally unless he really worked for it. There would be no unlimited expense account and no possibility of dipping into the petty cash once his little brother was in charge. It was bad enough that the stupid little coolie man was tightening the purse strings. Everything he bought would soon have to go through Carter and the cheeky little shit would take great pleasure in denying his requests.

Carter, the golden boy who was not golden. Surely Miss Ida must have suspected Carter had a drug habit and was not addicted to just any drugs, but to hard drugs? Yet there she was, planning to put the Chinchillerz reins into the hands of a junkie.

If Carter hadn't been so frazzled, he would have noticed Lester's closeness to that gorgeous girlfriend of his. Instead he had seemed quite happy to watch his sibling making friends with his high-maintenance woman. Lester knew from the moment he set eyes on Zadie that he could take her. He enjoyed the chase thoroughly and surprised himself by actually falling for her. It did not stop him from playing the field, but she was such a nice sweet girl, or at least she had been. He touched his sore left shoulder gingerly nursing the purple bruise. If Zadie could aim a gun as well as she could gyrate it would have been curtains for him. Never in a million years would Lester have thought that the lovely, leggy beauty would try to kill someone. Especially someone she loved. And with the gun he gave her. He and Zadie were obviously more alike than he knew.

He had seen the police cars earlier, racing in the direction of Bluefields Bay while he headed towards Negril aerodrome and he was certain that the officers would now be navigating Buddles Mountain. The simple-minded gardener better be worth his pay.

The tiny remote airstrip was quite dark, but Lester could see a light in the watchman's small hut and he wondered whether the man was inside or if it was derelict and the lights were always left on all night. Either way it would not be that easy to get into the grounds. The aircraft hangar itself was not that sturdy having been damaged in the last tropical storm, and he could see the nose of at least one plane from where he stood. The shelter could only hold two planes, one of which was the four-seater family plane that he was determined to board.

The gardener's clothes felt loose on him and billowed around his waist so he paused briefly to secure another notch of the leather belt. The sturdy chain-link fence above him carried trails of mean-looking barbed wire at the top. He moved slowly alongside the fence, pressing it every few seconds, trying to find the weakest link.

On and on he crept pushing at the fence and pulling at its roots while keeping an eye out for the watchman. Eventually, he found a spot at the bottom of the fence where the ground felt soft and he attempted to lift it, but the embedded fence did not give way. Breathing heavily with sweat pouring down his face, Lester knelt beside it and put both hands to work. The task was not easy and he stopped to rest several times before exerting another spurt of energy. Finally, he managed to prise the wire far enough upwards, and he crawled underneath like a snake, snagging his thin shirt as he did so.

"Hey, you! Stop, man!"

Lester jumped up and spun around to see a burly security guard making his way towards him, baton in one hand, two-way radio in the other. In a flash the fugitive pulled out his gun and pointed it at the guard's chest. The man spotted the glint of gleaming metal and stood still.

"Listen, boss, me no want no trouble, you hear. No money no deh pon de premises."

Lester stared back coldly, ignored the pleading look in the man's eyes and pulled the trigger. The guard's face registered shock and disbelief as he crumpled to the ground writhing in agony. Lester sprinted past him without a backward glance and darted toward the hangar.

* * *

Harris pressed his phone to his ear. "Man down at the aerodrome. Bullet tae the chest."

"Rass. Where de hell are de Sav people?"

Preddy stepped on the gas pedal and eventually caught up with, then raced past, two local police cars, followed by Rabino and Spence. As they covered the journey mile by mile shortening the distance between themselves and the aerodrome, Preddy thought about Lester's latest inane move. If the guard died, he would go down for double murder and even if the man survived it was one more charge to add to the sheet and make life that much tougher for him. Lester had been given plenty of opportunity to surrender and had chosen the coward's way out. It was time to bring an end to this once and for all, and if it took a gun battle so be it. Negril was not Norwood. At least this time Preddy was sure that his opponent was fully armed and ready for violent action.

* * *

Lester cursed under his breath as he spotted a chain attached to the landing gear with one end firmly anchored in the ground by a solid metal peg. He crouched and pulled at the thick metal, sweating profusely, every sinew standing upright in his arms. It shifted slightly so he stopped and rested for a few seconds before giving it another tug. The peg would not be moved and Lester finally let go, breathing heavily, temples throbbing.

He picked up a large rock and bashed at the peg from the side, hoping that it would lean over so he could prise it free. It moved marginally but remained firmly anchored. In frustration he fumbled around in the dark until he found a large toolbox and, using a hammer, he smashed away at the peg until it gave way. He clambered up into his plane and was dismayed to realise that the keys must have fallen out of his pocket. There were no spare keys anywhere in the plane. He jumped out and ran over to the unlocked key holder cabinet where he took up a handful of keys searching in vain for the right duplicate key. In the distance came the wailing of police sirens and what sounded like a much nearer police helicopter which he hadn't reckoned on.

The police cars screeched to a halt outside the aerodrome. The injured guard stumbled to the gate and unlocked it swinging it open and allowing them to stream through. Preddy heard the distinct whirring of rotor blades, yet there was no police helicopter in use in Western Jamaica, unless Harris had managed to pull off a major miracle.

He leaned out of his window and squinted up at the chopper as it came in to land. The detective swore under his breath as he was just able to make out the tense pale face of Terence Chin Ellis who swung the cabin door open.

"Lester! Come son!"

The fugitive sprinted towards the swaying machine. Preddy leapt from his vehicle and started to run towards it too. The other detectives followed suit, but Lester kept well ahead of them.

Terence lowered the helicopter precariously and again called to his son, encouraging him to quicken up his pace. Dust thrown up from the aircraft's propellers went into the detectives' eyes and they blinked desperately while trying to see ahead. Each had their guns drawn, but could not see well enough to identify a target.

Preddy moved back from the aircraft's dust stream, took aim as best he could and fired repeatedly. Some bullets grazed the chassis, yet Terence managed to set it down on the ground relatively unscathed. Preddy backed away even further and fired two more shots. The windshield cracked, but did not shatter. The detectives all retreated as far back as they could out of the dust and wind pressure before firing another round. Bullets ricocheted from the metal and punctured the fuselage.

Lester stayed low and managed to scramble into the chopper, avoiding injury. As he did so his father screamed in pain. A bullet had entered Terence's right shoulder and he lost control of the aircraft as it started to lift. Lester clambered into position reaching across his father for the controls, trying to settle the bucking movements. The helicopter lifted a few feet off the ground and started to move along horizontally. It weaved dangerously as the landing skids barely clipped a stationary police car. One glance at the gas indicator told Lester it would never lift off to even tree height. The aircraft spun wildly, increasing the distance between itself and the stunned police officers. Preddy reloaded and fired at it again causing a rotor to splinter, yet it fought its way along for a considerable distance bypassing the runway completely before it jack-knifed and came to rest in the sand, beside a clump of bushes. A huge cloud of sand particles enveloped it and hung suspended in the air, temporarily impairing the officers' view.

The detectives sprinted back to their vehicles and sped down the runway towards the dust cloud. They surrounded the dilapidated aircraft which was making a muffled sound as if panting from exhaustion. The tank was crushed and the strong smell of the remaining gasoline permeated the night air and mixed in with salty sea odour. Preddy was covered in sand up to his ankles, and his legs felt heavy from trying to run on the moist sinking ground.

"Lester!" he bellowed.

Rabino squinted at the bushes. "Don't be a fool, Lester!"

"Terence! You better dan dis!" cried Spence. "Give him up!"

"Lester Chin Ellis! Come out with yer hands up!" shouted Harris, raising his gun.

Preddy bent almost double and crept in closer with his gun cocked and ready to fire. "Don't make dis any harder dan it needs to be. De two of you need to get out now!" He peered inside the mangled cabin. "Dem gone!"

Spence spun around and detected a movement in the foliage behind Harris. She pointed her weapon and silently motioned to the Glaswegian to get down. Harris crouched low while spinning, his eyes following the direction of her studious gaze. Preddy motioned to Rabino to hold her ground, while he approached the bushes carefully, gun held at arm's length.

"Lester! Terence!"

"Here, Detective," said a weary voice. Terence Chin Ellis emerged from the dense brush land with his own gun held out and glinting in the moonlight.

"Put down de gun!" ordered Preddy.

"Drop the weapon, sir!" shouted Harris. "We dinnae want tae hurt ye."

"I'm not dropping it. Leave my son alone!"

"You are making dis very hard, Terence," said Preddy. "Just put down de gun and you and Lester come out wid your hands over your head."

Terence let out a hysterical laugh. "Boy, you hurt my right arm. It can't raise at all. And I'm not putting up my one good arm for you to take it too."

Rabino tried to creep past the clearly disturbed patriarch, but her foot became entangled in dry seaweed and she stumbled. Terence swung around in alarm and released an untrained shot in her direction. Without hesitation Preddy opened fire again. Terence yelped in pain and fell to the floor clutching his thigh, the gun discarded at his side. Preddy ran towards him and kicked away the weapon, then crouched down to inspect the damage.

"You lucky, you will live."

Harris moved to check that Rabino was unharmed.

"I'm okay. That bullet sounded close though." Rabino reached for her phone. "Better get an ambulance for him."

"Right," said Preddy. "Let's go get Lester."

Spence cocked her weapon. "Yes, sir."

They searched the compact overgrowth, prodded deep holes with sticks and even shone their torches up into the trees. The sound of waves crashing on the shore mingled with the sound of boots trampling dry branches.

"He's been spotted on de rocks, sir, up by de caves," said Spence turning to look at Preddy as she replaced her radio in her pocket.

"Rass." Preddy frowned. Lester could certainly move and the fugitive knew the western coastline better than any of the detectives. He must have covered at least a mile of white sandy beach in order to reach the hazardous caves. The detective doubted that even Lester would enter the treacherous terrain in pitch blackness where some of the rocks were as sharp as machetes and hidden under water.

"We dinnae have our own helicopter, do we?" asked Harris.

"Ah wha' wrong you?" Spence snapped. "Dis is not Glasgow."

"Detective Spence," said Preddy.

She kissed her teeth and strode off briskly without looking behind her.

"I'm worried she'll shoot me," Harris said with a frown, watching as she stormed away.

"She might." Preddy walked past him and headed back towards their jeep.

As the officers turned into the driveway of the remote boutique hotel the porter met them and used his kerosene lamp to highlight the spot where he had seen the strange man crawling. The detectives left their vehicles and walked towards the rocks. Preddy leaned over the precipice and peered into the usually clear blue water below, which was now almost black. The light of his torch picked up what appeared to be a torn white shirt which lay floating on the waters.

"Can we get a rope?" asked Harris, looking at the porter.

Rabino arched an eyebrow. "Who is going down there?"

"We don't need a rope," Preddy said as he turned around and surveyed the surroundings. "Nobody not going down dere."

"Naw?" said Harris, as the veins in his forehead began to throb.

"No," said Preddy.

The porter hesitated and raised his lamp, illuminating their faces. All these guns were making him nervous. He wondered which of the men was in charge. The white man had to be the boss, they always were, but the Black man sounded more authoritative and looked like he meant business. There were plenty of ropes available if these men would just make up their minds, although their expressions said "lynch each other" not "capture a wanted man."

"What's dat over dere?" Preddy indicated a tiny structure in the distance.

"Is one old pit toilet," said the porter. "Nobody uses it. Dem soon going take it down."

Preddy drew his weapon and walked towards the derelict latrine, which appeared to be held together by rusted zinc. He stopped a few feet away and listening keenly. The only perceptible sounds were roars of strong waves buffeting the sharp rocks below.

"Lester Chin Ellis!" Preddy shouted.

The detectives circled the hut while the porter quickly backed away, but remained transfixed by the goings on.

From inside the hut came a drawn out creak that grated on the nerves of everyone who heard it.

At first the strangled creaking meant nothing to Lester. In the instant that it took for realisation to set in he was falling and clutching at air. Human excrement enveloped his body right up to his neck. Lester screamed at the top of his voice like a wounded animal, over and over. The smell was ten times worse than he could have imagined. He felt, rather than saw, cockroaches flying near his head and heard a rushing sound as hundreds of them scuttled on the walls.

Preddy kicked at the hinges of the dangling door which capitulated immediately and fell to one side. He teetered over the edge of the broken wooden floor and peered inside the deep hole. The flashlight picked out Lester's disgusted face and the detective allowed himself to smile as he backed away from the stench. The other detectives holstered their weapons and walked up to the hole. Rabino held her flashlight with one hand and her nose with the other. Spence covered her nose and mouth with both hands. Harris just leaned over and peered in with his hands at his sides as if oblivious to the odour.

"Don't shoot!" Lester cried. "Help me!"

"Lester Chin Ellis, you are so full of shit," said Preddy as he sat exhausted on the dry rocks.

"I think ye mean 'ye are under arrest'?" said Harris with a broad smile.

Preddy wiped his brow and grinned. "Dat too."

"How's he going to get out of that nastiness?" asked Rabino, trying not to retch.

Spence shook her head firmly. "Not wid my help."

"Over to you, sir," said Preddy, turning to face his boss. "Be careful how you hold de rope now."

CHAPTER 36

Saturday, 15 August, 9.28 a.m.

The sun appeared to form a halo around Pelican Walk police station. The media learned about the successful apprehension of Lester Chin Ellis as Commissioner Davis had insisted they be told immediately. Good news would be reported for once rather than the usual doom and gloom littered with scurrilous attacks on his marvellous men and women. The short official press release explained Lester was a person of interest who was assisting with enquiries in a murder investigation, but rumour said he murdered his own brother, and the public trusted rumour.

Lester sat silently in the interview room, watched through the one-way viewing glass by Harris's team of detectives. After being thoroughly hosed down outside the boutique hotel, Lester was transported to Pelican Walk clad only in a threadbare gown kindly donated by the proprietor. The on-call doctor had given him an analgesic as a precaution and declared him fit and well. His demands to see Doctor Sherman were ignored.

A request to have clothes brought from home was denied and so Lester had to suffer the indignity of wearing the ill-fitting gown. He was placed in a solitary cell for the few hours until daylight with two armed officers standing guard. The short rest did not appear to have done him any good as he still generated aggression, but Preddy had no intention of trying to make the murderer feel calm or comfortable. A cup of coffee was as far as he would go in that regard.

Preddy wanted to question Lester immediately, but the young man had demanded a lawyer and it was their duty to accede to the request before the interrogation could begin. Bets had been taken as to whether their prime suspect would willingly give up any information. Spence and Harris believed that he would not and Preddy was relieved to see that the two detectives could agree on something. Rabino sat on the fence unable to make a firm choice although Lester's increasingly hostile behaviour suggested that he would remain tight-lipped. Preddy avoided getting dragged into the bet, mainly because he needed to give this interview the best shot possible. It was prudent to avoid anything that would prejudice the outcome in his own mind.

"How is de watchman doing?" asked Preddy.

"The man's still in shock, but the doctor says he'll be okay," said Rabino. "The bullet went straight through the right side of his chest and out through the back."

"What about Terence?"

"Him shoulder not so bad," said Spence. "Him still a bawl for him leg. Him not going walk good for a while."

"The lawyer is here, sir," said the secretary, walking towards the detectives. "Says he wants to see his client right now."

"Good," said Preddy. "Bring him come."

The four detectives watched as Neville Higgs entered the interview room. They recognised him as the same pushy lawyer who had spoken at the Chin Ellis press conference. He glared at them as he walked past.

"Today must be zoo day or something," he said, and closed the door behind him, promptly rearranging the chairs so that both he and his client had their backs to the watching eyes.

"Dat's nice," said Spence in annoyance.

"Och, ma lip-reading skills were never good anyway so he didnae have tae do that," muttered Harris.

"Those two will need to make up some damn good lies," said Rabino.

Preddy shook his head. "Dem don't have enough time for dat."

"Let's give them ten minutes," said Harris. "Then it's our time."

When the ten minutes had elapsed, Harris knocked on the door and entered, followed by Preddy carrying a large briefcase. Higgs reorganised the chairs into their original positions so that the two parties faced each other.

"Mr Higgs, I'm Detective Harris, this is Detective Preddy. Mr Chin Ellis, we've all met before."

The lawyer acknowledged them. His client did not. Preddy proceeded to read the suspect his rights and asked him if he understood. Lester remained silent. His lawyer leaned forward and whispered something in his ear.

"Yes, I understand," drawled Lester.

"Well Lester, I must tell you dat de evidence we have against you is substantial," said Preddy. "I'm going to ask you some questions and your co-operation will be greatly appreciated. You should be aware before we begin dat we have already spoken to Marcus Darnay and we have a sworn statement."

The lawyer said, "Remember you are not obliged to answer any questions. Let them bring the evidence."

"Please dinnae interrupt, sir," retorted Harris. "The questions havenae even begun yet."

The lawyer sat back. He was not used to criminal investigations, but he knew that silence was nearly always the best strategy when under suspicion. Let the detectives go chase their tails without his client's help.

"We have a number of items in our possession, one of which is a bracelet," said Preddy, as he opened the briefcase and took out the transparent bag which he pushed towards the suspect. "Have you seen dis bracelet before?"

Lester said nothing although he allowed himself the briefest of glances at the bracelet.

"I should tell you dat we took it from Zadie Merton and she claims you gave it to her days after Carter's murder. But you knew dat already, right?"

"I don't know anything about any bracelet. Zadie just likes to talk foolishness."

"She took a shot at ye yesterday," said Harris. "So she just likes tae shoot too?"

The lawyer chimed in, "My client has already said that he doesn't know anything about the bracelet. Miss Merton is a lovesick prostitute."

Lester gave his lawyer the side-eye. "Don't call her that."

"Yer client hasnae really looked at it," said Harris, pushing the bracelet firmly towards Lester. "Look closely. Carter was wearing it the night he got killed."

"I don't know anything about what he had on," Lester maintained. He peered at Harris with fake concern. "You need to stay out of the sun, it's not good for people like you."

The lawyer pushed the bag back towards the detectives. "Detective, anyone could have given that bracelet to Zadie Merton. Maybe Marcus Darnay gave it to her, although I'm sure he forgot to put that in his statement. Any of the crime scene officers could have done so. It wouldn't be the first time that victims have been separated from their property by officers of the law. I'm sure that when Miss Merton gets around to giving her statement she will tell you about all of her police clients."

"Same way," said Lester smugly, folding his arms across his chest.

"We also have another object with which I'm sure ye are familiar," said Harris.

Harris removed the black balaclava from the briefcase, straightened the plastic enclosure and spread it in front of Lester, who blinked involuntarily. His thin eyes grew even thinner.

"There's saliva and sweat on this hood," said Harris. "Are ye willing tae give us a DNA sample?"

"No, he is not," said Higgs. "You can go get a court order."

Lester smirked. "What my lawyer said."

"Dat is only a matter of time," replied Preddy. "Co-operation at dis stage can only help you."

The lawyer's eyes bored into Preddy. "I only hope your chain of evidence is rock solid, because I know your Officer Nembhard gave my client a handkerchief to wipe his face that night, and I am sure it will not be difficult to establish reasonable doubt as to how any of my client's DNA came to be on that hood."

"We can place you inside Darnay's car, Lester," Preddy lied. "De car dat you picked up from de Orchid and drove in pursuit of your own brother."

Lester shook his head. "I never did that."

"Ye murdered Carter in cold blood," said Harris.

"That's a fucking lie!"

"That's enough, Detectives." The lawyer stood up. "If you have hard evidence, bring it. Lay your charges. Your witnesses have zero credibility. I've seen Marcus Darnay's rap sheet, or should I say rap blanket? No jury will take him seriously."

Lester stood up too. "Looks like we're done for now then?"

"Lester, dis is your chance to help yourself," said Preddy, feeling the air go out of his lungs. "Once you go back to your cell, what next?

"My client cannot help you any further, Detective." Higgs reached for Lester's plastic cup, crushing it under his fingers. "And I'll take this."

"Lester, you going sit in prison maybe for years waiting for a trial?" asked Preddy. "You must know dat no way you are getting any bail, no matter what Miss Ida or Mr Higgs say."

"I will get bail," predicted Lester confidently.

"Never mind the murder. Ye shot at police officers and ye injured a security guard," said Harris. "Ye didn't get bail last time and ye certainly won't be getting any bail this time."

"My client has, with good reason, lived in fear of officers for some time now," said Higgs. "The court will be told that his fears are well-founded as there is plenty of documentary evidence to support that claim. Ask any man on the street and see if they don't agree that my client is safer on the street than in jail. He will get bail."

Preddy felt a mixture of despair and frustration overwhelm him and he sought to regain control of the proceedings. "You don't think your mother and father deserve closure, Lester?" he asked. "You going let dem sit and fret maybe for years and not know de truth?"

Lester's smirk faded. "Don't talk about my people. You don't know them."

"Why not talk about dem? Dey talk about you a lot," said Preddy. "Your father even risked his life to help you. We going have to charge him too. Him have a licensed firearm, but dat don't give him de right to shoot after police."

"You better leave Mas Terence alone!" snapped Lester, wiping his palms on his gown.

"A wealthy, Chinese businessman in prison. He might not get on so well wid de food, de environment, de neighbours . . ." Preddy shook his head. "Bwoy, de neighbours."

"Aye, the neighbours won't like Terence," agreed Harris. "Never heard any of them say a nice word about Chinese people. You know Terence doesnae believe ye could've killed Carter. He said you relied on Carter for help, couldnae make a good business move without him."

"I never relied on Carter for anything! Carter fooled lots of people, but he never knew more about the business than me!"

"Well, let's talk about it and maybe we can also talk about what we can do for Mas Terence," said Preddy encouragingly. "You really going leave Miss Ida by herself?"

"I would advise you not to talk anymore," said the lawyer rapping on the mirror and beckoning to whoever was now outside the door.

"Don't advise me of nothing!" said Lester angrily. "What do you know? From day one you've just been milking money from us for legal fees. I can just imagine how you're gonna try and take away every penny that Miss Ida has once Mas Terence is in jail. Don't talk to me!"

Preddy looked at the lawyer. "If you really want to go you can gwaan, but I think your client wants to stay."

"He is here tae advise ye, Lester, but ye make up yer own mind," said Harris.

Lester stood staring down at the balaclava and the bracelet. His bruised face had long returned to its bronzed colour, but it now carried small scratches from the previous night's escapades. His shoulders slumped as all arrogance drained from his body.

"Your chauffeur, Officer Nembhard, will be looking for a deal, and if he gets in before you, you'll be out in de cold," said Preddy. "Ida and Terence are becoming old people, Lester. Dey have looked after you all your life. Don't do dis to dem."

Lester crumpled back into his seat while his lawyer frowned and resumed his own seat.

"They were going to take my empire from me," he whispered quietly. "Can you imagine that? Me the older one and they were going to make Carter run things. I couldn't let it happen. And then there was Zadie. He used to treat Zadie badly, slapped her in the face more than once. I warned him about it."

"Are ye giving us a statement willingly, Lester?" asked Harris.

"Yes, you can take my statement."

Outside the door, Rabino and Spence cheered and high-fived each other. There was nothing like a long-awaited confession to lift their spirits. Rabino reached for her phone and placed a call to the superintendent.

* * *

Detective Harris contemplated Commissioner Davis's question as he sat with the leader and his deputy in a secluded room at Pelican Walk. It was not the first time he was having a private meeting with the khaki mafia. These were the men in the top roles who remained remote from the action, but whose shoulder straps were adorned with laurel wreaths of promotion and position.

"Well?" Commissioner Davis sipped delicately from his glass as he waited on Harris.

Harris ignored the bottle of imported champagne and his brimming glass remained untouched. "Nothing on him, sir. He feeds the homeless, has only one girlfriend, a nice daughter and a lovely son. Doesnae mix with any undesirables."

"Did you observe any corners being cut, anything unethical?" asked the deputy commissioner.

Harris shook his head. "He's a clean officer and a great guy."

The commissioner raised an eyebrow. "I would like to know more about his on-the-job methods."

"With respect, sir, he has done a tremendous amount of good work with inadequate facilities and a small team of officers," said Harris. "His methods may naw be the same as mine, but they do work."

"So you don't think we have any cause for concern?" pressed the deputy.

"Everything has been fully laid out in ma reports for ye, sir." Harris stretched over the desk and picked up a sheet of paper. "Listen: 'He demonstrates an outstanding level of proficiency at tasks requiring investigative skills.' And aye, I did take it from the textbook because it's an accurate representation. There isnae much I can add."

The commissioner ran his fingers down the paperwork in front of him. "Here you say, 'At first I was unsure about the subject's interview techniques when dealing with fellow officers.' Would you like to elaborate?"

"I did further on, sir. Ye'll see I said it was firm but effective, 'displaying mental agility with outstanding analytical skills' is what's written there. Also 'is open and honest, demonstrating considerable integrity and high ethical standards.'"

"What about his team? What was the interaction like particularly with the female officers?" The deputy took a sip from his glass and licked his lips.

"He has earned their respect, sir. It's a 'harmonious work environment' as I say here. They listen, make valid suggestions and take directions. He hasnae been overly familiar with anyone. All in all there is a very good dynamic within the team. In fact I think he could teach other people a thing or two."

The commissioner looked thoughtful. "Is there anything else you think we should know?"

If ye cut out the champagne and the soirées ye could fix the CCTV and upgrade the officers furniture. "Naw, sir."

"We thank you for your efforts, Detective." Commissioner Davis reached over the desk and shook Harris's hand.

Harris nodded at the deputy and stood to leave the room. "Ye have a very valuable asset on the force, sir, and ye need tae keep him."

As Harris closed the door and started down the corridor, Preddy stepped out of the shadows and stood opposite him.

"Dat took a while, Detective Harris. I thought you said you were on de way to de canteen?"

Harris looked momentarily embarrassed. "Um, aye. I got distracted."

"Davis and his sidekick are some distraction. Is dere anything you want to tell me?"

Harris sighed. "Ye'll hear about it soon enough, no doubt."

"Now is soon enough for me."

The door opened again and the commissioner put out his head. "Ah, I thought I heard your voice, Detective Preddy." He turned and muttered something to his deputy, before reappearing and smiling brightly. "Come in Detective, we need to have a chat."

* * *

Harris took a mouthful of cold beer and admired the bottle before placing it back on the bar counter. "That's good local stuff. I'm impressed."

"Wait till you try our special tea," said Preddy.

"What special tea?" asked Harris, taking another long swig.

Preddy smiled and stared at his own half-empty bottle. "Pace yourself."

"I can handle it, ye dinnae need tae worry."

"You cannot even handle Spence and Rabino, let alone beer!"

Harris grimaced. "Aye, ye noticed then. I thought Spence was sure tae shoot me. Accidentally, of course. And I knew Rabino was giving me plenty of deadly looks beneath those long lashes."

"She hides things well," Preddy chuckled. "Dey are very loyal. You'll never know how many times I had to have pep talks wid dem when you took over."

"Ye know they really believed ye were up tae no good, the bosses I mean."

"De commissioner hinted as much, although knowing him I didn't get half de picture."

"Naw, I'm sure you didnae." Harris said. "If ye hadnae pulled this off I'm sure they'd have sacked ye, then told me ma work here was done and I could go back tae Glasgow."

Preddy laughed, relief apparent in his shining eyes. "It was a close call. De media would have thought all deir Christmases came at once."

"It's the image problem that's scaring them," said Harris. "They're looking for the rogue leaders at the top and that's where ye came in unfortunately, especially after Norwood. Ye can see where they're coming from though. Even in Scotland there's a suspicion that we've got people at the top teaching the younger ones how tae get away with cutting corners and ignoring the law."

"I know," said Preddy. "INDECOM cleared me and de public supported me by and large. What happened was tragic, but I have never, and could never work against my badge."

Harris nodded and beckoned to the barman to bring more beers.

"Sometimes I see de Norwood men, you know . . . dead and alive, in my sleep."

Harris looked at Preddy closely. "Counselling is nae a dirty word, sir."

The detective's eyes twinkled. "You forget you don't have to call me 'sir' anymore. You don't have to call me 'arsehole' either, though."

Harris winced. "Ye should have knocked me out!"

"You don't know how close I came to it. You really don't."

"Ye have tae believe me I'm sorry about saying that."

Preddy allowed himself to laugh out loud. "Well, I was being one! You didn't lie."

Harris laughed too and clinked his newly-arrived beer bottle against Preddy's.

"Seriously though, ye should talk tae someone, someone independent. It's not easy tae talk tae family and friends about things like death. I know it from personal experience."

"You've been involved in a shootout where someone died?"

"No, it wasnae a shootout but someone died alright." Harris wiped his lips. "About a year ago. Some drunken fool drove his car right off the road and in tae the station, took out all the glass and ploughed through the desks. I mean this guy must have been airborne at the speed of light. Ye have never heard such a noise! We all thought it was a terrorist attack. I was absolutely petrified. He missed killing a group of us by about a metre and ended up breaking his own neck."

"Man, dat must have been some shock."

"I couldnae talk tae anyone. I didnae want tae go tae counselling. Fought against it for months on end, but when I finally did . . .man, it was good tae talk. I still think about it sometimes, see his snapped neck, but ma nerves are all in one piece again and I can certainly sleep."

Preddy nodded. "You're right, I know. Valerie has told me as much too. I'll talk to de superintendent about it."

"Ye'll get anything ye want now ye know, Golden Boy. Ye saved the government millions that they'd have had tae pay out for Lester's fake injury lawsuit." Harris grinned. "I suggest ye put in for a five-star holiday in Hawaii and do it quickly. They wouldnae say naw."

"I need it. Is two year now I don't take a holiday, too much work. You know how it is."

"Aye, but the truth is the crime will always be here naw matter what we do. We have tae take a break from it sometimes."

"True. I tell myself dat every time I take de day off to rest, or take de kids out," Preddy said. "It should be depressing. Sometimes it is, but I just can't imagine doing another job."

"Me neither."

"We are strange people." Both men laughed.

"Ye wouldn't happen tae fancy a stint in Glasgow by any chance?"

"No occasion could be special enough to get me in a skirt."

Harris smiled and his green eyes shone. "Never mind the kilt. We have night vision goggles, helicopters, technology galore and plenty of officers. We dinnae have mosquitoes."

Preddy smiled. "You got used to de mosquitoes in de end though."

"Och naw, I can assure ye there ain't naw getting used tae the little buggers. I got bitten from head tae toe in the mountains last night."

"You never said anything."

"I was really going tae say in front of Spence and Rabino that I was being eaten by mosquitoes? We're all racing along, guns drawn, hunting a murderer and I'm going tae stop and say 'pass the bug spray!' Spence would've rightly shot me!"

The two men laughed heartily. Harris dabbed his eyes with his handkerchief and wiped the perspiration from his brow.

"So, definitely naw chance of a placement in Glasgow for ye then, Preddy?"

"Dat cold place? Not at dis time, thank you, sir!" said Preddy with a mock shudder.

"If I can put up with ye heat, ye can put up with our snow."

"Well, Sean Harris, you are a better man dan me," said Preddy, draining his bottle. "But don't tell de Super I said so."

THE END

ACKNOWLEDGEMENTS

A great big thanks to Joffe Books for publishing this Murder series.

To those who were always ready with sound words of advice or encouragement, I thank you: Virginia Bailey Plowright, Doreen Bailey, Elaine (Pat) Harris, Carol Harris Simpson, Sharon Thompson, Gwendolyn Thompson and Juliet (Lavern) Ingram Reid.

And because you never forget great teachers, I thank those who were dedicated to the cause at Clarendon College, Chapelton, and those who still are. *Perstare et praestare.*

Thank you for reading this book.

If you enjoyed it please leave feedback on Amazon or Goodreads, and if there is anything we missed or you have a question about, then please get in touch. We appreciate you choosing our book.

Founded in 2014 in Shoreditch, London, we at Joffe Books pride ourselves on our history of innovative publishing. We were thrilled to be shortlisted for Independent Publisher of the Year at the British Book Awards.

www.joffebooks.com

We're very grateful to eagle-eyed readers who take the time to contact us. Please send any errors you find to corrections@joffebooks.com. We'll get them fixed ASAP.